A D

Also by Stephen Davis

The Tsar's Banker
I Spy the Wolf

A Duty to Kill

Stephen Davis

To Rosie with all my love

Stephen

A Duty to Kill © Stephen Davis

ISBN 978-0-9955423-5-8
eISBN 978-0-9955423-6-5

Published in 2018 by Peakes Place Publications

The right of Stephen Davis to be identified as the author of this work has been asserted by him in accordance with the Copyright, Designs and Patents Act 1988.

A CIP record of this book is available from the British Library.

All rights reserved. No part of this book may be reproduced, stored in a retrieval system, or transmitted in any form or by any means, electronic, mechanical, photocopying, recording or otherwise, without the prior written permission of the copyright holder.

Printed in the UK

I cannot fully express my gratitude to two people for their invaluable help with this story.

First to Father Bernardo, a Roman Catholic priest who, over a delightful lunch one hot afternoon in Rome, described how a few priests within the Vatican as well as some members of the Franciscan order helped prominent Nazis escape justice after the Second World War.

The second, to whom I am equally indebted, is the FBI Special Agent who pointed me towards relevant bureaux documents detailing the people and locations within the Roman Catholic Church that made possible the disappearance of Nazi war criminals.

PRATI DI CASTELLO
Castel Sant' Angelo
St. Peter's
VATICAN CITY
Piazza Navona
ROME
MONTI
AURELIO
R. Tiber
CAMPITELLI
Forum
The Colosseum
TRASTEVERE
MONTEVERDE
S.SABA
TESTACCIO
Ostiense Station
0
1 mile
0
1km
OSTIENSE

Cast of characters

The Tagleva Family and Tagleva bank employees

Philip Tagleva, Head of the Tagleva banking family and chairman of the bank

Sophie Tagleva, Philip's wife and runs the Tagleva charitable foundation

Michael Tagleva, eldest son of Philip and Sophie

Juliette Tagleva, Michael's wife

Matislav and Halinka twins

Dorothy, adopted daughter of Philip and Sophie

Jean-Claude Moreau, Managing Director of the Tagleva bank and based in Paris

Sébastien, Jean-Claude's partner

Nicole Labranche, secretary at the bank in Paris

Katherine du Bois, Head of Department in the records floor of the Tagleva bank in Paris

German and Swiss

Julius Halder, Major der Polizeito in the Gestapo attached to Department D, responsible for the policing of the occupied territories

Carl Bernstorff, tank commander and SS Sturmbannführer (Major)

Heinrich Himmler, Reichsführer of the Schutzstaffel (SS)

Matteo Keller, Swiss banker based in Zurich

French Resistance

Alain, member of the Liferaft resistance organisation

Luc, member of Liferaft

Matthieu, member of Liferaft

Samuel, the forger for the Liferaft organisation

Jacques, French resistant and leader of a group in Paris

Vincent, member of Jacques' resistance group

Vatican

Bishop Alois Hudal, head of the Collegio Teutonico (German seminary) at the Vatican in Rome

Domenico Tardini, Head of the Secretariat of State at the Vatican for external affairs

Father Marius, priest at the Collegio Teutonico

Sir D'Arcy Osborne, British Envoy Extraordinary and Minister Plenipotentiary to the Holy See.

Father Armando, priest who worked for Sir D'Arcy Osbourne's resistance group during and after the German occupation of Italy.

British and members of the Special Operations Executive (SOE)

Colonel Tim Wilson, Michael Tagleva's commanding officer and member of the Special Operations Executive, SOE

John Masterman, Senior intelligence officer in MI5

Captain Peter Maclean, member of SOE

Sergeant John Evans, member of SOE

Private Nigel Begg, member of SOE

Private Edward Daniels, member of SOE

Charles Sydney Gibbes, Russian orthodox priest and friend of Philip and Sophie Tagleva

Prologue

Vatican City, October 1945

Just west of the Piazza Navona in central Rome is the beautiful church of Santa Maria dell'Anima and the adjacent priests' seminary, commonly referred to within the Vatican as the Collegio Teutonico. Both church and seminary are peculiar in that, despite being located outside the walls of the Vatican City, they still constitute part of the territory of the Vatican State. The most notable architectural features are the distinctive slender bell tower, an internal courtyard with gardens and a high wall that surrounds the property, which guarantees the privacy of the church and the seminary from undesirable observation.

For five hundred years the seminary has ensured that the Catholic Church has suitable young men of German origin studying for the priesthood. For the past twenty-one years its head has been Bishop Alois Hudal, a round-faced man with piercing blue eyes, thin lips, bushy eyebrows and, despite his sixty years, a full head of hair.

It's been two hours since the sun disappeared below the hills of Rome and, as usual, Bishop Hudal is working late in his office on the second floor of the seminary. He's composing a letter to a cardinal expressing his fear that, now that the German Third Reich has been defeated, there is nothing to prevent communism's relentless march across Europe. The letter informs the cardinal that an invasion of Italy from communist Eastern Europe would be unstoppable and that such an action would inevitably result in the destruction of the Church in Rome.

The bishop yawns, takes off his steel-rimmed glasses and rubs his eyes with thumb and forefinger. There's a gentle knock on the door.

'*Eingeben*,' he responds in German.

A priest dressed in a black cassock enters the room carrying a small brown leather attaché case.

'I'm sorry to disturb you, Your Excellency,' says the bishop's secretary. 'The package you have been expecting has arrived and, as instructed, I've brought it to you.'

'Yes, I remember, thank you. Could you please put it on the side table next to my biretta?'

The attaché case is carefully placed next to the purple square-shaped hat with its four ridges, called horns, denoting the bishop's elevated rank among the Catholic priesthood. The young secretary bows his head to the bishop and leaves, closing the door quietly behind him.

Placing his glasses on his nose, the bishop stands up and walks over to the side table. Taking a key out of his cassock pocket he inserts it into the lock. The catches spring open. Lifting the lid Bishop Hudal sees the brown paper package. Inside are two hundred and fifty bearer bonds each worth a hundred thousand Swiss francs. Taking the package out, he carries it to a picture of the Virgin and child on the far wall. Pulling at the picture-frame, it effortlessly swings on its hinges, revealing a wall-safe. Once the paper package is safely locked away Bishop Hudal returns to his letter.

Chapter One

Paris, seventeen months previously, 15 May 1944

The waiter poured a glass of wine and slid the menu onto the table.

'Is there anything else I can bring to sir?' he asked.

'No, I'll wait for my guest to arrive. Thank you.'

Julius Halder sipped his wine. He liked dining at the Tour d'Argent with its view over the rooftops towards Notre Dame Cathedral and in the distance the Eiffel Tower. Before the war its fine food and wines had attracted the rich and famous, and Julius thought it fitting that the day Paris was occupied the restaurant had been reserved for the exclusive use of the German victors. Julius looked around the room and noticed every table, except one, was filled with men in uniform enjoying meals with colleagues. The man in civilian clothes, no doubt a German officer, was probably entertaining his French mistress. Halder leaned back in his chair and stared out of the window. He was looking forward to meeting his luncheon guest. The reports in his police file described his guest as trustworthy, discreet, diligent, eloquent and highly intelligent. Halder hoped the reports were true, it would make the next few weeks more interesting.

He took another sip of wine and thought back to the day he had decided to become a policeman: his fourteenth birthday and the same day his mother died. That morning, for another unexplained crime, his father collected the cane from the cupboard on the landing saying, as he always did on such occasions, 'The most important lesson a father can give his son is the importance of the enforcement of law'. That afternoon, when Julius arrived home from school, he discovered the undertakers had already removed his mother's body. He listened to his father tell the policeman that the tear in the carpet must have caught her foot sending her headlong down the steep flight of stairs. Throughout his mother's funeral Julius didn't cry; he spent the time wondering how the slightly worn stair carpet had developed its lethal tear in the few hours he'd spent at school. As he watched the coffin being lowered into the cold sodden earth Julius set his mind to solving the mystery. On the regular occasions his father was drunk on schnapps and asleep in his favourite armchair Julius would investigate his mother's death.

Julius worked hard at school, passed his exams and gained a place to study law at the Université de Paris. He was pleased to escape the suffocating atmosphere his father created at home and cared little that on the same day he travelled on the train to Paris his father moved his mistress in. After graduating from university he took his mother's maiden name; instead of returning home to Munich he applied to join the Schutzpolizei and was accepted into the police academy in Berlin. That day he posted an anonymous letter to the Bavarian chief of police enclosing some of his father's love letters to his mistress that he'd discovered hidden in a secret drawer in his father's desk. Julius followed the trial in the *Coburger Zeitung* newspaper; when he read his father and his father's mistress had been sentenced to death and guillotined he felt nothing but satisfaction.

Julius enjoyed being a policeman. He worked hard and promotion came quickly. When the war started he had risen to the rank of Major der Polizeito attached to Department D, responsible for the policing of the occupied territories. When France was defeated he was posted to Paris. The eight thousand, five hundred marks salary gave him an excellent standard of living and the work was not too onerous: to investigate and bring to justice those guilty of treason, sabotage and criminal attacks on German forces in the Paris area. At the start of the war there had been very little resistance but as the years of occupation rolled on he found himself investigating more serious crimes and in the past month he had taken into 'protective custody' fifteen resistants. He smiled at the uniquely Nazi euphemism that allowed the imprisonment of suspects by requiring them to sign a statement declaring they had requested their own imprisonment, presumably out of fear of personal harm, which in a way was true. His thoughts were interrupted by the arrival of his guest. Halder stood up, waved the managing director of the Tagleva bank to the chair opposite him and poured his guest a glass of wine.

'Thank you for giving up time to have lunch with me,' said Halder.

'My pleasure. I'm always anxious to help the Gestapo in their investigations.'

'And it's much appreciated, but before we talk about business, let's order some food.'

The waiter brought over some menus. They both chose rabbit fricassee and once the waiter left Halder looked across the table.

'While we wait for our meal let me explain why I invited you to lunch and how I think you can help me.'

His guest said nothing and Julius continued. 'When France made peace with Germany we anticipated there would be some resistance from a small part of the population. Much as we expected, it began with children scribbling V for victory onto the backs of café chairs and on walls. A silly prank, harmless one might think, though extremely annoying to us Germans. Initially we were pleased the children's parents were not so adventurous; they correctly assumed we would be less forgiving of petty lawbreaking by adults. So they listened to the BBC as their own act of resistance. However, we Germans were not stupid enough to expect that as time passed, petty rules such as the curfew, food rationing and general shortages wouldn't cause general disgruntlement. Then, in my opinion, we made a mistake.'

Halder looked at his guest, there was no reaction to his criticism of German policy, and he took a sip of wine before continuing.

'Germany needed workers. We encouraged the French Vichy government to send French men and women to work in Germany in return for releasing French prisoners of war. I don't think my superiors anticipated that so many young men would prefer to flee to the foothills of the Pyrenees and the mountains of the Jura than to work in Germany for two years.

The unintended consequence of that mistake has been to create an army of resistance, now popularly referred to as the Maquis. Did you know it's a Corsican term for scrubland?'

'I didn't,' replied his guest.

Halder took another sip of wine.

'The Gestapo estimates there are around thirteen thousand *maquisards* scattered around France. Virtually all of them under twenty-five, many of them communists, petty criminals and thugs, and they're making a nuisance of themselves.'

'I don't know about such things.'

'Oh, I'm sure you don't. But I'm hoping Jean-Claude Moreau, the managing director of the Tagleva bank, will be able to help me answer some questions I have, but let me finish my story. Over time the Maquis has become more daring. Helping Allied pilots shot down over France to escape capture, vandalising trains and telephone lines, stealing German uniforms and equipment and so on. However, the Gestapo has had some successes. We arrested fifty terrorists in Lyon a few weeks ago. Their interrogation has been most informative.'

Julius paused and leaned back in his chair.

'As a matter of fact we are to execute two of the terrorists this afternoon. I don't suppose you'd like to come to Gestapo headquarters and witness the execution, to see German justice in action? There would be plenty of time to finish our lunch and arrive in good time.'

Jean-Claude looked away. 'Thank you, no,' he mumbled.

'No, you're probably wise. Executions are not for those with a sensitive disposition, particularly after a good lunch.'

The policeman smiled and took another sip of wine before continuing.

'So, let me come to the point of our meeting. Everyone anticipates, any day soon, the Allies will begin their liberation of France. As that day draws closer we expect the Maquis to become increasingly involved in serious acts of terrorism as a way of helping the Allies.'

Julius looked hard at his guest before continuing.

'The aspect of the Resistance that interests me is how it's financed. Resisting an army of occupation requires lots of money, possibly millions of francs… I wondered, as a banker, if you might have some thoughts on how such large amounts of money are being obtained and distributed?'

They were interrupted by the arrival of their food. Rabbit flambéed with cognac was expertly served onto their plates, a dish of braised lettuce hearts cooked in white wine and chicken stock and another of potato purée placed between them. It had been a long time since Jean-Claude had seen such a lavish meal and the smell of the caramelised onions, braised meat and rich stock intoxicated him. As their wine glasses were being refilled, Halder studied Jean-Claude carefully, once the waiter was content that everything was in order he turned his attention to another table.

Jean-Claude looked up from his plate of food. 'To answer your question, I'm not sure I can help much, but I'll try by giving you some background that might be useful. In 1940 Germany informed the French government it was obliged to pay for the costs of the occupation and those payments amount to many millions of francs each week. To do this, the French government in Vichy has increased taxation, issued bonds and printed money. It has led to enormous inflation reducing the value of the French franc. For most families that would be manageable if income matched the inflation but almost a third of all French households work for the German occupying forces, in one form or another, and the wages paid are pitifully small.'

Julius Halder adopted a disinterested expression on his face as he cut into the rabbit on his plate and despite this Jean-Claude continued his explanation.

'The result is that most households have very little income. Those who had savings before the war have seen them disappear due to inflation, and the painfully low interest rates being offered by banks do nothing to relieve the pressure. Anyone with spare money needs it to buy food. So, to answer your question, I would say that no one in France has spare money, certainly not enough to finance the needs of the Resistance. For that reason alone I'm surprised they manage to function at all.'

Julius Halder put down his knife and fork. 'So if there's no money in France to finance the Resistance, where's it coming from?'

'You would know better than I, but I'm told some banks and post offices have been robbed. Still probably not enough to finance all the activities of the Resistance so I assume the rest is dropped to them by the RAF or the American air force,' answered Jean-Claude.

'I'm sure you're correct, though the source of the money is of less interest to me. Far more important is the *identity* of the person or people that distribute it. My thought is, if I can find and arrest those who act as the bankers for the various Resistance groups then the most serious acts of terror will be forced to stop for lack of finance. What's your opinion?'

Halder reached for his glass and sipped some wine.

'That would be logical. Have you any thoughts on who you're looking for?' asked Jean-Claude as he carefully transferred a piece of rabbit from his plate to his mouth.

'Not at this time. I was hoping you could tell me where I might begin to look.'

'I'm afraid not. But if I hear of anything you'll be the first to know.'

Halder smiled again. 'I know I can rely on your co-operation. Changing the subject for the moment, I was reading your SS file yesterday and was most impressed how diligently you have worked for the German Reich ever since the Tagleva bank was requisitioned by the SS. We are most appreciative. It's one of the reasons why your friend and companion... Sébastien isn't it... hasn't been conscripted into the programme providing two years labour in Germany. Being the *sensitive* individual I suspect he is I don't suppose building roads in Germany would be too agreeable to him. It's why I'm in no doubt your co-operation will continue, particularly as I extend my investigations into finding those people who act as bankers for the Resistance.'

Halder looked at Jean-Claude looking back at him. Experience told him his guest would be calculating that if he was suspected of a crime he would not be eating in the Tour d'Argent but in an interview room at Gestapo headquarters on the Avenue Foch. At the same time Halder wondered if his reference to Sébastien had Jean-Claude's brain screaming, if his heart was hammering inside his chest and if the saliva in his mouth had thickened and was turning the food rancid. But Jean-Claude looked the picture of calm, there seemed to be no adrenaline surge shutting down his ability to think logically and this calmness confirmed to Halder that Jean-Claude's police file was accurate. It would make the next few months even more stimulating.

The end of the meal arrived all too quickly. Jean-Claude didn't finish the rabbit, claiming the portion of meat on his plate had been too generous. He refused a coffee, not surprising thought Halder. Since America entered the war the coffee in France, due to the absence of coffee beans, had become a revolting beverage made from chicory. But the result was that the time he'd spent with Jean-Claude had been shorter than he had hoped.

As Halder's guest stood to depart he said, 'I'm sorry I haven't been able to be of much help to you.'

'On the contrary, I've found our meeting most informative. I'm sure we'll see each other again, very soon, I suspect,' replied Halder.

After leaving the Tour d'Argent Jean-Claude arrived on the street and gulped in the fresh air as he quickly walked in the direction of his apartment. He wanted to be as far away from the policeman with the piercing green eyes as possible. Once inside the apartment Jean-Claude rushed into the bathroom and was violently sick.

Chapter Two

London, 16 May 1944

Michael Tagleva was waking from the first good night's sleep he'd had in a couple of weeks. Even in his drowsy state he was conscious of the soft duck down pillow and the crisp cotton sheets, a luxury when compared to the camp bed in his office. He opened his eyes and saw the blonde hair covering the pillow in front of him, nestled into the naked body and kissed the nape of her neck.

'Morning,' he whispered in her ear.

'Mmm,' came the sleepy but contented reply.

He kissed her again and moved an arm around her waist and she pressed her naked body into his. Michael glanced at the carriage clock on the bedside table.

'Sorry, my love, I don't have time. I have to go to work.'

'Ohhhh, then don't be such a tease,' she complained sleepily.

Hearing the French accent, Michael was tempted to stay in bed for another half hour, but nevertheless pushed back the bedclothes, swung his legs out of the bed and walked to the bathroom. He chuckled at a second moan of complaint coming from the bed as his absence was felt.

Twenty minutes later, washed, shaved and still naked Michael walked back into the bedroom to find Juliette wide awake propped up by pillows, wearing a nightgown and with her long golden hair brushed. As he noticed her studying his athletic body he gave her a slightly crooked grin that was immediately contagious. She continued to watch him as he threaded his arms into a clean shirt and put on a dark suit and tie. As he tied up the shoelaces of his handmade shoes from James Taylor & Son in Paddington he thought about how they had met and ended up living with his parents.

Their romance began at the Tagleva bank in Paris before the war started. He still felt embarrassed at the clumsy way he'd asked her out on his first day at work and her immediate and firm rejection. It was only later, when Juliette suggested he take her to the cinema that he'd learned the reason for her rejection. 'Just because you're the chairman's son I didn't want you to think I'd fall at your feet.' The first date was quickly followed by others, and as they spent more time together Juliette changed from being a complete stranger to someone who never left his mind, and he resented any time spent apart from her. When the war started it became a rude intrusion into their private little world and, of course, it had parted them. The day war was declared Michael had been in London on business with his father; Juliette was stuck in Paris and it was a miserable interlude for them both. It was only when Michael had been sent on a secret mission to Paris he had, against all orders, used the opportunity to be reunited with Juliette and bring her out of occupied France to Britain. The journey hadn't been without its dangers. Twice they had nearly been caught and on one occasion Michael had to kill a man to prevent him betraying them to the Germans. Back in Britain Michael was given a severe dressing down by his superiors for involving a civilian in his mission.

Initially he and Juliette moved in with his parents. But they craved their own independence and found a terraced house at the Fulham end of the King's Road. The house may have been small, but the reception rooms had beautiful proportions with high ceilings and it benefited from a south-facing garden. Juliette set about furnishing the house in a minimalist French elegance that wartime restrictions and ration coupons allowed. Being French, and very patriotic, it was with a sense of amusement Juliette learned that further up the road, at No. 215, had once lived Thomas Arne the composer of 'Rule Britannia' and Michael taught her the chorus which would be loudly sung as they washed the dishes after dinner.

One evening during the Blitz they were in central London at His Majesty's Theatre watching the musical *The Lilac Domino*. The cast were coming to the end of the first act and had just begun the song 'This Seems to Me a Tricky Business', when the undulating sound of the air-raid siren was heard. The curtain came down and, with the rest of the audience, they rushed out of the theatre to take shelter in the underground station at Piccadilly Circus. Despite missing the end of the play it had been a fun evening sitting on the underground platform with the few hundred other Londoners protected from the Luftwaffe's bombs singing 'When I'm Cleaning Windows' and 'The Siegfried Line'. In the morning they turned into the King's Road to discover their small house, along with a few others in the street, had disappeared in the bombing and a pile of rubble was all that remained of their home and most of their possessions. They moved back in with Michael's parents.

Michael looked up from tying his shoes. 'You look happy.'

'How could I not be when I'm married to the most handsome man in England?'

He chuckled at the exaggeration.

'Will you be home again tonight?'

'I hope so.'

'So, we can have another early night,' she said conspiratorially.

'If you're a good girl.'

'Good girl! What opportunity do I have to be anything but good, living in this large house with your family and a few servants?'

He walked over to the bed and sat down. 'I'm sorry. I know how much you loved the house in the King's Road. We'll find another place soon.'

'I'm not complaining. Your family's lovely, but I'll never forgive the bastard Boche. First they invade my beautiful France and when I come to England they bomb our lovely new home only a few weeks after we had moved in.'

'Are you working today?' he asked changing the subject.

'Not until tomorrow, I intend to spend the entire morning in bed. It'll be lovely to be able to relax.'

He leaned over to give her a final kiss on the lips. 'Then have a nice day.'

She wrapped her arms around him and pulled him close to her.

'Give the Germans hell from me,' whispered Juliette in his ear.

Michael descended the stairs, walked into the dining room and took his usual place at the table. His parents Philip and Sophie were sitting at each end, opposite him Dorothy, a young orphan his parents adopted when her orphanage was bombed at the start of the war. The two empty chairs next to Dorothy were reserved for Michael's twin brother and sister, Matislav and Halinka, both at boarding school in Wales. Michael liked Dorothy and discovered after she joined the family that he'd been blessed with a second sister who more than filled the absence of his other siblings. Her infectious laughter and her ability to mimic, with merciless accuracy, every member of the family and the servants sent him into convulsions, which only served to encourage her.

'Good morning,' he said.

'Good morning, Michael,' they chorused back.

As he spread a slice of toast with margarine, his mother poured a cup of tea and passed it to him.

Looking at his mother he said, 'I was given a gift yesterday and I was wondering if my sister had been good enough to have it.'

'She has been very good,' smiled his mother.

Mimicking her nanny's northern accent Dorothy said, 'And I suppose I'll be expected to be *canny good for another day* after receiving your lovely gift.'

'I couldn't expect you to be good for *two days* in a row.' Michael laughed and pulled out a block of Hershey's chocolate from his pocket. There was a squeal of delight as the precious chocolate was slid over the table to Dorothy.

'Thank you, Michael,' said Dorothy with a broad smile.

As he was leaving the house his mother said, 'That was very generous of you. Dorothy will love the chocolate.'

Michael laughed. 'I don't see how. My GI friends give it away because it tastes only slightly better than a boiled potato. They tell me it's made like that on purpose to keep them from eating it in non-emergency situations. But I hope she enjoys it. By the way, could you arrange a breakfast tray for Juliette? I think she intends spending the morning of her day off in bed.'

He kissed his mother goodbye and walked up the street to the underground.

As Michael walked up Caxton Street towards the St. Ermin's Hotel he knew, what most Londoners could not, that the hotel conveniently located near St. James's Park underground station, close to Buckingham Palace and the Houses of Parliament is the London headquarters for clandestine operations. The Special Operations Executive occupied the entire second floor, MI6 was stationed two floors above and guerrilla warfare classes were run for operatives in one of the meeting rooms in the basement. The hotel's Caxton Bar was a convenient place for London's secret intelligence officers to meet agents from other secret organisations, including MI9 also located in Caxton Street, the Government Communications Headquarters in Palmer Street, SIS head office in Queen Anne's Gate and the MI8 listening post on the roof of an office building in Petty France.

Major Michael Tagleva walked into the hotel lobby and up the stairs to the highly theatrical and undulating balcony covered in rich plasterwork. He continued to the second floor and nodded to the plain-clothes policeman sitting on a sofa reading the *Daily Herald*. Michael opened the door of room 202 and walked in. Standing at the far end of the room studying a map of France was a tall man with a moustache, prematurely receding brown hair and a scar, which ran from his left ear to his mouth giving him a sinister look.

'Good Morning, sir,' said Michael to his boss.

Colonel Tim Wilson replied, with his usual greeting to any subordinate who happened to be younger, 'Morning, old man.'

Michael's discreet enquiries had revealed that his commanding officer, only a few years older than himself, had adopted the characteristics of an older man after leaving Sandhurst where his nickname was Babyface because he didn't ever need to shave. It had been a long time since anyone had dared use the name.

They barely had time to exchange another word before the door opened and John Masterman walked in. Dressed in a three-piece suit with a gold watch chain spread over his waistcoat many people mistook the senior intelligence officer in MI5 for a bank manager. Educated at the Royal Naval College in Dartmouth and at Oxford, when the war broke out Masterman was drafted into the Intelligence Corps and soon became somewhat of a legend within the secret service. No introductions were needed and once they were seated around the meeting table Masterman began to speak.

'Gentlemen, currently three hundred thousand troops, fifty thousand vehicles and over one hundred thousand tons of equipment are camped along Britain's southern coastline waiting for the order to begin the liberation of France.'

Masterman paused to pour some water into a glass and took a sip.

'But there's one aspect of the plan we have less control over than I would wish for: the French Resistance. Much of it is made up of small groups who decide for themselves what they should be doing. But come D-Day we need the Resistance to bring the French transport system to a standstill by destroying railway tracks and bridges. It's a key element to the success of the D-Day landings. That means having our people on the ground to liaise with the Resistance leaders and ensure their efforts are directed and co-ordinated.'

Michael suspected his orders were coming next.

'Major Tagleva we're sending you back to France. Having lived in Paris for much of your childhood you can pass as a native, and you also speak German which may be an added advantage. Your mission is quite specific. You're to meet up with a leader of a French Resistance group in Paris and act as the group's co-ordinator. The colonel will brief you on the details and the exact targets we expect the group in Paris to destroy in the run up to D-Day. I can't emphasise enough the importance of your mission.'

'Thank you, gentlemen.' Masterman stood up and left the room.

Chapter Three

17 May 1944

Paris's 8th arrondissement is situated on the right bank of the River Seine and is a place of political and business power. It hosts the Élysée Palace, the Arc de Triomphe, the Place de la Concorde and the shops, hotels and financial institutions that serve the upper bourgeoisie. In its centre and connecting the avenues George-V and the Champs-Élysées is the Rue Pierre Charron and halfway along the street is the five-storey headquarters of the Tagleva bank.

Jean-Claude was sitting at his desk in his fourth-floor office. He picked up the ornate English art deco onyx paper knife topped with sterling silver he'd bought in the Burlington Arcade when on a trip to London a few years ago. He played with the trinket, a habit he'd adopted when thinking through a problem, and began to contemplate his lunch with the policeman a couple of days ago.

His thoughts returned to the day the Germans marched into Paris and the SS requisitioned the bank as part of the German Economic and Administration Department. He remembered being upset as he'd watched men in SS uniforms strut around the bank's corridors, occupy its offices and order the staff to manage the financial affairs of the SS in France. In those early days of the occupation Jean-Claude had contemplated resigning from his job. It was Sébastien who'd persuaded him that such an action would be a meaningless gesture and the Germans would simply appoint another chief administrator. Sébastien's advice had been right; he would have hated to abandon Tagleva to people who cared nothing for the bank, its staff or its French clients and to have watched from afar as the business he loved slowly died. So for the past four years he reluctantly rubbed shoulders with the German victors, becoming increasingly aware that there were some advantages to his schizophrenic situation. As managing director he had contact with the upper levels of the German administration in Paris and, as a result, was able to peep inside the mechanism of German occupation and view secrets hidden from ordinary citizens. On more than a few occasions the information he'd learned had saved a couple of Resistance networks in danger of discovery. However, as Jean-Claude thought through his meeting at the Tour d'Argent with Halder, it was obvious the lunch had potentially dangerous implications. He knew there were some decisions he had to take, and one, in particular, would be very painful.

Arriving home Jean-Claude found the apartment empty. He could think of nothing more indulgent than to pour himself a large drink and collapse on the sofa, but the last bottle of champagne in the kitchen cupboard waited for the day of liberation and he was reluctant to waste it. He gazed out of the window towards the Eiffel Tower and the dark rain clouds hovering over the city. He thought back to the weeks before the war, when Paris had never looked so colourful, when the gardens and balconies were a mass of flowers. When Sébastien and he had watched the German infantry as they first marched down the Champs-Élysées, Paris seemed to lose its colour as well as its pride. The Germans changed everything. He had been appalled when the Vichy government replaced the French maxim *Liberté, Egalté, Fraternité* with the Germanic and hollow, 'Work, Family, Fatherland'. He was outraged when the street signs were Germanised and the Germans confiscated fuel and private cars vanished from the roads, when rickshaws replaced taxis and deliveries were made by horse and cart. As if these changes weren't enough, within weeks German propaganda informed the population there was to be food rationing. A necessity, they said, to ensure food supplies reached everyone. That's not how it turned out; food soon became scarce. Working for the Germans at the bank allowed him a slightly larger food ration but he resisted using the privilege, preferring to live the same way as every other Frenchman. Such resolve was difficult as the shortages resulted in surviving on a few handfuls of pasta, split peas, a single slice of meat once a week, a gluey inedible concoction somehow described as bread and possibly an egg every six or seven weeks. Like most Parisians Jean-Claude and Sébastien usually ended the month with unspent ration coupons because there was no food to buy. The only way to stave off starvation was to buy essentials from the black market. Cigarettes could be traded for food, a pound of butter exchanged for an hour's private piano tuition and a new chest of drawers bought for a couple of eggs. Everyone, including Jean-Claude, used the black market while at the same time condemning it for causing the shortages but in the past months things had got worse. If food could be found, there was no guarantee there would be cooking fat to cook it in, nor the electricity to cook it with. For the past six months Jean-Claude heard of households that had been forced to use candles as a fuel – now there was even a shortage of candles.

Each morning, as Sébastien searched the city for food, Jean-Claude walked to the bank and past queues of people holding on to their overused shopping bags with threadbare handles, waiting for meagre provisions. He knew the women whispered to each other that he worked for the enemy, was a collaborator, and on more than one occasion he'd arrived at the bank to find spittle on the back of his overcoat. He didn't blame them, had their circumstances been reversed he might have drawn the same conclusions as the women in the queue.

He heard the front door open and a tear crept down his cheek as he thought of the conversation he must have with the man he loved.

Later that evening, after Jean-Claude had recounted his meeting with Halder and the decision he had come to, Sébastien looked at him.

'Jean-Claude, I love you. How can you be so cold as to send me away?' Sébastien kept his eyes steady, resting on Jean-Claude's face. 'I won't go,' he said angrily as he looked away.

Jean-Claude's features buckled just slightly before he spoke. 'You must. This policeman will use my love for you against me, force me to betray the network. If the Gestapo arrest you, torture you, we both know I would tell them everything to save you from the pain. You must get away from Paris, away from the Gestapo, where I know you'll be safe.'

Sébastien's gaze rested on the wall behind Jean-Claude. 'I would suffer any torture for you, to protect you…' Then his shoulders slumped, his eyes cast down and he began to sob.

'I belong here with you, in your arms, not skulking in some mountains far away while you're in danger. I understand that if I were not here you would have less to worry about.'

Jean-Claude enveloped Sébastien in a tight hug.

'I'll be sorry to see you go. Our love will keep us together even when you're far away. But right now it's time we were apart, to protect each other.'

'Will you send me some messages to say you're safe?' asked Sébastien.

'You know I can't and you mustn't send me any messages either. The Germans might find them. When this is all over, we'll be together again, I promise.'

Breaking free from Jean-Claude's arms Sébastien wiped away a tear. 'When must I go?'

'Tomorrow, I've arranged for you to be escorted down the line and through the network until you reach a safe house in the Massif Central. I won't know exactly where, it's best that way.'

Sébastien nodded, he knew Jean-Claude had picked the least accessible part of France for his exile. The Massif Central has just three large cities, Saint Etienne, Clermont Ferrand and Limoges, all of them lying on the edge of the area. The remainder is a huge area of open spaces, small villages, hamlets and isolated farmsteads. The highest parts and the plateaux are used during the summer for grazing cattle, the south for sheep, and the remainder is forested and large enough to hide an army. Sébastien knew that in the Massif Central he would spend the rest of the war in isolation, lonely, worried for Jean-Claude but, unlike the man he loved, he would be safe.

'I will miss you so much,' sobbed Sébastien.

'And I you,' replied Jean-Claude his eyes bloodshot from tears.

Chapter Four

London, 18 May 1944

Philip Tagleva was in his study preparing for the day's meetings. Despite approaching his seventh decade, the lenses in his reading glasses becoming increasingly thicker and the slight stiffening in his hips when he walked, he refused to contemplate retirement and sit out his remaining years in quiet comfort, not while his country was at war. He made a final scribble in the margin of the paper and took the pocket watch from his waistcoat pocket; he decided he had a few more minutes before he needed to leave for his meeting. As he did so often, he glanced up at the portrait of his wife hanging above the fireplace. He smiled back at the picture of the beautiful woman holding a white rose in her hands. *Where had the time gone* he thought. Twenty-seven years ago he first met Sophie at the Hotel European in St. Petersburg and had been captivated by her looks and charm. As a result he delayed his departure to England by a couple of days and became trapped in Russia by the revolution. Without that delay he and Sophie would never have travelled one thousand three hundred miles across Russia to escape the Bolsheviks. He would never have met Prince Felix Youssoupov, nor escaped on the same British battleship that took what remained of the imperial royal family into exile, and the Bank of Tagleva would never have existed to become one of the wealthiest financial institutions in Europe. *Strange,* he thought, *how it is that wars and revolutions change our lives.* Just as he and Sophie had been discussing his retirement, the war with Germany had begun. On the day Winston Churchill became prime minister, Philip received a letter from Downing Street asking if he would advise the government on financing the war against Germany. Naturally, he was flattered but asked Sophie's opinion. He was not surprised, in fact secretly pleased, by her answer.

'Winston's eight years older than you... if he can work for Britain's victory, then so can we, and I'll help in whatever way I can. Besides you never *really* wanted to retire, you were only doing it for me.' So he continued to work and Sophie continued to run the Tagleva Foundation.

Philip discovered that working for Churchill resulted in long days and often long nights but he never tried to hide the truth from the great man and soon felt that Churchill appreciated the candour of his reports. A month after being appointed, Philip met with Churchill in the cabinet room of 10 Downing Street and gave the prime minister his assessment of the country's financial situation.

'Britain began the war by paying for its war materials in gold under a "cash and carry" system but so many assets have been liquidated that the country is running short of cash.'

So in September 1940, while the Battle of Britain raged over the skies of London, Churchill dispatched Philip, with a group of other experts, to the United States. Officially it was a technical and scientific mission. Unofficially the main purpose was to share with the US military Britain's secret research in exchange for supplies of food, oil and war materials. Britain gained some worn-out, but desperately needed, warships, planes and some food; the Americans the technology they so desired: the cavity magnetron that allowed radar to detect enemy aircraft and ships, the plans to Frank Whittle's jet engine, gyroscopic gunsights, submarine detection devices, self-sealing fuel tanks and plastic explosive and a memorandum describing the feasibility of an atomic bomb. When Philip and his colleagues returned to Britain and informed the government of the results of their negotiations, some members of the cabinet coughed and spluttered. They said that the United States had demanded and obtained Britain's secret technology in return for 'a few rusty ships and food to feed the population for a couple of months, when the Americans could have spared a billion dollars, or two, as a gift.'

Turning away from his wife's portrait Philip bent down and picked up his bag, placed the paper inside and closed it.

He was now ready for his meeting with the prime minister. It would not be an easy meeting. Philip had to explain to Winston Churchill that Britain's debt was fast approaching a figure when it would be bankrupt. A situation last reached when it had been at war with another corporal who thought he could unite Europe, one Napoleon Bonaparte.

The study door opened and he looked up to see his daughter-in-law walk into the room. Philip liked Juliette. She had been an efficient and hard worker at Tagleva's office in Paris. When his son arrived in London from France it seemed natural his future daughter-in-law should become his secretary. It was a decision he had never regretted.

'Good morning,' Juliette said in her soft French accent.

'Thank you for preparing my papers for today's meetings. Doubtless I'll have lots of work for us both to do when I return, so I suggest you take the rest of the day off. What will you do?'

'Sophie's off to the East End to meet some families the Tagleva Foundation has been helping. So, as I'm free, I'll go with her and see if I can help.'

'That's fine then. I'll see you later and hope you both have a good day.'

Twenty minutes later Philip left the house in Mayfair and walked the short distance to the Cabinet War Rooms and his meeting with the prime minister.

After Philip left, Juliette spent a few minutes tidying some papers before closing the study door and walking across the hallway to the sitting room. Juliette saw her mother-in-law with straight back and perfectly coiffured golden hair with just a hint of grey sitting on the sofa reading the *Daily Express* newspaper.

Juliette smiled as she remembered how nervous she had been when first introduced to Michael's mother. Her only experience of mother-in-law relationships had been her mother's with her paternal grandmother and she dreaded the thought that her own might be as fractious. She need not have worried. After she addressed Sophie using her correct title of Countess

Tagleva, Sophie replied, 'My dear, let's not worry about all that nonsense. Just call me Sophie.'

From that moment onwards it seemed Sophie delighted in spending time with her future daughter-in-law. Their days would often start at Le Dôme Café where Sophie introduced Juliette to the painters, sculptors and dealers that supplied the Tagleva Foundation with works of art, including Jean-Paul Sartre and Pablo Picasso. In the afternoon they would walk along the Place Vendôme and pop into the fashion houses of Chanel or Schiaparelli. The excitement of being engaged to be married came to an abrupt end when Britain declared war on Germany and the Tagleva family were in London while she was still in Paris.

Separated from Michael, Juliette had been desperately lonely, not helped by the unwelcome attention she attracted from German soldiers who worked at the Tagleva bank. The first she knew of Michael's involvement in clandestine operations was when, months after the Germans had occupied it, he appeared in Paris. A few weeks later they were both travelling, with false papers, through France into neutral Spain and Gibraltar and from there by ship back to England. Once in England she discovered that her mother-in-law was an expert at extracting gossip from even her most tight-lipped friend, and Juliette stood no chance of keeping their escape from occupied France secret. It was not long before she was recounting their adventures to Sophie. Sophie listened attentively to how Juliette and Michael spent a night in a convent, slept in a haystack and hid in a farm building as it was being searched by the French police. But the story Sophie most enjoyed was their crossing the Pyrenees on donkeys and how Michael's beast, a particularly ill-tempered animal, had thrown its saddle depositing her son in the middle of a large gorse bush. When Juliette told her how Michael had cursed the animal all the way to Spain, regularly whispering in the animal's ear that any repeat of the deed would result in its immediate dispatch to the knacker's yard, Sophie had to wipe the tears of laughter from her face.

The morning Michael and Juliette married, in the Russian Orthodox Cathedral in Knightsbridge, Sophie presented her with a pair of sapphire and diamond bracelets with matching earrings made by Bolins, the family of Swedish jewellers who had settled in Russia several decades before Fabergé.

When Sophie saw Juliette walk into the room, she put down the newspaper, smiled and asked, 'So what are you and I doing today to help the war effort?'

Chapter Five

Paris, 20 May 1944

Jean-Claude left the bank early, walked through one of the Palais-Royal's arcades and joined the queue outside a boulangerie that baked bread during the afternoon. After queuing for over an hour there were still eight people in front of him. The time spent waiting fed his anxiety that he might arrive at the counter and there would be no bread to buy; it made him increasingly intolerant of the others in the queue. When a woman opened her purse as she arrived at the counter and then fiddled with out-of-date ration coupons he clenched his teeth, when a man asked inane questions of the shopkeeper he made a tight fist of his hand. He approved when an old man, wearing his old military decorations in an effort to cut into the head of the queue, was firmly dispatched to the back of the line by the others. Through all this he became fixated by the man in front wearing a jacket with the right elbow a shade lighter than the left and decided he would check his own jackets to see if they were the same. After finally collecting his bread, he pulled his jacket collar up to protect him from the chill wind of the evening and with drooped shoulders and his chin clamped firmly to his chest tramped home angry that the past hour could have been spent more usefully. As he opened the wrought iron and glass front door to the apartment block, entered the white marble-clad lobby and called the elevator he decided that he would advertise for a housekeeper to undertake the chores of daily shopping and keeping the apartment clean. It was with relief that once inside his apartment Jean-Claude was able to close the door on the outside world.

After putting the bread in the kitchen, Jean-Claude went to the bedroom and changed his shoes into more casual slippers trying to ignore the holes that were beginning to form where his big toes were. He walked to the living room, sat down on one of the art deco sofas and stared out of the window towards the Eiffel Tower in the distance. It had only been a couple of days since Sébastien left Paris, but he felt the ache of his absence and wanted so much to have him to talk to that for the past two nights he had comforted himself by pulling Sébastien's pillow to him and cradling it until the morning. The tranquillity was disturbed by a loud knock on the front door.

Jean-Claude sighed, rose out of his chair and walked towards the intrusive noise and opened the door.

'May I come in?' asked the police inspector.

A flicker of a smile played on Halder's lips and Jean-Claude was convinced the policeman had seen the surprise that must have registered on his face, but he managed to gather his composure and usher the policeman inside.

'I'm sorry I can't offer you a drink, I have nothing in the apartment.'

The Gestapo man removed his trilby hat saying, 'Refreshments won't be necessary, I won't be staying long. After our lunch the other day I've been thinking and I have one more question.'

Jean-Claude raised his eyebrows and waited.

'How much money do you think is needed to finance a Resistance group?'

'I haven't thought about it… a lot I guess. I really couldn't speculate. Thousands, possibly hundreds of thousands of francs,' answered Jean-Claude.

'You're probably right. It's interesting because it occurs to me that vast quantities of bulky cash would be difficult to hide. It therefore surprises me that when we arrest groups of resistors so little money is ever found. It's a problem. Still, there it is.'

Halder began to walk out of the room and back towards the hallway.

'Was that all you wanted?' asked Jean-Claude surprised by the brevity of the meeting.

'Oh, yes. I was just passing and thought I'd ask your opinion. I hope I haven't disturbed you.'

'Do you live near Rue le Tasse?'

'No, in fact I live in the opposite direction but the rain has stopped for the moment and I fancied a walk around the Eiffel Tower,' came the reply.

Jean-Claude escorted him to the front door.

Before stepping into the hallway the policeman paused. 'By the way, did you hear about the arrest of two radio operators in Lyon, part of the Michelle Group? After their interrogation the Gestapo was able to arrest twenty more members of the group. I probably don't need to tell you, as you will have guessed, that when the Gestapo arrests one member of a gang of criminals it inevitably leads to others.'

Jean-Claude felt the policeman's green eyes bore into him.

'I don't suppose you will have heard of the Michelle Group?'

Jean-Claude shook his head.

'And you won't, in the next few days most will be shot. But I mustn't keep you any longer. I'll bid you goodnight. And be careful, monsieur, we live in dangerous times.' The policeman put his hat on and walked towards the elevator.

As Jean-Claude watched the policeman leave, he thought a housekeeper who could inform the authorities of his movements and visitors might be a danger best avoided, he would do his own shopping and laundry.

That night Jean-Claude had a troubled night's sleep and despite feeling tired rose early to prepare to go out. On one corner of a street he bought a copy of *Le Figaro* and, hunched against the rain, walked to Café Floré. The German's occupation had done nothing to dent the Parisian café being a centre of social life in Paris, as a rendezvous spot, a place to relax, to refuel and pick up some gossip. Jean-Claude particularly liked Café Floré on the Boulevard Saint-Germain because it was well heated and not frequented by the Germans who preferred the Café Deux Magots further up the road. As he walked into the café Jean-Claude spied an empty table near the kitchen and sat down. A waiter, dressed in his uniform of white shirt, black waistcoat and a white apron to his ankles, approached to take Jean-Claude's order. After ordering a coffee he opened the newspaper and began to read the headlines. The coffee arrived with a glass of water and the waiter pushed a small piece of paper with the bill under the sugar bowl that hadn't contained sugar for over two years.

Despite the newspaper being open Jean-Claude wasn't reading the news, he was thinking of Halder's comment the night before, the words that had played in his mind all night, *a group of resistors is vulnerable if one member of a group is captured and talks*. Jean-Claude drank some of the coffee and took a sip of water to take away the revolting taste of chicory. He was also troubled that the policeman was chasing the money that financed the Resistance. Resistance is an expensive business. People had to be compensated for not working, safe houses had to be rented, officials bribed and there had to be money to pay the hundreds of other minor expenses. If Halder could cut off the money that financed a network, then any serious resistance against the Germans would collapse.

Jean-Claude saw the man he was expecting enter the café. He drained the cup of the bitter liquid and replaced the cup, not in its saucer, but upside down on the table then stood, picked up his raincoat, tossed thirty centimes onto the table and left. The man Jean-Claude was to meet took a seat at a nearby table.

With his coat collar pulled up around his ears to protect him from the rain, Jean-Claude walked past the Louvre. He was not sure what alerted him to the presence of someone else, but he was aware of the distinct creeping sensation when you know someone's following you.

He turned a corner and hurriedly stepped into the large entrance of an office building and pressed himself into the shadows. Seconds later the man following him rushed past. Jean-Claude waited a short while and when he was sure he had lost his tail doubled back. After checking a number of times he was no longer being followed, he eventually turned into Rue Chabanais and, ignoring the brothel at number 12 said to be the most luxurious *house of tolerance* in Paris, walked into one of the buildings opposite. Climbing the stairs to the second floor he waited on the landing. Satisfied no one had entered the building behind him he climbed to the third floor and knocked the code onto the door.

The door was opened by Alain; Jean-Claude entered the apartment, removing his trilby hat he shook off the rain, took off his overcoat and hung them on the coat-hook by the door. Once done he shook hands with the only other person to know all the secrets of the network. Jean-Claude had been friends with Alain, and his lover Luc, since they had rescued a young man called Helmut Becker from Nazi persecution in Germany before the war. Having successfully saved one person it was not long before a regular stream of people considered non-Aryan were being rescued. Once the war started, the network changed their operation to hiding Jews from the Germans and, eventually, Allied airmen shot down by the Luftwaffe, to return them to the United Kingdom so that they could fight again.

'After you left the Café Floré a man followed you, by the way he was dressed, I would guess he was a Gestapo agent,' said Alain.

Jean-Claude smiled. 'He was a Gestapo agent and I managed to lose him around the streets near the Louvre, but I also had the strange impression he wasn't making much of an effort to hide the fact he was following me. No doubt my actions will only serve to heighten the Gestapo's interest in me. Anyhow, it had to be done if I was to speak to you.'

Jean-Claude watched Alain prepare himself for bad news.

'Last night I had a visit from the Gestapo and we now know I'm being followed, which means I'm under suspicion and it's too dangerous for me to be in contact with anyone involved with Liferaft.'

'What do you want me to do?' asked Alain.

'You have to take charge of the network. No one is to contact me and everyone involved must be prepared to initiate the plan to scatter. If I'm arrested Liferaft's work must continue but it's vital that even under torture I can't reveal where our people are.'

'I'll make the necessary preparations.'

'Secondly, make sure Samuel and his family are safe. He's too valuable to Liferaft. The forged documents he produces are essential to running the escape line and he knows too much about us to have the Gestapo capture him. I want you to move Samuel and his family to a safe house, one I don't know about.'

'I'll do that, but I must tell you Samuel's not well. He's very stressed by the continual round-ups. As a Jew, he knows there's only one destination for him and his wife and children if he's captured.'

'I know it's hard on them being hidden away. See if you can get a doctor to him, but you must avoid his capture at all costs.'

Jean-Claude changed the topic. 'How many strays is Liferaft currently caring for?'

'In all twenty-seven aircrew, twenty-two British, four Americans and one Canadian, then there's six escaped prisoners of war, all somewhere along the line. Apart from Samuel and his family, there are seven Jews hidden in safe houses.'

Jean-Claude nodded. 'Move the airmen down the line as fast as you can. The further down the line the less likely they are to be captured if Liferaft is broken by the Gestapo.'

'The ones we have now can be moved but each day brings more aircrew needing to be rescued. If Liferaft is broken, some will have to get used to spending the rest of the war as German prisoners.'

'You're right, but see what you can do. Next I want you to get a message to London. Inform them the Michelle Group has been broken by the Gestapo and most of its members have been arrested.'

'I'll tell Luc to send the message tonight,' said Alain.

'Lastly, you need a signal so you know if I'm still free or if the Gestapo have arrested me. There's a large glass vase in the window of my living room. Each evening I'll change the vase for one of a different shape and colour, either blue or red. If the colour remains the same for two days in a row, you'll know the Gestapo have arrested me or that they're controlling me. If that happens, no one's to contact me, no matter what the emergency.'

Alain nodded. 'It's only a few people who know you're the head of Liferaft but I'll make sure they all know your orders.'

Jean-Claude pulled a brown envelope from his jacket pocket and passed it to Alain.

'Here are French francs and German deutschmarks. It's more than usual, but it may be some time before I'll be able to get you more. I'll leave you to distribute it.'

They hugged each other and Jean-Claude left the apartment and walked into the driving rain once more.

Chapter Six

21 May 1944

Julius Halder stuffed the paper into the envelope, sealed it, placed it against the inkwell on his desk and stared at it. Two months ago he'd attended the conference in Rome to discuss defeating the Resistance in occupied territories. The police chiefs from important territories including Prague in Bohemia, the general government area previously known as Poland and Brussels in Belgium, had all spoken on the problems of population control, but the man Julius had found most interesting was Lieutenant Colonel Herbert Kappler. Kappler's problems were unique in that he had to prevent escaped Allied prisoners, Jews and refugees seeking refuge within the neutral territory of the Vatican. Julius paid close attention as Kappler detailed how the underground organisation was run and financed by senior members of the clergy and some members of the diplomatic corps within the Holy See. Kappler had told the conference that, despite the Vatican's neutrality, he had managed to recapture escaped POWs, deport Jews to concentration camps and exploit the general population. However, in a private meeting Kappler had admitted to Halder that he'd failed to bring an end to the network and the activities of the rescue organisation was still up and running.

'The problem is my inability to arrest the priest who acts as leader and banker to the group. If I could stop the money, I could easily defeat him,' Kappler had confided to him.

'Couldn't you ignore Vatican neutrality and arrest the priest?' asked Julius.

'If only I could. But there are too many Catholics among the German High Command and senior members of the Nazi party. They'd be outraged at such an act against the sanctity of the Church and I'd probably end up being shot.'

On his return to Paris, Julius Halder began to pay increased attention to how the Resistance was financed and those people most likely to be controlling the money. It was a frustrating task because whenever a resistant was arrested it never led him to the source of the money or anyone who distributed it to the organisation.

He was about to give up his line of investigation until one evening when he was invited to dinner with a group of Gestapo and SS officers at one of Paris's grand brasseries, Le Grand Colbert. A couple of the SS men brightened what might otherwise have been a boring evening by bringing their French mistresses. One, Nicole Labranche, a pretty girl who worked as a secretary was particularly effervescent and kept everyone amused with her flirtatious stories. At one point in the evening the German officers began to discuss the name of the most intelligent man in Germany, after the Führer of course. One officer proposed Alfred Baeumler, the German philosopher, another Ernst Rudolf Huber, the lawyer who created the legal structure to anchor Adolf Hitler's dictatorship as the source of all legitimate power in Germany, a third proposed Emile Burnouf, the racialist whose ideas had led to the theosophy of Aryanism. The debate was interrupted by Nicole Labranche who laughingly stated there was one Frenchman who ranked equally among all the Germans mentioned. The SS officers paused their debate and playfully indulged her opinion by asking which Frenchman she would nominate, expecting her to suggest Maurice Chevalier, the popular cabaret singer and entertainer or René Descartes or perhaps Jean-Jacques Rousseau. Instead she said, 'Jean-Claude Moreau, the managing director of the Tagleva bank.'

The SS officers looked at each other with incredulous expressions.

'Why, what's so special about this banker?' asked one German officer.

'I work at the bank and know he has a brilliant mind for finance and could, quite possibly, run two or even three organisations without having to commit a single fact to paper,' she replied.

Every man at the table laughingly dismissed her idea as fanciful and continued the debate, except Julius Halder who made a mental note that if the man was as brilliant and intelligent as she said then he was worth investigating further.

Over the following weeks Julius looked into Jean-Claude's career and connections. To all appearances Jean-Claude Moreau seemed to be a useful servant of the Reich and model citizen his only crimes being his homosexuality and occasionally using the black market, neither of which interested the policeman. He seemed above suspicion… until the previous day when he appeared to have purposely lost the man ordered to follow him. That act in itself could be an excuse to arrest Jean-Claude. Julius knew he didn't have Kappler's constraints to prevent him walking into the Tagleva bank and arresting Jean-Claude Moreau. Nevertheless, the banker worked for the SS and developed some powerful contacts among senior German staff officers for whom he had arranged profitable investments. Julius knew he had to be sure of his facts before taking action. He picked up the envelope containing the arrest warrant and placed it carefully inside Jean-Claude's file that had started with a single sheet of paper and was now three centimetres thick.

Chapter Seven

London, 26 May 1944

For the past ten days Major Michael Tagleva knew he had to leave for France and was not looking forward to explaining to Juliette the war was to part them once again. When they fell in love, like so many other couples, they promised never to have secrets from each other. As he walked home the fact he would have to lie about being sent to occupied France irritated him more than anything else; it made him feel deceitful.

Michael entered the drawing room. His mother and Juliette were sitting on the sofa by the fire with his father standing with his back to the unlit fireplace. As he entered his mother stood up. 'I have to go and check on dinner, Philip why don't you come with me?'

'Oh, yes, of course,' his father said placing a half-full glass of whisky on the mantelpiece and following his wife out of the room.

When they were alone Michael said, 'My parents are behaving very strangely, is there something wrong?'

Juliette smiled and tapped the seat next to her. 'I have something to say to you.'

'This is all very serious. Are you're divorcing me so soon?' he laughed.

'Don't be stupid. I just want us to have a talk.'

'So it's *that* serious,' he said adopting an expression of playful sternness as he sat next to her.

'Now do behave,' said Juliette. 'I went to the doctor this morning, just for a check-up.'

Michael's playful look was replaced by genuine concern. 'You're keeping me in suspense.'

'I would have told you first but your mother's very observant. So I'm afraid your parents know before you. You're going to be a father.'

'Oh, my darling, how wonderful,' he said enveloping Juliette in his arms.

The news he was going away would be even more difficult to deliver now. How he hated this war.

On 29 May 1944 Michael received his final briefing from Tim Wilson. Afterwards they inspected the equipment Michael would parachute into France with.

First he checked the weapons. The Welrod bolt-action pistol with a sound suppressor, perfect for a silent kill, the Fairbairn-Sykes fighting dagger with its razor-sharp point, a four-inch thumb dagger designed to be hidden in the lapel of a jacket and boot laces with metal thread running through them that could be used to silently garrotte an enemy. Michael checked the biscuit tin that cleverly disguised a radio and paid particular attention to the civilian clothes ensuring labels such as Marks & Spencer or Army and Navy, which would betray him if found by a German intelligence officer, had been removed; he found none. He picked up his identity card. In the top left corner was a poor black and white photo of him in profile, an official stamp from the Prefecture de Paris correctly covered part of the photo and in the space provided, was his thumbprint, it was an excellent forgery. Next he turned to the *Carte de Vêtements*, the clothing ration card, with some pink clothing ration coupons glued to the inside left edge. Finally, he studied the *Certificat de Recensement*, his exemption from the requirements of compulsory labour service in Germany, if stopped by the police it would be the one document that would save him from immediate deportation to Germany.

'It all looks good,' he said.

He picked up a small bottle of pills off the table, Benzedrine to keep him awake when necessary. Then the small metal cylinder with a little rubber cover, his 'L' tablet. He opened it and looked at the cyanide suicide pill. If captured he need only bite down on it and he would be dead within fifteen seconds. He passed it to the man next to him.

'I won't need this.'

'Are you're sure?'
'I'm sure,' replied Michael.

The following day as the Halifax bomber crossed the coast of France it steadied itself at an altitude of four hundred feet to avoid detection by enemy radar. As the plane approached the drop point the dispatcher handed Michael a hot toddy with a liberal amount of rum in it. Michael drank it down in one, and followed him to the back of the plane. The dispatcher attached the top of Michael's D-Bag to the static line that would pull open the parachute immediately he left the aircraft and went to great trouble to show Michael that he was well attached. Through his headphones the dispatcher heard the call from the pilot and opened a trapdoor in the floor of the fuselage. Michael felt the cold night air rush up to meet him and was thankful for the drink of hot rum. When the red light came on, he sat with his legs dangling over the edge of the hole, looking steadfastly at the red light and waiting for it to turn green. The red light began to flash. The plane's engines were cut to slow the speed and ensure Michael would go out straight down through the hole and not get caught up in the aircraft's slipstream. There was a loud buzz, the red light turned green, Michael raised himself up on his hands and dropped into the darkness. His face was lashed with rain, the goggles steamed up. Suddenly he felt the static line become taut, pull the D-Bag and he looked up to see the parachute blossom open above him. Then Michael felt an upward jerk and the harness cut into his armpits and crotch and his breath left him. Fifteen seconds later and hardly having recovered his breath Michael hit the muddy ground. There was no time to delay, landing was the most dangerous time and he began gathering up the parachute silk so it could be buried, along with his 'striptease suit', the nickname given to his flying suit because it wasn't worn long after landing. The two metal cylinders containing his clothes, radio and weapons landed a few hundred yards away. They were already being collected by some of the reception committee that signalled the landing site to the pilot.

A tall man in a heavy coat, wearing a beret approached and held out a hand.

'Welcome to France, monsieur. You can call me Jacques. Don't worry about your parachute and flying suit, my men will dispose of them for you, but we must move you away. The Boche have patrols in the area and will have heard the plane.'

The next few hours were a complete confusion to Michael. First he was driven to a farm where he was given a meal of an omelette and some bread by a middle-aged woman who didn't reply when he asked her name.

Jacques smiled. 'If she tells you her name and you're captured, you can tell the Germans. Anyway you won't be here long enough to make friends or romantic liaisons. We leave for Paris in an hour.'

'Paris? I thought you operated from this farm,' said Michael.

Jacques looked around the farmhouse kitchen as if the prospect wouldn't displease him.

'No. We're just here long enough for the German patrols to stop looking for you.'

As he ate, Michael studied Jacques. He was a thick-set man with large thighs gained, Michael guessed, from thousands of kilometres he'd cycled as a youth. Most noticeable and theatrical was a nose that stuck out from his red face like a beak, hooked, not in a regal way, but protruding above an unkempt grey beard covering the lower part of his face and falling to his chest. The vision reminded Michael of a bearded Mr Punch.

Later the following afternoon Jacques and Michael left the farmhouse and travelled to Paris. Michael carried a small bag with some clothes and his weapons. He was told by Jacques the remainder of his equipment would follow piece by piece so as not to run the risk of it all being found by a police patrol. A couple of hours later, they arrived near the railway station of Belleville-Villette in the 19th arrondissement of Paris. Jacques walked Michael down the Rue de Crimée and into a small restaurant called Le Gasconne. Once inside Michael found himself in a narrow room wide enough to accommodate a single table on either side with a small bar at the far end. Michael estimated the restaurant would accommodate around twenty diners. As he followed Jacques towards the bar he glanced at the walls covered in green ceramic tiles framing a few tiled scenes of old Paris. Michael thought it might have once have been an impressive room, but years of little investment had taken its toll. A few of the tiles on the walls were chipped, the tables and chairs were of different styles, the red and white check tablecloths seemed faded and the gilded mirror above the bar betrayed a thick layer of dust.

'Welcome to my restaurant,' said Jacques.

At that moment, a girl in her twenties, wearing a blue floral patterned apron, appeared from what Michael assumed to be the kitchen.

'This is my daughter, and our chef,' said Jacques.

Michael smiled at the girl whose pretty face was a complete contrast to her father's and she smiled back in a disarming manner, which Michael assumed she gave to all the customers, before picking up a plate from the bar and returning to the kitchen. Jacques collected a bottle of wine and two glasses from the bar, motioned Michael to a table and sat opposite him. The two glasses were filled with the red liquid and Jacques indicated to Michael to drink.

'It's safe here. The Boche tend to avoid the place. Now and again a couple might wander in, but most take one look at the place and walk out. If ever they are brave enough to stay, my wife takes their order and serves at table, but as she doesn't speak German it usually takes a very long time. Then when the food eventually arrives, the Germans always complain, some say the food is so bad they refuse to pay. I can't blame them – my daughter's a terrible cook.' Jacques shook his head and laughed.

Michael smiled. 'I have some instructions for you from London and we need to discuss them.'

He was interrupted by Jacques' daughter arriving with two bowls of soup and chunks of bread, which she placed before them.

'There will be time enough to discuss plans tomorrow. First, we eat.'

Jacques lifted his glass of wine, took a gulp and refilled his glass.

Michael looked at the soup, remembering what Jacques had said about his daughter's cooking.

'Go on, eat,' encouraged his host.

He hesitantly picked up his spoon and dipped it into the liquid.

'This is delicious. How can the Germans not like it?' asked Michael after the first spoonful.

'My daughter reserves a large pot of rancid butter which she uses to cook food ordered by our glorious occupiers. For some reason they don't seem to enjoy the taste.' Jacques laughed again.

Chapter Eight

The Atlantic Wall, France, 1 June 1944

Carl Bernstorff stood on the dunes above the beach, his coat collar pulled up to protect him from the lashing rain. Despite the summer month the weather had been foul for weeks, but it didn't worry him – the weather in Russia had been far worse.

So far Bernstorff's war had been a mixture of ambition and luck. Ambition had motivated him to join the Waffen-SS and luck that he'd been attached to the elite tank division the 2nd SS Panzer Division Das Reich. The first time Bernstorff climbed into a panzer tank he felt an immediate affinity for the machine as if it were a living thing to be cherished and would often stroke and pat it as if it were a prize stallion. He loved the power emanating from deep within the engine, the vibrations as it rumbled over the ground, the smells of gunpowder from the shells after they were fired and the odour from the sweat that ran off the other men in the cramped space during the heat of battle. It was during the first battles in France, as his tank ripped through the French and British infantry, that he first noticed the tingling sensation run through his entire body, a sensation he had never experienced in the bedroom. It was a sensation he craved again and again, and when the battles in the west were won the yearning for it made him volunteer his unit to fight on the eastern front. In Russia Bernstorff never complained about the spring mud that could pull a man's boots off as he waded through it; the clouds of flies that fed on every bead of sweat in the summer; the bitter cold of the autumn wind as it ate into the very marrow of one's bones or the winter snow that would blind a man if he lost his goggles. To Bernstorff these hardships only served to heighten his lust and the satisfaction he felt as his panzers ploughed an orgiastic furrow through Russia, laying waste Sniatin, Kharkov and all the land between until his unit finally arrived at Stalingrad.

Those he commanded saw him as a Herculean leader and talked about his exploits between themselves with the same veneration that the Roman legionnaires had once spoken about Julius Caesar and his victories in Gaul and Egypt. The story most often recounted was the incident outside Vinnitsa when Bernstorff's panzers had become stuck in mud and a group of Russian infantry decided that the predicament left the panzers vulnerable. As the Russians approached, Bernstorff recognised the danger to his beloved steeds. Leaping down from his panzer onto the leading Russian, he thrust his dagger into the soldier's neck and, picking up the dead Russian's Simonov AVS-36 rifle, shot two others before fighting hand-to-hand with three more, the only surviving Russian ran away. For his bravery, and in a glittering ceremony, Adolf Hitler personally pinned the Close Combat Clasp, Silver Class, to his chest. His reputation for bravery and as a leader was such that, if he so ordered, his men would follow him through the gates of hell itself.

If there was one piece of bad luck Bernstorff would have changed it would be the silver Wound Badge he wore on the lower left breast of his uniform. A Russian grenade had resulted in the loss of his left arm, a wound to his leg causing him to walk with a limp and disfigurement to the left side of his face. No longer fit to fight on the Russian front he and his panzers had been transferred to France, to await the invasion by the Allies.

In France Field Marshal Erwin Rommel appointed him to use his experiences in Russia to supervise construction of the defences along part of the Atlantic Wall on the French coast. Like Rommel, Bernstorff knew the war would be won or lost on the landing beaches, that if the Allies gained a foothold on the continent their manpower and air superiority would eventually overwhelm the German forces. Bernstorff threw himself into the task of building the defences for the French beaches knowing that the best chance to prevent a German defeat would be to cut down the Allied troops while they were in the water, struggling with their rifles and equipment to get ashore. Bernstorff designed obstacles to snare landing craft as they approached the beach, and ordered German engineers to lay millions of anti-personnel mines in the sand. Behind the mines tank traps were constructed and at the top of the beach Bernstorff ordered labourers to pour thousands of tons of concrete to build pillboxes, observation bunkers, communication trenches and machine-gun nests with interlocking fields of fire. Squinting through the rain he looked with satisfaction at the rivers of barbed wire and the gun emplacements with their guns pointed out to sea. He'd seen enough and, turning to the three junior officers, smiled his approval. He looked at his watch. If he delayed longer he would be late for the war games exercise and began to walk to the staff car. Passing a machine-gun pillbox Bernstorff saw three men huddled together in a vain attempt to stay warm from the cold wind sweeping in from the Atlantic. Their bare feet, shaved heads, striped jacket and trousers identified them as Russian prisoners from the Lager Norderney slave labour camp on Alderney.

'What are *they* doing here?' Bernstorff asked one of his men.

'I don't know,' came the reply.

'They should have been taken back to Alderney – somebody's been inefficient. But there's no point in having a boat waste everybody's time taking them back now. Find somewhere quiet where the French labourers won't see or hear, and shoot them. Then dump their bodies into the concrete completing the final gun emplacement. They may as well be more useful in death than ever they could have been in life.'

As the Russians were marched away Bernstorff walked to the staff car. Before ordering his driver to take him to his meeting he sat in the back, picked up his briefcase from the passenger seat, took out a syringe and a glass vial. He steadied the vial containing morphine sulphate between his knees, broke the cork stopper and inserted the syringe into the liquid. Once the syringe was full, he pulled aside his breeches to expose an inch of flesh and injected it into his thigh. The relief to the pain in his leg was immediate.

Chapter Nine

Gestapo headquarters, Paris, 4 June 1944

Halder had spent the past couple of hours watching the interrogation of a young man suspected of having links to a Resistance group. The interrogation took the familiar pattern. The prisoner's resolve had been weakened by isolated incarceration for a couple of days with nothing to do except look at the walls; the intention was that the young man would become increasingly fearful for what was to come. When finally dragged from his cell he would be questioned by teams of interrogators for the next twenty-four hours without food or rest. It started with a continuous bombardment of questions interspersed with threats and the examiners appearing to lose their temper, a form of mental violence. Halder admired the length of time the young man had resisted answering the questions put to him. He stayed to watch as the second, more physical, stage began. The prisoner was forced to stand for more than an hour with his hands over his head as the questions continued. Still he refused to speak and so he was hung from the ceiling by handcuffs with spikes inside them and was beaten with a rubber truncheon. Halder didn't entirely support the cruder methods of interrogation used by the Gestapo and when the young man fainted Halder left. He didn't want to watch the final stage, when the prisoner would be stripped naked, his legs tied to a bar attached to a chain in the ceiling and his body lifted into a tub filled with freezing water. The interrogators had only to pull on the chain for the prisoner's head to be pulled underwater by his feet. It was usually at this point even the most stubborn prisoner began to talk.

Julius returned to his office and leafed through the file of the young resistant. He looked at the photograph of the fresh-faced boy, only seventeen, arrested for handing out communist leaflets outside the Gare de l'Est railway station. *What a waste of a life,* Halder said to himself. After satisfactorily answering the questions put to him, the boy would then be executed the following day. Halder replaced the photograph into the file and closed it. He glanced at the wall-clock above the doorway; it was time for him to go to the Tagleva bank in Rue Pierre Charron. He would have preferred to walk, to clear his lungs of the stale air of the interrogation room, but it was still raining and so he donned his leather coat and trilby hat and walked down the stairs to the car. Arriving at the Tagleva bank he was immediately shown into Jean-Claude's office.

'We meet again, and so soon,' said Jean-Claude shaking the policeman's hand. As he sat down in the seat proffered by Jean-Claude, Julius noticed the blue silk of the chair was worn at the edges. It prompted him to look around the office, the leather on the antique desk was covered in water stains, one edge of the blue and white Persian carpet on the floor had been attacked by moths and some of the gilding on the mirror over the mantelpiece had begun to turn black. Looking behind Jean-Claude he saw the familiar portrait of the Führer on the wall.

'It's a good likeness,' said Halder indicating towards the picture.

Jean-Claude didn't turn around.

'It replaces a particularly fine scene of domestic life by the Dutch artist Anthonie Palamedes. I'm informed the masterpiece is to hang in the Führer's art gallery that's planned to be built in his hometown of Linz.'

Julius chuckled. 'I'm sure you consider the Führer's portrait a more appropriate and pleasing adornment for your office than a Dutch representation of domestic bliss.'

Jean-Claude forced a smile.

'I've come to see you because I'm told your friend Sébastien hasn't been seen for some time.'

'He's left the apartment. We had a disagreement,' answered Jean-Claude.

'Oh, I'm sorry. Will he be returning?'

'I doubt it, it was a serious argument.'

'I won't be impolite as to enquire what the argument was about, but do you know where he's gone?'

'No, and I don't much care.'

'I see. Then I'll come to the real reason for my visit. I want your opinion of these.'

Julius Halder passed over two banknotes.

Jean-Claude picked up a magnifying glass and studied them.

'These are twenty-Reichsmark notes,' he said, 'introduced in 1939 with the design and engraving taken from an unissued Austrian note. The front depicts a young woman holding edelweiss and, as I would expect, there's a large swastika under-print. As far as I can tell, it's not a forgery.'

'Oh, they're real banknotes all right. We recovered over a hundred of them from a man stopped at a checkpoint yesterday. He's currently at Gestapo headquarters and will be interrogated in the morning.'

'That's a lot of money,' said Jean-Claude

'Equivalent to forty thousand French francs at the official occupation fixed rate. The question is how does a Frenchman get hold of such a large amount of money?'

'I've no idea. Perhaps he's involved with the black market.'

The policeman pursed his lips. 'His name is Antoine Desforges and I don't think he's a black marketer.'

'Could this be the Resistance banker you're looking for?' enquired Jean-Claude.

'No, he's small fry, a cobbler with little education, almost illiterate. The banker I'm looking for would be far more intelligent than Desforges. He's more likely a courier, moving money about Paris for the Resistance.'

'Can I ask, Inspector, why are you telling me this?'

'Oh, I'm sorry, I didn't explain. I was wondering if you might know this Antoine Desforges.'

'Not personally. Would you like me to check if he has an account at the Tagleva bank?'

'That would be most useful.'

Jean-Claude picked up the phone and spoke to his secretary. Julius and Jean-Claude sat in silence looking at each other. After a few minutes the secretary entered the office and handed Jean-Claude a piece of paper.

'I'm sorry, there is no such account at the Tagleva bank under that name,' said Jean-Claude passing the note to Julius.

'I would have been surprised if there had been. As the Tagleva bank manages the SS finances in Paris it would be too ironic if the Resistance banked here too. Never mind, I'll keep looking. Once again, thank you for your help.'

****

The following day Antoine Desforges was taken from the cell he shared with a rat and more than a few cockroaches and dragged to another room. As his head was pushed backwards into the water he took a deep breath. Through the water he could see the distorted shapes of his tormentors hovering above him. He held onto the precious oxygen as long as he could; when he couldn't hold his breath any longer his mouth opened. The precious air escaped and icy water streamed into his lungs, he was drowning, losing consciousness. He was dying and began a desperate struggle, but was held in a vice-like grip by the metal pole strapped to his ankles. Suddenly he was pulled out of the water. Coughing up some water from his lungs he desperately gulped in some air. Then, without warning, he found himself under the freezing water again.

Chapter Ten

5 June 1944

Michael, Jacques and three members of his resistance group were sitting in a room above the restaurant. It was late into the evening and they were discussing the targets London expected Jacques' group to attack when the Allies landed in France.

'When the Allies begin the invasion we should announce a general strike. Every citizen must attack the Germans,' said one of Jacques' men.

Michael shook his head. 'That would be a mistake. The Allies will be fighting to get off the beaches and consolidate a bridgehead; it may be weeks before they're able to liberate Paris. If you organise an uprising before the Allies are able to give support, the Germans will take massive reprisals and people will sacrifice their lives for no reason.'

'But we've waited too long not to fight,' another of Jacques' men protested.

'I understand your frustration and it's not a question of fighting or not fighting but having a gradual, phased insurrection, in line with the advance of the Allied force,' argued Michael.

'I know you're right, Major. But after four years of occupation we're all impatient to take our revenge and kick the Boche bastards out of France,' said Jacques.

'You'll get your wish and soon enough, I promise.'

Michael looked at the three resistants in turn. They seemed to have reluctantly accepted his argument against an insurrection.

Michael continued the briefing. 'Ninety per cent of the German army and its equipment are transported by rail. When the Allies begin their liberation of France, London wants us to attack the railways. By crippling the railway network the Germans will be prevented from bringing up reinforcements and the Allies will be given vital hours to fight their way off the landing beaches.'

'I suppose you're right,' said one of the men and the remainder nodded.

Relieved, Michael spread out a map over the table and began to point out the targets they would attack.

It was late when he finished the briefing. As Jacques opened a bottle of wine one of the men brought over the radio to the kitchen table and they huddled around it to listen to the news from London. Through the crackle they strained to hear the words of the BBC announcer. Once the news finished they heard the phrase they were waiting for, *'Ici Londres! Et voici quelques messages personnel.'* There followed fifteen minutes containing over two hundred coded messages, *'The chair is against the wall… John has a long moustache… It's hot in Cairo…'* In the middle the announcer spoke seven words from Paul Verlaine's poem 'Chanson d'Automne': *'Wounds my heart in a monotonous languor'.*

At the end of the message everyone around the table looked at each other. Someone asked if they had heard the message correctly, and once it had been confirmed Jacques' men began to sing and dance. He had to shout above the noise to calm the enthusiasm.

'It's too early to celebrate. Now the Allies are coming there's work to do.'

****

Bernstorff poured himself a large cognac and sat in one of the leather chairs near the empty fireplace. He thought that attending the war games conference was a waste of his time and achieved nothing. Middle ranking officers talked endlessly of how easily the Allies would be thrown back into the sea if they tried a landing on the beaches of France. Bernstorff listened patiently until it was his turn to speak and then told the audience the reality, as he saw it.

'The Allies won't easily be pushed back into the sea because there aren't enough battle-hardened troops to prevent an

Allied landing. In addition the Luftwaffe can do little to help prevent the Allied invasion because it's withdrawn nearly all its fighters to counter American daylight bombing operations over Germany. A landing by the Allies is likely to succeed for lack of defences.'

He ended his assessment of the situation. 'Fortress Europe is in fact, a sham. It's a thin line of garrison troops from which the fittest and most able men had been combed to feed the meatgrinder of the Russian campaign.'

Most at the conference loudly rejected his views and some had angrily accused him of being a defeatist. Were it not for the Knight's Cross with oak leaves that hung around his neck he might have expected someone to accuse him of being a coward and a traitor who should be arrested and shot. He wouldn't have cared had they done so; he cared little for the opinions of middle ranking administrators. His regret was that the people he had intended should hear his assessment of the situation were absent from the conference. Rommel had taken the opportunity of the bad weather to return to Germany to celebrate his wife's birthday and most of the other senior commanders had followed his lead and were enjoying the attractions of Paris.

Leaning back into the leather chair Bernstorff took a sip of the after dinner cognac and thought how much he missed the Russian vodka that helped to numb the constant pain in his leg. He closed his eyes and thought of the phial of morphine in his bedroom that would give him a good night's sleep. It was then that he heard the distinctive drone of Allied aircraft overhead, *another bombing raid heading for Berlin* he said to himself. However, as the evening progressed it seemed different, the Allied planes flying in their thousands close to the ground made the sound deafening. German officers peered into the sky, marvelled at the discipline of the endless rows of bombers and tried to figure out what was happening.

'Is this it?' a few of them asked each other.

Bernstorff continued to sip his cognac as he observed an increased activity within the chateau. The situation seemed to become increasingly confusing as orderlies began to deliver communications reporting bombing raids, landings by Allied parachutists and time and again Bernstorff heard shouted orders, 'Send a situation update to Field Marshal von Rundstedt, inform Rommel's headquarters, radio the Führer's headquarters in Rastenburg.'

After a couple of hours Bernstorff felt the tingling sensation in his groin and decided to make plans to return to his unit.

****

Kneeling by the side of the railway tracks Michael pulled out the Explosive 808 from the shoulder bag. He smelt the distinct odour of almonds as he carefully opened the oiled paper protecting the yellow, putty-like explosive. After softening the explosive in his hands he moulded it around the railway track. Placing the explosive on a bend Michael hoped not just to destroy the track but to derail a train and make hasty repairs almost impossible. Once satisfied he pushed the detonator into the explosive so that it would explode as soon as the train's wheels ran over it. In case the first explosive wasn't effective, Michael placed another a few feet further up the rail. Then he waved to the two men keeping watch further up the track to indicate that all was ready and all three withdrew into the safety of the trees lining the railway and waited.

Twenty minutes later Michael heard the distinct flange squeal of a locomotive's wheels turning on the rails. He peered through the darkness as the locomotive approached the bend and heard a dull thud as the first explosive charge dislocated the track. The train shuddered and Michael wondered how many of the passengers understood its implications. As the wheels hit the second charge the rails buckled and the inertia of one hundred tons of locomotive could not prevent it leaving the rails. The engine slowed down as it bumped over the sleepers while the carriages immediately behind were lifted into the air, twisted onto their sides and then dragged along the ground. There was a sound, like a clap of thunder, followed by the scream of metal scraping against metal as the locomotive slewed off the tracks plunging down the bank pulling two carriages behind it. Coming to a halt at the bottom of the muddy earth bank the engine gave a loud hiss as steam escaped. Michael watched as the last carriage, propelled by inertia, continued to move along the track until it hit a stationary carriage and pirouetted into the air coming down on top of the carriage in front of it. Even though he was a few hundred yards away Michael could distinctly hear the screams of the soldiers inside as seats were torn from their fittings, and splintering wood and buckling metal flew through the air causing horrific injuries. A fire began in the second wagon; against the red glow of the flames Michael saw silhouettes of survivors emerging from the wreckage. He was transfixed by the frightful scene and the screams of the badly injured but was, nevertheless, caught between conflicting emotions: his natural desire to help fellow human beings in danger and distress and his duty as a soldier to destroy the enemy. After a minute or two he knew the rail track had been destroyed and with the other resistants withdrew to move on to their next target. Before the night ended Jacques' group would destroy another railway track and a dozen telephone lines.

Chapter Eleven

7 June 1944

In London Juliette heard the BBC's news broadcast announcing that the Allies had begun to land on the beaches in France. She had never believed Michael when he'd told her he was being posted to Southampton as an administrator of some sort. She convinced herself that ignorance of the dangers Michael was placing himself in would be less stressful than knowing the truth. *I bet Michael's in the thick of D-Day. I hope he's being careful.*

Deciding not to dwell on the news from France and the dangers Michael might be in Juliette busied herself with her work for Philip and the Tagleva Foundation. That day she was due to go the East End of London with Sophie and visit a family made homeless by the bombing earlier in the war. It was the third visit they would make to this one family because Sophie insisted the Foundation maintained contact with those affected long after the other organisations had moved on.

'People's problems don't end when they've been given temporary accommodation to live in. Besides they like to talk, it gives them some sort of release,' Sophie had told Juliette.

So Juliette and Sophie would hand out blankets, toys for the children and hold the hands of the young and old, as they recounted their experiences.

It was a familiar story. 'After sirens wailed you could 'ear the German planes overhead. Me room would shake from the anti-aircraft guns, not too far away, next street almost. It were awful… I was in shelter when my house caught fire. Lost everything I 'ad, even baby's clothes… After Germans had gone you could see fires all around – scores of 'em, perhaps 'undreds. Fires were so close you could even 'ear the crackling, feel the heat of the flames and the yells of firemen, know what I mean?'

Often at the end of the story Juliette would be told, 'Then Countess Tagleva helped us out, wonderful she be, I'm so grateful to the Countess…'

Juliette would watch Sophie offer support to people and was impressed by her natural empathy. Sophie always seemed to know just when to listen, when to provide that word of comfort, and in turn those made homeless hung on her every word. Perhaps it was no surprise people loved her so much Juliette thought. Sophie had a kind of understated beauty; whenever she spoke to people her skin glowed and her eyes lit up and, despite her age, was disarmingly unaware of how beautiful she was. Juliette knew how lucky she was to have married into the Tagleva family.

****

It had been two days since news of the Allies landing in France had reached Paris, and walking through the corridors of Gestapo headquarters Julius Halder couldn't avoid hearing the rumours that the Atlantic Wall had failed to contain the invasion. He heard the whispered criticism of the troops defending the beaches; 'eastern troops, conscripts from Russia, Turkestan and other European nations, with no desire or will to fight for Germany.' Halder was angry that the Allied invasion had increased the acts of sabotage and, as a result, he had been ordered to give up hunting for the Resistance's banker and instead investigate the acts of sabotage. He was in his office reading a communication from his superiors:

After it became common knowledge among the French population that the Allies had landed in Normandy some seemed to assume the war would be ended within a few days. A belief encouraged by General de Gaulle, broadcasting over the BBC, inciting the population to violence and criminal acts of sabotage. All over France misguided groups heard the broadcast and took to the streets. There are reports of German soldiers being attacked in Paris, military supplies stolen and the French Tricolour has been flown over some buildings. All such acts against German occupation must be curtailed and retribution must be swift and 'understood' by the population. It is vital that any act of terrorism is severely punished. The Gestapo, SS and all military units are authorised to use whatever means necessary to facilitate this position. HQ recommends hostages be taken to ensure civilian compliance with legal German orders. Following any murder of members of our armed forces by civilian groups or the Resistance, retribution is recommended. A figure of twelve civilians for each German soldier murdered is to be rounded up at random and hanged from balconies and telegraph poles around the district to discourage other members of the community taking similar acts of terrorism.

Halder put down the report and sighed. He donned his hat and coat and walked down the stairs to the waiting car.

Chapter Twelve

Afternoon in Paris, 7 June 1944

Samuel looked up from the work permit he was working on and smiled at his guardians Mathieu and Luc. He liked Luc, a young man in his late twenties that always had a kind word for his wife and would smile and ruffle his children's hair. Since the start of the war Samuel had forged all the documents needed by Liferaft that allowed the Resistance group to function effectively: the army discharge papers, the travel permits, ration books and the certificates of exemption from forced labour in Germany. Samuel knew his importance to the group but also understood the purpose of his guardians. Their job would be to move him to safety in the event of a German raid. Though he enjoyed his guardians' company, and they were someone other than his family to talk with, he had no illusions that, while their job was to protect him, if he were in danger of being captured by the Germans, Mathieu would draw the Browning pistol he carried in his jacket pocket and shoot him dead. Samuel accepted it would be a necessary act, to protect the information he knew and the identities of those in the Liferaft network. He didn't worry about his friend killing him, it would be a quicker and less painful path to eternal peace than being tortured and finally shot by the Germans, and he was comforted by Jean-Claude's promise that his family would continue to be protected by the network even if he was captured or killed.

Samuel placed two and a half teaspoons of ground coffee powder in the centre of a towel and folded over the edges to trap the coffee in the centre. Walking over to the sink he poured the contents of a kettle of boiling water over the towel. Once satisfied the colour draining from the towel was the correct colour for what he wanted he squeezed it to remove the excess liquid, returned to the workbench and gently stroked the cloth over the paper. After a few strokes the paper took on a soft brown hue. Satisfied the paper had aged correctly and the document had taken on an authentic look, he repeated the process on the other side. In a day or so the *Arbeitsbuch*, that German law required all workers to carry, would be ready.

****

As he sat in the passenger seat of the Mercedes 260D sedan following the two troop carriers, Halder thought his superior's orders were a waste of time. A show of force by conducting a house to house raid in one of the poorer arrondissements of Paris to check identity papers and arresting those who were not to their liking would achieve very little and only serve as a recruiting call to the Resistance. Looking out of the car window he noticed a couple of pedestrians give the convoy the briefest of glances before looking away. Every Parisian knew a Mercedes 260D sedan arriving outside your apartment building meant trouble and probable arrest: for being a Jew, working for the detriment of the Reich, refusal to work, sexual intercourse with a non-Aryan, spreading religious propaganda, having been overheard speaking defeatist statements, belonging to an illegal Resistance organisation or a dozen other crimes.

****

Mathieu was sitting in the window looking down the street. It was almost the end of his shift when the responsibility for Samuel's safety could be handed over to the next bodyguard. He was looking forward to walking home, having a meal and reading a book until he fell asleep. He closed his eyes for a moment and began to drift into an unpleasant daydream, or was it paranoid fantasy that he could hear engines? He shook himself awake from the daydream and peered towards the corner of the street. The distinctive noise could only be from German vehicles, there was no petrol for private ones. Luc also heard the rumble of German trucks. He walked to the window and glanced at Samuel who seemed to be concentrating so hard he hadn't heard the commotion. Mathieu and Luc watched the covered troop carriers and the Mercedes sedan turn the corner into the street. As the trucks began to disgorge German infantry Mathieu felt a tightening in his stomach and for a moment it robbed him of his senses replacing them with a freezing of his muscles. There followed the sound of leather boots on the cobbles, shouted orders and rifle butts banging on doors up and down the street demanding entry. Mathieu and Luc turned away from the window to see that Samuel had heard the commotion and began to stuff documents, the inks he used for official signatures and the official rubber stamps he had painstakingly recreated into a small satchel. Then they heard the banging on the front door three storeys below, someone opened it, heavy German boots began to climb the stairs.

'Quickly, they're coming,' Mathieu cried out to Samuel as he pulled the Browning pistol from his jacket. He would use it as a last resort only when it was inevitable that Samuel would be captured. Until that time Mathieu's job was to protect Samuel as much as he could. He pointed the weapon at the door knowing that despite the heavy metal bolts it would not stop the Germans for long.

'Quick,' Luc pleaded to Samuel who was still filling his satchel with papers.

Luc walked to a bookcase set against one wall and pulled it forward on hinges to reveal a hidden staircase. Luc admired the ingenuity of the man who, long ago, had built the secret passage that allowed him to visit his mistress in the building next door and avoid any scandal. Carrying his satchel Samuel rushed past Luc and down the secret passage. Mathieu watched as the handle on the metal door turned and then he entered the staircase pulling the bookcase back into place behind him. The three of them began to descend the stairs, but they had not gone far before they heard rifle butts against the wooden door in the room behind them. There was a crash and Mathieu guessed the doorframe had given way. He pictured the Germans storming into Samuel's workshop and knew it wouldn't take them long to discover the false bookcase that hid a second set of stairs. Rushing as fast as they could down the narrow winding staircase the they arrived at another door. Luc pulled the key off the hook on the wall but before he could fit it into the lock, he fumbled and it fell from his grasp onto the floor. Luc cursed as the metal key clattered on the stone steps and the sound echoed around the staircase. Both Luc and Mathieu bent down to retrieve the key. Mathieu grasped the key and passed it to Luc. This time Luc managed to insert it into the lock and turn it. The door opened and they found themselves on the first-floor landing of the apartment in the adjacent block of apartments. As they locked the door behind them, muffled shouts could be heard. It meant their escape passage had been discovered and the Germans were in pursuit. The three continued their descent to the cellars.

Mathieu looked at Samuel. 'Are you OK?' he asked.

'I'm fine, it's just as we practised.'

'We aren't safe yet, we must hurry,' said Mathieu.

They rushed down the stairs to the cellars that in better days would have stored hundreds of bottles of wine but now housed empty racks. The lightbulbs in the cellars had been removed long ago so that the darkness would delay their pursuers; the three of them made good progress as they followed the route they had rehearsed so often. A minute later they arrived at a small flight of steps and access to a courtyard two streets away from the workshop. They walked across the courtyard to a door they knew gave access to the relative safety of the street. Mathieu gently opened the door and looked out; there were no Germans to be seen.

Once in the street Luc spoke to Mathieu. 'Now the Germans have discovered the workshop it won't be long before they call for reinforcements and start searching the whole area. You take Samuel to the safe house. I'll follow at a short distance and distract them if I need to.

'We're meant to stay together,' said Mathieu.

'I need to find out if the raid was a coincidence or if they knew about Samuel's workshop. So just do as I say, make sure Samuel's safe. Now go,' ordered Luc.

He watched as Mathieu and Samuel disappeared along the street.

****

When Halder was informed that a forger's workroom had been discovered, he was delighted. *Perhaps the raid had not been a waste of time after all.* Arriving on the top floor of the building he found a door off its hinges and a bookcase pulled away from the far wall that revealed a hidden flight of stairs. He looked around the room and at the chemicals, papers, discarded ink bottles and a couple of rubber stamps on the workbench. He picked one up, pressed it onto a piece of paper and saw a perfect copy of a Polizeidirektor stamp authorising a civilian to travel around occupied France. On one table were mugs of liquid. He touched one; the liquid was still warm. They had missed the forger by seconds.

Halder was distracted by a piece of paper poking out under his shoe. He bent down and picked it up. It was a photograph of a young man. He looked at the face staring back at him and carefully placed the picture in his wallet.

Turning to a soldier he said, 'Everything in this room is to be photographed and then moved to Gestapo headquarters. Everyone in this building, and the ones either side, are to be detained and questioned. They are all suspects.'

Chapter Thirteen

18 June 1944

Michael, Jacques and some others from the resistance group were clustered around the kitchen table in the restaurant in Paris listening to the news from the BBC. They heard John Snagge report that a bridgehead had been established and then Richard Dimbleby, broadcasting from a beach in Normandy, told listeners that British, American and Canadian troops were moving off the beaches and into the French countryside. When the news finished the radio was turned off and Jacques and Michael began to discuss the night's targets to be attacked when Vincent walked in. Michael glanced up and recognised him as one of the men that had been with him when the troop train was destroyed. Looking at his face Michael knew something was seriously wrong, Vincent's cheeks were flushed, the eyes narrow, rigid and cold.

'What's the problem?' asked Jacques.

Vincent looked daggers at Michael. 'Have you heard of Oradour-sur-Glane?' he said through bared teeth.

'It's a village twenty miles north of Limoges,' Jacques informed Michael helpfully.

'The bastard Boche believed the Maquis were holding a German officer captive in the village. Nine days ago SS soldiers drove into the village and ordered all the men to parade in the marketplace. The women and children were taken to the church and locked inside. The SS found no Maquis, no German officer being held prisoner. Yet, despite that, they machine-gunned all the men to death and set the village ablaze. Then they went to the church and began shooting. Over six hundred villagers have been murdered including two hundred children.'

Jacques clenched his fists and Michael closed his eyes trying to hide the picture of the massacre.

Vincent leaned onto the table so that his mouth was next to Michael's ear.

'The BBC told the population to rise up and fight the Boche. But there would be no help from the Allies. If there had been all those women and children would still be alive. What have you to say to that, Englishman?'

'Calm down, Vincent, it's not Michael's fault,' interrupted Jacques. 'The only people responsible for the massacre are the Boche.'

'Isn't his fault? He's here to organise us to attack the Germans, blow up their trains and attack their supplies. But the Germans don't attack us; instead they take revenge on innocent French women and children for the acts of sabotage ordered by London. All over the country people are being arrested and shot simply for being on the street. And the British and Americans aren't hurrying to liberate us, it's as if the Allies want us all dead so that there'll be no French left alive to liberate, just our land to occupy,' he snarled.

'Perhaps we should stop the sabotage,' sighed Michael.

Jacques shook his head. 'No, that would be an act of compliance. It would give the Germans what they want, and it won't stop the killing. We always knew the occupation would turn into a nightmare for innocent civilians before they could be liberated. The only way to stop the atrocities is to throw the Germans out of France, and before it's over we'll have our revenge.'

Vincent gave Michael a scowl and left the room.

Jacques looked at Michael. 'Don't worry, he'll calm down. Now, let's work out how we're going to attack this weapons store.'

****

Arriving home Jean-Claude saw the chalked 'Z' on the side of his apartment block. Its position, near the entrance to the apartments, meant the signal could only have come from Alain. The following morning Jean-Claude rose early, washed and, just after the end of the curfew, gathered up his coat and hat and left the apartment block. To ensure he wasn't being followed he walked for half an hour before arriving at the gardens opposite Rue le Tasse.

Alain was waiting at the pre-agreed place. 'I saw your signal, what's wrong?' Jean-Claude asked.

'Luc's been arrested by the Gestapo.'

'Damn, how did it happen?'

'He was at Samuel's workshop when the Germans raided it. Samuel only just managed to escape with Mathieu, but then Luc separated from them and was unlucky enough to bump into a German patrol. Despite having all the correct papers the Germans detained him.'

'How do you know all this?'

'When Luc didn't come home I went to Samuel's workshop but Germans were crawling all over the area. I didn't go too close but assumed it'd been discovered. I spoke to a concierge in a building nearby that I know. She saw Luc being arrested.'

'What about Samuel?'

'Mathieu's contacted me to say that he and Samuel are safe.'

'Do you know where Luc's been taken?'

'The Gestapo arrested all the residents in the building and those either side and took them to Gestapo headquarters.'

Jean-Claude looked into Alain's face. The eyes were red and bleary, he had obviously been kept awake all night by a carousel of ideas swirling around inside his mind, each one more worrying than the last.

Alain spoke. 'Luc isn't the strongest of men. He knows too much about Liferaft, he knows you for God's sake… If the Gestapo torture him he won't be able to hold out for long. You know he won't.'

Jean-Claude placed a hand on Alain's shoulder. 'Luc's stronger than you think. We've planned for this happening for a long time. It's why each of you were assigned a separate safe house, so if either was arrested the other would have somewhere to move to and hide. I trust you kept the address of each safe house secret from each other?'

'It's the *only* secret we've kept from each other.'

Jean-Claude smiled. 'Good, then go there and stay as quiet as possible. I don't know where the safe house is, so if either of us needs to meet the other we'll chalk a sign on the side of the building at the end of Rue de Montmorency. Now you go to the safe house, and be careful.'

After watching Alain walk away Jean-Claude returned to his apartment. In his sitting room he sat down to think. Thoughts trundled through his brain like a train. Half an hour later Jean-Claude came to a conclusion; he knew what he would do and it meant visiting Julius Halder at Gestapo headquarters.

Chapter Fourteen

London, 18 June 1944

Philip arrived home from his meeting at Whitehall. It had been two months since the prime minister, Winston Churchill, had asked him to chair a committee of bankers, economists and civil servants to draw up plans for financing the United Kingdom once Germany had been defeated. Philip knew the war had many more months of fighting before it would be over but Churchill had insisted that the plans for the rebuilding of the economy, the destroyed cities and the factories be in place early.

As Philip walked into the drawing room Sophie looked up from her book and asked, 'How was the committee?'

He gave his wife a kiss on the cheek. 'Bent on revenge, I fear.'

'Oh dear, I take it the committee doesn't share your opinion that *we shouldn't be beastly to the Germans when our victory is ultimately won.*'

Philip smiled at her reference to Nöel Coward's popular song as he sank into one of the armchairs and looked at his wife. Since meeting in Russia they had rarely been apart and in all that time the years had been kind. She was as slim as the day they met, her violet eyes still sparkled with enthusiasm for life and the soft lines spoke more of the laughter they had enjoyed than of old age. After twenty-seven years of marriage he still thought she was the most beautiful woman he had ever seen.

'So tell me what did you men talk about?' Sophie asked.

'Much of the time the committee insisted on talking about Germany's reparations after the First World War and what penalties should be imposed on it this time.'

'But that's the same mistake the Allies made after the Great War.'

'That's what I told them. I reminded them that when Germany was defeated, the Allies demanded a payment of thirty-three billion dollars and the German people considered it a national humiliation. I even emphasised the point by saying a weak Germany was a contributory cause for the rise of Nazism.'

'I take it they didn't agree with you?'

'Some argued against me, saying Nazi Germany is responsible for starting the war and must pay. When I argued against it a few of the committee said London, Southampton, Manchester, Cardiff, Portsmouth, Hull, Plymouth, Clydebank and even Belfast had all been damaged in the Blitz and will need millions of pounds spent on them. They insisted that Germany must be made to pay. One economist estimated that Germany owes the Allies up to three hundred and twenty billion dollars and he had lots of support from other members of the committee.'

'That's difficult to argue against. So what do you think will happen?'

Philip sighed. 'The argument is going to be protracted. However, the committee and the government must accept any payment of reparations by Germany must leave enough resources for the German people to subsist. Punishing Germany will simply repeat the mistakes of the past... They'll come round to my way of thinking, eventually,'

'Doesn't everybody?' Sophie laughed.

Philip smiled. 'There was one person on the committee who raised an interesting point. He said the money the Nazis confiscated from Jews, both before and during the war, should be treated as a separate condition to reparations and that Germany must be made to repay what they've stolen.'

'Does it amount to lots?'

'Millions, he said. He also said that much of it has already been transferred to Switzerland.'

'The war's not over so how does he know about such things?' asked Sophie.

'Even in wartime it's difficult to keep secrets. It's fairly common knowledge in the banking and diplomatic circles that Germany's been sending large amounts of gold to Switzerland.'

Changing the subject Philip asked, 'Are you in the East End again tomorrow?'

'Every day this next week. With the doodlebugs doing so much damage in London there are many new families that need help.'

****

In Paris Luc regained consciousness. His head throbbed and his entire lower body ached. He tried to move to make himself more comfortable and felt a sharp pain from the broken ribs. It made him gasp. As his head cleared panic coursed through him as he remembered where he was, in the interrogation room in Gestapo headquarters. He felt something cold hold his hands and wrists, preventing him being able to move. He looked down and saw his hands sandwiched between two metal plates forcing his fingers flat and leaving the nails exposed. Luc groaned, he couldn't take much more pain and needed some sleep. He was close to telling them everything. But then another thought entered his head. If he could remain silent, even for another hour, then Alain would have more time to escape. A tear fell down his cheek as he pictured his lover, *I will not betray you my darling* he said to himself. His mind repeated their favourite line of John Donne's poem, so often repeated to each other when times had been difficult, *Our love hath no decay; no tomorrow, nor yesterday, but only keeps his first, last, everlasting day.*

The door opened and was slammed shut, making Luc jump a little. The interrogator had arrived. It was the same black SS uniform but it was a fresh face, with fresh energy to interrogate him further. The man sat in the chair opposite.

'What's the name of the Resistance group you work for?'

Luc stayed silent.

'Tell me,' the man repeated sternly.

'I don't belong to any Resistance group,' mumbled Luc through bruised lips.

The interrogator clicked his fingers. Luc watched as a small table was positioned in front of him. A chair was dragged across the concrete floor. The door opened and another man entered the room, sat down in the chair and took what looked like a roll of cloth from inside his jacket. He placed it on the table, untied the ribbon and unrolled it revealing thirteen pockets, each containing a surgeon's medical instrument. Luc stared at the instruments and an icy coldness passed through him.

'Tell me who leads your Resistance group,' demanded the inquisitor.

Luc remained silent.

The inquisitor nodded to the man who extracted a scalpel. With no expression on his face he made an incision into Luc's finger. Putting down the scalpel he extracted a pair of surgical pliers.

Luc watched in disbelief as his nail was slowly pulled away from the finger. Once the flesh had been exposed the pain hit him. He let out a piercing scream, a scream of uncontrolled panic bordering on terror.

Another question was put to him but Luc gritted his teeth and shook his head.

The scalpel was picked up again. The pain sent an electric shock up his arm and through his body. Luc had felt nothing so agonising and he screamed once more. As the torturer finished with each fingernail another question was put to him by the SS interrogator. Still Luc refused to answer, thinking only of Alain as he whispered out loud, over and over again, *'Il n'y a qu'un bonheur dans la vie, c'est d'aimer et d'être aimé.'*

The SS man translated the words from George Sand's poem, 'There is only one happiness in life: to love and be loved.'

'What does the poetry mean?' Luc's interrogator demanded.

'A Nazi wouldn't understand,' whispered Luc.

On a signal from the interrogator the torturer picked up the scalpel once more and Luc screamed.

After all the nails on his left hand had been removed a film of oily sweat covered Luc giving his skin a glossy shine, his greasy hair was glued to his face and drops of sweat invaded his eyes making them sting.

The SS man spoke. 'You're a brave man, stupid, but brave. We will stop now, but will start on your right hand if you continue to remain silent. Until then, think on this. I know you're a member of the Resistance. You can't deny it. We found your photograph on the floor of a forger's workshop. So, save yourself from all this unnecessary pain, tell me what I want to know and I'll stop your pain and you'll be able to go to sleep.'

As Luc was unshackled and hauled from the chair by two SS guards he looked into the face of the man packing away the surgical instruments.

The man looked up. '*Désolé monsieur, c'est mon travail.*'

Luc stared in disbelief at the man who had so expertly pulled out his fingernails. He was a Frenchman, apologising to him, making the excuse that it was his job. Luc felt sick and began to faint, but the soldiers held him up and dragged him from the room.

Thrown onto the floor of his cell, Luc studied the bloodied hand that throbbed with pain. It took him half an hour to remove his shirt and tear one sleeve off so he could use it as a bandage. Once the bloodied mess was wrapped in the bandage he lay on the wooden planks that doubled as a bed, clutched his injured hand by the wrist and held it comfortingly close to his chest. Clamping his eyes shut he whispered through his tears, *I'm sorry, Alain. I can't take much more. I love you and feel so lucky to have been loved in return, but I can't take any more of this.*

Chapter Fifteen

The same day

Carl Bernstorff was in a good mood. The SS panzer division his unit belonged to had been ordered to fall back from Caen to the Verrières Ridge to entrench and form a strong defensive position. During a break in the fighting he was with his second in command studying a map of northern France and explaining his plans for the fight to come. Bernstorff was convinced that strict adherence to a defensive doctrine with strong and effective counter attacks by his panzers would result in heavy Allied casualties. If his plan succeeded, it would hold up the British and Canadian infantry north-west of Caen so effectively that any liberation of the Calvados region would not be possible for several weeks.

An orderly entered the room and handed him an envelope. Bernstorff placed the envelope under his left armpit and used his right hand to tear it open and pull out the note from inside.

To: SS-Obersturmbannführer Bernstorff.

Immediate: Report to Reichsfüehrer Himmler at SS headquarters Prinz-Albrecht-Straße in Berlin.

Bernstorff fixed a murderous stare at the far wall, crunched up the note, threw it onto the floor and ran his hand through his close-cropped hair.

He snarled. 'Why order me to Berlin now? What's it for? Are they so fucking incompetent they can't see I can win this battle? But not if I'm in Berlin.'

The tingling sensation he had so enjoyed over the past days disappeared.

****

Luc was sitting on the edge of the wooden bed in his cell, with no strength to move. His good hand cradled the bloodied bandage to his chest in the hope it would somehow ease the throbbing, it hadn't. His body craved sleep, relief from the pain and he would give anything for a cigarette. He imagined taking a long draw and feeling the hot smoke hit the back of his throat and the comfort as the nicotine coursed through his bloodstream. *Was it too much to have a cigarette?* He gazed around the cell illuminated by a strong light bulb set high in the ceiling that he guessed was designed to prevent sleep. There was no furniture, not even a bucket to act as a toilet; the walls were brown and dappled in one corner with mildew. Luc bit down on his lip trying not to burst into tears.

He was startled by the bolt being drawn back on the cell door. An SS guard walked into the cell. Luc stared at the familiar grey service uniform with the black belt that he knew would escort him back to the interrogation room. The guard indicated for him to get up. Luc slowly stood, his hip hurt and he staggered a little as his bruised muscles complained at having to move, and hobbled out of the cell. Luc knew the familiar route along the corridor to the interrogation room was thirty-two paces and he plodded along trying to eke out the relatively pain-free seconds while the German guard pushed him forward every few feet in an effort to make him walk faster. Luc looked ahead, at the end of the corridor was a window, the panes crudely painted over in a faded white paint and taped to prevent flying glass in the event of a bomb. He pictured that beyond the whitewashed glass was a large garden filled with flowering jasmine and roses and in its centre a small lake, with pink and white lilies with a wooden bridge, painted red. Luc imagined that if he were to stand on the bridge he would be able to look down at the koi carp zigzagging calmly through the water.

He looked at the window, and suddenly no longer felt the pain in his body. He ran forward and a few feet from it jumped. He flew through the air. He crashed into the slightly rotten wooden frame that gave way under the assault. Luc felt the rush of clean air on his face and was sure he could smell sweet jasmine.

****

Jean-Claude turned the corner of the street and heard a woman scream. He looked towards the sound and saw a man falling from the top of a building. The man tumbled, like a rag doll, in slow motion until landing with a soft dull thud. Joining other passers-by Jean-Claude ran forward to look through the railings that separated the building from the street and at the limp body surrounded by broken glass. The sight was hideous. Jean-Claude closed his eyes so he would not to have to look at Luc's contorted and bruised face and then, hoping the image had disappeared, opened them again. It was still there. He was momentarily distracted by a woman a few feet away bent over with warm cream coloured liquid spilling from her mouth and splashing into the gutter. Then Jean-Claude looked back and studied his friend's lifeless body. He noticed the bloodied and bandaged hand, the torn, dirty, sleeveless shirt. At that moment three SS soldiers ran out of the building and began pushing the growing crowd back from the railings. Jean-Claude felt a rifle pressed against his chest and he took a few steps backwards. Suddenly, despite the crowd and the commotion, he became aware of someone standing next to him. Jean-Claude turned; it was Halder.

'You're a long way from the Tagleva bank. Were you on your way to see me?' asked the policeman matter-of-factly.

Jean-Claude had walked to Gestapo headquarters intending to bargain for Luc's life. He had even considered giving himself up to Halder if it would set Luc free, knowing it would result in his own death.

'I don't know... No, I was walking, clearing my head...' he said, his head in a spin as he continued to stare at Luc's limp body.

'I'm sorry you had to see this,' said Halder. 'He was no one important, just someone helping us with our investigations.

He threw himself out of the window, it's to be regretted, such a waste of a life.'

As Jean-Claude looked at the limp and contorted body on the ground two soldiers began to remove it from the courtyard and carry it back inside Gestapo headquarters. The crowd started to disperse. Within minutes Jean-Claude was alone on the pavement.

Jean-Claude must have walked for hours and didn't know how he managed to arrive home. Finding himself at the front door of his apartment he pulled the key from his coat pocket. As he tried to insert it into the lock his fingers shook, as if in spasms, and he had to hold the key with two hands to keep it steady. Once inside he took off his coat and threw it onto the hallway chair then walked into the living room. For a few minutes he stared out of the window, without seeing anything through the glass. The apartment felt cold, empty of the life it once had and his thoughts turned to Sébastien. Before Sébastien left, he imagined the feeling of loneliness would pass, but the coldness of Sébastien's absence stayed with him and at this precise moment it felt like a chill wind, eating into the marrow of his bones.

His thoughts returned to Luc and wondered if he had talked under torture. He felt caught between opposing needs: a desire to go to Alain and comfort him over the loss of Luc and the necessity to keep his distance to protect the other members of Liferaft. Then there was a fear of his own impending arrest that had begun to gnaw at his insides. Jean-Claude gritted his teeth as he sat down on the sofa, placed his head in his hands and began to sob.

Chapter Sixteen

Berlin, 25 June 1944

The stated duty of the Reich Security Office on Prinz-Albrecht-Straße in Berlin is to fight all 'enemies of the Reich' and is headed by Heinrich Himmler in his dual capacities as Reichsführer-SS and chief of the German police. As Carl Bernstorff walked into the building the two SS soldiers guarding the main entrance came to attention. At the reception desk he presented his identification and was politely requested to surrender his pistol, which, he was informed, would be returned to him on his departure. Twenty minutes later he was escorted to the top floor of the building and into the Reichsführer's office. At the door Bernstorff came to attention and raised his right arm. *Heil Hitler.* Without looking up, the man behind the desk waved him into the room and to a chair. Once he was seated Himmler put down the file and looked up. It was the first time Bernstorff had seen the commander in chief of Germany's home forces up close and he looked at the youthfully slender man, the two grey-blue eyes looking back at him from behind a glittering pince-nez, the trimmed moustache below the straight, well-shaped nose and pale skin. Bernstorff thought there was nothing outstanding or extraordinary about Himmler and it struck him that the Reichsführer looked more like an elementary schoolteacher than the man who led the feared SS.

'Thank you for coming to see me, Obersturmbannführer. I see from your personal file how much you relish a fight so I hope my orders didn't displease you.'

Himmler broadened the constant set, faintly mocking, smile to display two rows of sparkling white teeth between pencil thin lips. 'You probably haven't heard the latest news of the war in the east? No… of course you wouldn't. You've been busy fighting in France and besides it's not yet been made public.'

Bernstorff guessed the news was bad. Good news would have been broadcast from the rooftops by the Propaganda Ministry the very minute it was received.

'Soon after the Allies landed in Normandy the Red Army mounted a counter-offensive and attacked our army group in Byelorussia. The latest information I have is that the Fourth Army has been destroyed, together with the Ninth Army and most of the Third Panzer Division. The Russians are exploiting our collapse and encircling our formations in the vicinity of Minsk... A more intelligent man than I might consider the war is lost. What's your opinion Obersturmbannführer?'

'I'm a soldier, Reichsführer. I follow orders. I leave opinions to my superiors.'

Himmler's smile widened. 'A sensible answer. I find opinions, in these uncertain times, can too often be a dangerous luxury.'

'Am I to return to Russia, Reichsminister?'

Himmler ignored the question. 'Nevertheless, there are some faithless traitors who openly suggest Germany has lost the war, but I have faith in the Führer who, only this morning, assured me of our final victory. The Führer told me that the wonder weapons such as the V1 pilotless bombs now raining down on London, and the other weapons of mass destruction he has in reserve will bring the Allies to their knees. So, to answer your question; as victory will soon be ours it will not be necessary for you to risk your life fighting in Russia. Yet, as we await these wonder weapons, one can't help but wonder that if the Third Reich should collapse whether the ideologies of National Socialism would survive, and if they did not what would history say of National Socialism and would we be condemned for not preserving those ideologies?'

'I'm not sure I understand what you mean,' answered Bernstorff.

'If the Third Reich is defeated then the world will be deprived of the Führer's vision and humanity would be impoverished as a result. It would seem to me that, even in defeat, the Führer's vision should be preserved for future generations of Germans to value as I do.'

Himmler picked up a paper from his desk.

'Yet the Propaganda Ministry seems to be preparing the German people for such an event. Goebbels is soon to broadcast to the nation saying that an enemy invading German territory will be taken in the rear by a fanatical population which will ceaselessly attack him and tie down strong forces, allow no rest or exploitation of any possible success.'

Himmler put down the paper. 'He will then announce the elite of the SS and Hitler Youth are being trained in guerrilla tactics under the code name Werewolf.'

'The Russians, Greeks and Czechs did the same, with great effect, when we occupied their countries. With our superior forces and technology Germans should be able to do the same,' said Bernstorff.

Himmler smiled. 'Quite so.'

'Is that why I'm here, to set up a guerrilla army?'

'No Bernstorff, the guerrilla army is an irrelevance, your task is much more important. It's to ensure that, in the event of the Third Reich's defeat, the Führer's legacy is preserved for all eternity. You will make plans to establish a Nazi government-in-exile... a government that in better times can resurface... unite and dominate Europe once more.'

The Reichsfüehrer's eyes stared through the lenses as if waiting to see Bernstorff's reaction.

'I assume the government-in-exile would be led by the Führer,' said Bernstorff.

'At this time you will not concern yourself with the names of the leaders that may or may not head the government. Your task is to set up the organisation that ensures the leaders and the resources needed to support such a government can be preserved and protected.'

Himmler passed him a file. 'Inside this folder are your orders and the arrangements that have been made to date. Go to the anteroom and study them. The file is not to leave this building. Once you've done that, ring the bell and someone will bring you to me so I can answer any questions you might have.'

Bernstorff left the room and went to the anteroom; he sat down at the table and opened the file.

An hour later Bernstorff closed the file and pushed the bell, an orderly walked in and ushered him back into Himmler's office. Himmler took the file.

'Do you have any questions?' asked the Reichsfüehrer.

'One. A substantial amount of money will be required to finance a government-in-exile.'

Himmler nodded. 'Money is available. Even as we speak, there are many who are contributing funds to support such a cause. In fact such is the support and generosity of some that they are even donating the gold fillings from their teeth.' Himmler chuckled, as if he'd made a joke.

Bernstorff didn't understand but smiled back nevertheless.

'All the money you need will be made available to you. Do you have any other questions?'

'No Reichsfüehrer.'

'Excellent, I knew I'd chosen the right man for this… delicate task.'

Himmler pulled out an envelope from a folder on his desk and passed it over.

'You might find this letter of some use.'

He watched impassively as Bernstorff placed it into the crease of his arm, opened it and extracted the paper.

Bernstorff read:

Führerhauptquartiere: Berlin

To whom it may concern:

This is to confirm Obersturmbannführer Bernstorff is on a vital and secret mission for the Reich. This letter instructs, in the name of the Führer, all military and civilian personnel to provide the Obersturmbannführer any assistance, military or civilian, he considers necessary for the completion of his mission.

Adolf Hitler

Himmler passed him a buff-coloured folder.

'In this file you will find the names of people, companies and organisations that have expressed support to Germany. It may be useful. That's all,' said Himmler.

Bernstorff stood, came to attention and turned to leave. As he reached the door he heard Himmler say, 'Oh, I forgot. One more thing, you will send regular updates of your progress and are to report only to me. You understand, Obersturmbannführer?'

Without turning, Bernstorff answered, 'Perfectly, Reichsfüehrer.'

Once Bernstorff had left, another door in Himmler's office opened and an ADC walked in.

'Did you hear everything?' asked Himmler.

'I did, Reichsfüehrer. You told him about the broadcast Goebbels is to make about the Werewolf organisation.'

'I thought it best. I don't want Bernstorff making the mistake of becoming involved with Werewolf believing it can help him with his own task.'

Himmler paused before continuing, 'Once the Allies hear Goebbels' radio broadcast about a guerrilla organisation they will pour resources into defeating it. That will allow Bernstorff to complete his mission without interference from the Allies and perfectly fulfils the purpose I envisaged for the Werewolf project.'

Chapter Seventeen

London, 29 June 1944

Following D-Day there had been a period of elation in London but when flying bombs, nicknamed doodlebugs, began to fall from the skies Londoners realised their part in the war was far from over. Launched from the Pas-de-Calais and Dutch coast the deadly payload of the doodlebug destroyed an area half a mile in diameter indiscriminately ripping apart streets, houses, churches, shops and factories and sending clouds of powdered brick dust into the air. After five years of war, not surprisingly, the population of London were close to panic. In a replay of the Blitz, thousands made plans to evacuate their children and squeezed them into overflowing trains for the safety of the countryside.

The evacuations meant that the Tagleva Foundation was busier than ever. Travel arrangements had to be made, accommodation found, schooling provided for the children and comfort given to the mothers who, once again, waved goodbye to their loved ones leaving from every main railway station in London.

It was early in the morning when Sophie and Juliette found the house they were looking for in Stepney Way. The door was opened by a young woman wearing a yellow scarf on her head that only partly hid her hair curlers. A bewildered-looking boy around five years of age, already dressed in his coat, peeped from behind his mother's skirts and a few feet away, sucking her thumb, stood his younger sister.

'Am I pleased to see you. The kids 'ave been murder dis morning, what wiv all this upheaval, the doodle bugs an' all, know what I mean?'

Juliette smiled at the phrase she heard so often in this part of London, 'know what I mean?' that seemed to end every sentence and which she discovered was not a question at all, but an exclamation of fact.

'I've packed up kids' clothes and their favourite toy,' said the woman pointing to a couple of small suitcases at the bottom of the stairs.

'Are you coming with us to see them off at the station?' enquired Sophie.

'Yeah, I'll come to kiss 'em goodbye, I'm going to miss 'em terrible I am, but it's better they're safe an' away from London.'

Juliette smiled at the boy and the girl, knelt down and held out a small bag of lemon sherbets she'd bought the previous day at the Woolworths store in the Strand. The children's faces lit up as they took one of the sweets, part of the eight ounces comprising the month's sweet ration.

When an undulating siren began, indicating another flying bomb was on its way, the children looked afraid. Sophie, Juliette and the family rushed to the back of the house and into the garden where they squeezed inside the Anderson shelter, the corrugated iron and earth structure that would offer protection from the bomb. With five of them in the shelter Juliette was conscious of the cramped conditions, distinctive smell of damp and the odour coming from the chamber pot, covered in a cloth, in the corner.

They heard the flying bomb's motor go quiet and fifteen seconds later the dull thud of the explosion some miles away. The all clear was signalled and they emerged from the shelter. Halfway back to the house a deep sound in the sky was heard, like a small engine, and looking up they saw the doodlebug with its flaming tail. When the engine cut out they were fascinated by the strangeness of the silence and watched as it began to glide towards the ground and disappear behind some roofs in the next street. Juliette shouted to them all to lie flat on the ground but at that moment she felt the blast. The sensation was like being punched in the back of the head while someone threw rocks in her face and at the same time she felt a searing pain in her ears. Her body was picked up from the ground and tossed through the air in the middle of a choking dust cloud and debris. She lost consciousness.

When Juliette woke her whole body was stiff, her ears were ringing, she had a splitting headache and her chest hurt. She coughed and tasted grit on her lips. Wiping the grit away she saw a streak of blood stain the dust that covered her hand as if she were wearing a white glove. She moved her head and a piece of ceiling plaster fell out of her hair. Looking around she saw the young woman lying next to her. She was looking at Juliette and she smiled back but the woman's face remained still. Juliette was perplexed. The woman continued to stare at her but didn't blink and the two children, still clutching their mother's skirt, also remained motionless. Juliette moved her hand forward and shook the woman. She was still and so were her children.

Juliette suddenly felt a sense of panic and called out to Sophie; she heard a moan beside her. Turning her head she saw a familiar face covered in dust, her eyes closed.

'Sophie, are you all right?'

Sophie moaned. Juliette pushed away some bricks and crawled towards her. Reaching out she took hold of Sophie's hand and her eyes opened.

'Thank God you're safe,' whispered Sophie.

Juliette pushed away a few strands of hair from Sophie's face and exposed a large cut on her temple; she noticed some blood trickling out of one of Sophie's ears.

'I have such a headache, I feel so tired,' whispered Sophie as she closed her eyes.

'Help will soon come,' said Juliette encouragingly.

'I think they'll be too late for me.'

'No they won't.' Juliette felt the dread swell up inside her.

Over the next few minutes Juliette talked softly to Sophie but noticed that Sophie's breathing began to change, turning ragged with shallow gasps. An icy numbness came over Juliette.

'Help will soon be here, you have to hang on.'

Minutes passed as Juliette lay there holding Sophie's head, whispering encouragement and begging her to hang on until rescuers arrived.

Eventually Sophie whispered, 'Tell Philip I loved him so very much.'

Juliette heard voices and turned her head to see people begin to swarm all over the rubble.

'They're here. I told you it would be all right.'

'Over here,' Juliette screamed as loudly as she could to the rescuers.

'See Sophie, I told you they would come to rescue you,' said Juliette through her tears.

'Over here,' she shouted again to the men clambering over the rubble.

A fireman and an air-raid warden in his white helmet arrived and bent over them.

'How do you feel, Miss?' asked the fireman.

'I'm fine, but this woman needs help and there's another woman and two children next to me.'

'I'll look after the children,' said the warden turning away.

'Please see to Sophie. She's injured and needs more help than I do,' Juliette said to the fireman.

The fireman bent down to look at Sophie and then turned his attention to Juliette.

'We'll get to her, but let's see to you first.' He pulled her hand away from Sophie's.

There was no urgency to attend to Sophie and as Juliette looked at her mother-in-law's face she knew why the fireman was paying her so little attention.

'Oh no, Sophie, no.' Juliette sobbed.

As Juliette was lifted onto a stretcher she felt a stabbing pain in her abdomen. She took a deep breath in an effort to control the pain but knew she was losing her baby.

Chapter Eighteen

London, 17 July 1944

In the first days after Sophie's death whenever Philip read the letters of condolence, or when friends held him tightly barely able to contain their own grief, he felt guilty because he was not crying. He had expected to feel so much, but he felt nothing except emptiness, a silence inside himself, as though he had nothing to contribute. *What's wrong with me? Why don't I feel anything?* he asked himself time and again. He worried that others might be questioning his love for Sophie but no matter how he tried he couldn't relate to the feelings and emotions of those around him.

Ten days after her death a large congregation of friends, staff from the Tagleva Foundation and the bank crowded into the church, waited patiently for the family to arrive and the funeral service to begin. At the entrance the Russian Orthodox priest, with a long grey beard and dressed in white and gold vestments, shook Philip warmly by the hand. Philip was one of only two people at the funeral who knew the officiating priest had been born in Rotherham. The other was the petite woman dressed in black who sat, with a companion, inconspicuously at the back of the church. Grand Duchess Xenia Alexandrovna of Russia, the elder daughter of Emperor Alexander III and Empress Maria Feodorovna and the sister to Tsar Nicholas II, had travelled by car from her grace-and-favour house in Windsor Great Park especially to attend the funeral. The Grand Duchess and Sophie had begun their long friendship twenty-six years previously in 1919, when on board the British battleship HMS *Marlborough* during their escape from Russia and the Bolsheviks. Xenia had especially wanted to say her farewells to Sophie and meet the officiating priest, Charles Sydney Gibbes, the English tutor to her brother's five children before their murder.

The congregation stood as Philip and his family walked to the front of the church and sat in the front pew leaving an empty seat for Michael, who was in France and did not yet know his mother had been killed. In the open coffin in front of them Sophie was dressed in her favourite peach silk gown. She held a silver cross in her hands, on her forehead lay a headband made of paper with the words 'Holy God, Holy Mighty, Holy Immortal, have mercy on us' written on it, and folded over the lower part of her body was a burial shroud.

The funeral service comprised a Psalm, readings from the Scripture and various hymns. At the end Father Gibbes read a prayer of absolution from a piece of paper and then placed it into the hands of the departed. As the choir began to sing funereal hymns Philip moved forward to the coffin and looked at Sophie's face for the last time. Whispering a final goodbye he kissed the cross and the headband. It was then that a departure was made from the usual burial service as Father Gibbes handed Philip a small wooden box. Philip opened it and poured into the coffin the earth they had brought out of Russia all those years before. As Philip knew she had wished, Sophie would be buried with soil from her homeland. After the twins, Dorothy and Juliette made their own farewells the rest of the congregation filed forward to do the same. Once all was done the priest covered the body with the burial shroud, sprinkled holy oil over the top and closed the coffin.

A horse-drawn hearse carried Sophie the short distance to the cemetery. As the coffin was slowly lowered into the ground Philip felt a small hand thread itself into his own. Looking down he saw Dorothy smiling up at him with a tear in her eye. Her small hand squeezed his as if to comfort him and Dorothy whispered, 'I saw a bright star in the sky last night. It wasn't there before, it was Mummy's star, looking down on us, telling us she loved us.'

It took all of Philip's self-control not to dissolve into tears.

Later that night, after the children were in bed, Philip sat in his study and read the many messages of commiseration. There were telegrams from Winston Churchill, Anthony Eden, Nöel Coward and one from Prince Felix Yusupov of Russia. There was a long letter from the South Wales Miners' Federation, a few from Jewish organisations and many individual letters from families the Tagleva Foundation had helped. All talked of their regret, how they had admired Sophie, how shocked they were at her death. He looked at the pile of letters, expressing their love and sympathy and would have exchanged all of them for the two he knew would not come, could not come: Jean-Claude's and Michael's. More than anything else he wanted to sweep his eldest son into his arms and comfort him and to be able to cry on his best friend's shoulder. He walked over to the fireplace and stared at the portrait above it. Sophie's death happened while he was in a meeting. He had returned home to find his anchor, his best friend, his confidant and the only woman he had ever loved was dead. Suddenly the emptiness engulfed him entirely, his legs buckled and his knees sank to the carpet. *I never got to tell you I loved you one last time. I didn't get to hold you close before you slipped away.*

He cried out, 'Please don't leave me, my darling. I love you too much to be alone.'

Chapter Nineteen

Paris, 25 July 1944

On the surface Paris remained surprisingly calm and people went about their business as usual, but it was obvious to everyone the German apparatus of occupation was beginning to crumble and the city's population hoped liberation would arrive soon, possibly within days. All over the city trucks camouflaged in black and green paint were being loaded with office equipment and furniture from buildings the Nazis had occupied for the past four years. Seeing this, the city's bravery in the face of the enemy increased with each hour. In defiance of German orders shopkeepers openly displayed goods in the colours of red, white and blue in their windows; women began to wear clothes with the same colours, and near one Métro station youths built a huge bonfire and placed an effigy of Adolf Hitler atop it before setting it on fire. While the population anticipated freedom was close at hand, many were concerned that if the Germans defended the city, it might become a battleground like Stalingrad or Warsaw. That France's capital, known for its culture, a centre for art, fashion, gastronomy, the Louvre, the Eiffel Tower and the twelfth-century Gothic Notre Dame cathedral, would be destroyed.

The Germans had begun a partial evacuation of the city and senior officers riding in their staff cars, some laden with antiques and looted treasures, were being driven east towards Germany. Ignoring the palpable tensions in the city Julius Halder paced around his office in Gestapo headquarters. Before leaving Paris he was intent on arresting the person who acted as the banker to the Resistance. Even when the strains of 'La Marseillaise' from an accordion drifted through the open window, instead of ordering the arrest of the musician, he closed the window to stifle the noise. He had more urgent tasks than to arrest people for petty acts of defiance.

Halder was impatiently waiting for a car to take him to the apartment of the resistant who had thrown himself out of the Gestapo HQ's window. Failing to search it was an omission of good police practice, and it had played on his mind. It was not entirely his fault, for the past few days, he had been ordered by his superiors to detain hostages to ensure the population's compliance to German orders and it had taken up all his time.

When the car finally arrived and drove him to the apartment block, he wasted no time in ordering the concierge to collect her spare keys and open the apartment. Inside it was neat and simply decorated. The living room held a couple of leather chairs, some scenic pictures on the walls, a small dining table and a bookcase stuffed with books. In the bedroom he found a wooden base double bed, an armoire containing a few clothes and some empty hangers. After the cursory inspection Halder sat down in one of the comfortable leather chairs in the living room and looked around him. *It's strange*, he thought. The apartment was absent of the usual clutter of life, no photographs, no trinkets, even the thin layer of dust one could have expected was missing. *The apartment has been sanitised.* It prompted Halder to make a more thorough search. He stood up and upturned the chair he was sitting on. Taking out a pocketknife he cut away the hessian covering the bottom of the chair, there was nothing. He turned his attention to the other chair but again found nothing. Next he went to the kitchen and pulled out the drawers, spilling their contents onto the floor. He looked underneath each drawer, again nothing. Turning his attention to the bedroom Halder pulled away the bedclothes and upturned the mattress then carefully inspected the four pillows. He opened the wardrobe and noted all the clothes were on one side with empty hangers on the other. It meant that at one time two people had lived in the apartment; the concierge would confirm it to him. He walked back into the living room and surveyed his handiwork. The room was no longer neat and tidy. His attention was drawn to the bookcase. There were the usual classics by Proust, Dumas and Hugo. He noted three books he would not have expected to find in an ordinary household; André Gide's semi-autobiographical novel *The Immoralist*, about a newly married man reawakened by his attraction to young Arab boys. Blair Niles's *Strange Brother* describing the platonic relationship between a heterosexual woman and homosexual man in New York City in the late 1920s. Finally he saw Thomas Mann's novella *Death in Venice*, the story of an ageing writer who becomes increasingly infatuated with a young Polish boy, a book banned in Germany. Halder pulled it from the bookcase. He stroked the expensive leather tooled binding. Opening the cover he read the dedication.

A Happy Birthday to a very dear friend. Best wishes Jean-Claude Moreau, 24 April 1939

Two minutes later Halder left the apartment with the book in his pocket.

Chapter Twenty

Paris, 6 August 1944

The Allies had planned to liberate the historic and operationally important town of Caen, located astride the Orne River and at the junction of several roads and railways, on D-Day. But the Allied plan had been too ambitious. The British and American advance encountered some of the strongest German defences in Normandy and stalled around the Caen area. Paris, as a result, remained under German control.

It was evident to Jacques that the Allies were in difficulty when his unit reported that fast-moving German transport, infantry and tanks had been seen moving through and around Paris as the Wehrmacht prepared to push the Allies back towards the beaches of the English Channel.

'The Boche are still running all over Paris,' sighed one of Jacques' unit in frustration.

'Someone told me that the Germans are arresting people at random, shooting them and burying them in the woods in the city parks on the Bois du Boulogne and the Jardin du Luxembourg.'

'I've heard that too,' said another.

'If the Allies don't come soon, we'll all be dead,' said someone.

'We have to be able to defend ourselves,' pleaded another to Jacques.

'We need weapons. We have two rifles and a few pistols between us. We need more,' said another.

'Every Resistance unit in Paris is short of weapons and explosives,' answered Jacques.

'But we must do something,' another member fired back.

Jacques knew the frustration was building among his men and continued inaction might explode with unfortunate consequences.

'Perhaps there are some preparations that can be done. If half the group can obtain petrol to make Molotov cocktails we might be better prepared when the fighting does happen. It's all we can do for the moment,' shouted Jacques in an effort to calm the mood.

Some of the group mumbled among themselves but most seemed satisfied with the answer. Jacques allocated tasks and the group dispersed.

****

Halder was in his office when a colleague walked in and said he had some news that might be of interest.

'When the Allies landed in Normandy the Resistance thought liberation would come within a few days and they encouraged all sorts of people to join them. The only qualification for a new recruit was that they were prepared to fight, and they relaxed their usual caution to people joining their groups. That carelessness gave us an opportunity to infiltrate some of the larger resistance groups with Abwehr agents. One of our agents has reported back and is in my office. He has some information you will find interesting.'

A few minutes later Halder was looking at a man dressed in a tweed jacket, shirt and beret.

The Abwehr agent repeated the report he'd made before. 'It was easy for me to join the group. My mother was born in Alsace-Lorraine and I speak French like a native. They were recruiting anyone that volunteered and no one checked my credentials. The other thing in my favour is that I've never been posted to Paris so there was no chance I'd be identified. I joined a resistance group formed from some striking railway workers. It wasn't well led and when I told them I'd served in the French army before the war I was put in charge of a group of men. That meant I was soon in contact with the leaders of other groups.'

Halder smiled and nodded for the man to continue.

'Three days ago I arranged for the group to meet up with another resistance group in a house in a north-eastern suburb of the city. It was a trap and we arrested dozens of resistors. In exchange for his life, one resistant offered us information about a group called Liferaft and the location of a forger.'

'So, have you arrested this forger?' enquired Halder.

'Not yet, we thought you should be told before we did so because the address of the forger's hideout is a building owned by the Tagleva bank.'

'Where is the man who gave you this information?' asked Halder.

'On a train to Buchenwald concentration camp, but all the information he gave us is in this report.'

Halder took the file and returned to his office.

****

Now that the war seemed almost over, like the rest of the city, Samuel was waiting for the liberation. He would have been happy to make some travel passes, but since D-Day the leaders of Liferaft had decided it would be safer to hide Allied pilots and escaping prisoners of war in safe houses and wait for the liberation rather than risk their capture, and those helping them, by sending them down the line to Spain. He sighed – he was bored with the inactivity. Despite his redundancy he was still kept company by his protectors, today a man named Marcel would move him and his family to safety should there be any danger. Samuel was grateful to Liferaft. It meant he'd avoided the police round-up three years before, when half the Jewish male population in the 11th arrondissement had been arrested, and again in 1942 when six thousand Jews had been herded like cattle into trucks. Samuel put down the book he was reading and looked at Marcel.

'Would you like a hot drink?' he asked.

'That would be nice.'

Samuel went to the kitchen. He placed the kettle onto the stove and turned on the gas tap, there was no gas, instead he poured himself and Marcel a cup of water. It was then he heard steel tracks on the hard surface of the cobblestones in the street below, a sound that would jar your teeth loose after only a few minutes. He put down the mugs and walked into the living room. Samuel and Marcel heard the jackboots on the stairs. The Germans were raiding the house and that meant they must suspect he was inside. Marcel pulled aside a rug on the floor, bent down and lifted the trap door to reveal the space where Samuel could be hidden. Samuel stepped down into the hiding place just as the pounding on the apartment door began; the space was small and cramped but it would hide him from the Germans. The front door splintered and came off its hinges and a German was framed in the doorway. Samuel had not yet been hidden and he expected his guardian to kill him as ordered, but instead Marcel pointed his pistol at the German. Marcel fired, and fired again. The infantryman slumped to the floor like a sack of potatoes. A second infantryman appeared and raised his Sturmgewehr 44 rifle. Samuel, half in and half out of his hiding place, watched as bullets ripped into Marcel and was transfixed to the spot as the SS infantryman walked into the room and looked at him for a brief second. 'Jew,' he sneered, raised the assault rifle and then everything went black.

Chapter Twenty-One

18 August 1944

The Tagleva bank in Rue Pierre Charron was a hive of panicked activity. Jean-Claude got up from his desk and walked to the window. In the street below an army truck was being filled with papers the Germans intended should not fall into the hands of the Allies. In the distance he heard the faint sound of rifle fire. It seemed to Jean-Claude that despite the war being close to its end and the Germans making preparations to leave Paris things had become more dangerous. Liferaft, the network he'd built up so carefully, was in danger of collapse. Luc had been arrested and committed suicide, Alain was in hiding, Marcel had been killed and Samuel captured and his wife and children taken into custody. With everything that had happened Jean-Claude couldn't understand why the Gestapo hadn't arrested him; the dread of it sat heavily on his shoulders leaving him a little giddy and with a constantly knotted stomach. All he could do was to wait and hope the Allies would come before his name was called out and he was taken to Gestapo headquarters.

Jean-Claude left his office and walked down the staircase. On the ground floor boxes were stacked, one on top of another, waiting to be loaded into the trucks. The faceless SS orderlies moving this way and that ignored him; after four years of occupation he was part of the furniture.

He walked down the stairs to the basement. Most of the safe deposit boxes were disordered and open, and emptied of the money and valuables that the German officers had accumulated during their stay. He looked at the open door of the bank's twenty-four-bolt Diebold vault. Jean-Claude walked inside. The vault was empty except for a few boxes containing broken pots from ancient Greece. The most important and valuable pieces from the Tagleva art collection:

a nineteenth-century enamelled cup made out of rock crystal and gold by the jeweller Reinhold Vasters; an emerald and diamond tiara, a gift from Napoleon Bonaparte to his second wife; a prayer book once owned by Catherine de' Medici had all disappeared. He recognised one empty container that once held an Egyptian cup four inches high, made of glassy faience, from the eighteenth dynasty reign of Thutmosis III. He turned away and climbed the staircase back to his office. Walking past the chairman's office on the fourth floor he heard Nicole Labranche plead with her SS boss.

'Please take me with you. I've been your secretary for four years and done everything you asked of me. If I stay in Paris, they'll kill me... how can you leave me after everything we've meant to each other, I beg you...'

Jean-Claude walked on past, he had no sympathy for her situation or her distress. Like so many others in the city she had colluded with the occupiers, denounced colleagues to the Gestapo and must now live with the consequences of her collaboration.

****

The men in Jacques' group continued to grumble about the lack of progress by the Allies in liberating Paris. Michael sympathised with those for whom Paris held a political and emotional significance; it did for him too. He felt it best not to explain that the delay was probably because the American commander in chief, General Eisenhower, felt Paris was of little military significance and but an ink spot on the map. Eisenhower's armies were doing what Michael thought strategically more beneficial, race towards the greater military prize of the Rhine. Though, he wished that Jacques' men wouldn't vent their criticism towards him for the Allied strategy.

'France was betrayed by the British when the Germans attacked at the start of the war. Now, at the end the British are betraying us again by not liberating the capital.' Michael was told more than once and was always thankful when Jacques came to his defence to cool tempers.

Despite the lack of Allied support Jacques and Michael knew it was time to make plans for the liberation of Paris. Judging by their unit patches, the Germans had weakened their forces in the city. All battle-hardened soldiers had been moved to Normandy to fight the Allies and those detailed to keep peace on the city's streets had been replaced by administrators, and even cooks. It was obvious that if a German soldier could carry a rifle they were being dragooned to show a presence on the streets. However, the unseasoned German troops seemed to make the streets even more unsafe than before, they were nervous, undisciplined and trigger-happy.

Jacques had been discussing his unit's plans to attack the Germans for over an hour when a man walked into the room carrying a few sheets of paper.

'What have you there?' enquired Jacques.

'The communists have started fighting and have distributed a list of collaborators to be arrested and executed.'

Jacques held out his hand and the list was handed over. He glanced at the top page and noticed that against each name was a description of the crimes held against them. Unsurprisingly the first name was:

Philippe Pétain: Chief of State of Vichy France

He gave a cursory glance at some of the pages and recognised a few names and many he did not:

Joseph Barthélemy: Signed the law giving the Germans the legal right to pass down life imprisonment and death sentences without right of appeal

Henry Charbonneau: Encouraged Frenchmen to enlist in German army*

Coco Chanel: Couturier and the mistress of a German officer

Maurice Chevalier: Entertained Germans

Gabrielle Jeantet: Chief of propaganda in Pétain's government

Jean Luchaire: Journalist: Head of collaborationist press in Paris

Jean-Claude Moreau: Managing Director of Tagleva bank. Financial collaborator*

Georges Oltramare: Director of German funded newspaper La France au Travail

François Spirito: Gestapo agent

André Tulard: French civil administrator and police inspector*

Xavier Vallat: Commissioner-General for Jewish Questions in the Vichy government

Jacques folded the papers and put them to one side before continuing the discussion with his men.

'We must take some of the hotels where the Germans have set up their administration,' said Jacques as he unfolded a map of the city and began to identify the targets. 'The Hotel Meurice, the Ritz...'

At the end of the meeting, out of curiosity, Michael picked up the papers beside Jacques and began to read the list of names.

'Who made up this list?' asked Michael.

'I presume the self-styled *Comité Perisien de Libération*.'

Michael continued to read the names until he came to the one he knew so well. Pointing to the name Jean-Claude Moreau he said, 'Why the hell is he on the list? This man isn't a collaborator, I know him. He runs a resistance group that's smuggled British pilots out of France.'

Jacques took the paper from Michael and looked at it.

'It says he's collaborated with the Germans. He heads the bank used by the SS to manage the money stolen by the SS. This mark says he's to be shot if he resists arrest.'

'Then we have to get his name taken off the list,' said Michael.

'And how are you going to do that? Every resistance group in Paris will have the same list by now. To get his name removed you'll have to contact every resistance group, and we don't know them all. They all work separately; they're suspicious and jealous of each other. Some groups will believe you and take his name off the list and others won't. They'll say it's your word against many that this man is innocent.'

'If we radio London they'll confirm what I say.'

'All right, we'll ask London to confirm what you say in tonight's broadcast. Then we'll know if he's innocent. If London confirms it we'll try to tell as many groups as possible but it won't mean we can get his name removed from all the lists in Paris. When the uprising begins people will have too much to think about to remove one innocent man's name from a list of collaborators. So I suggest you forget about him.'

'I can't,' said Michael and he got up from the table and walked outside.

As Michael stood on the street a car passed, and from the window was thrown some leaflets. They scattered over the cobbles and Michael bent down to pick one up. It called for the population of Paris to rise up against the Germans. A minute later Jacques joined him on the pavement. He took out a cigarette, passed one to Michael and lit it.

'This Jean-Claude is important to you?'

'He is,' replied Michael. 'His network sent secrets and information to London about the German plans since the start of the war. He's saved hundreds of pilots shot down over France and helped them escape back to England.'

'He sounds like a good man. I've told the radio operator to get a message to London. If the information comes back that confirms your story I'll do what I can. But, I warn you, news has come through that the Germans killed every resistant prisoner in Caen prison, even the teenagers. Many in Paris are out for revenge. If he's captured he may be killed without a second's hesitation.'

Michael took a deep draw on the cigarette and threw it into the gutter in frustration.

****

Halder put on his coat, opened a drawer of his desk and took out the semi-automatic Browning pistol. Checking that the grip frame accommodated all nine bullets, he thrust it into his coat pocket, the arrest warrant he tucked inside his jacket. Halder knew he had waited longer than he should have before arresting Jean-Claude but he also knew the reason. He admired Jean-Claude and, in other circumstances, he would have given anything to have been his friend, but fate had conspired that they would support opposing sides, because of that any chance of friendship was impossible, and now he had a duty to perform.

He ordered a junior Gestapo officer to drive him to Rue Pierre Charron. It would be his final opportunity to arrest the banker. Halder had been told that Hitler had given orders that Paris was to be destroyed and German demolition groups were setting explosive charges on the Pont Alexandre III, Paris's most elegant bridge, Notre Dame Cathedral, the Arc de Triomphe, the Opéra and even the Eiffel Tower.

Riding in the passenger seat, Halder looked out of the window at the sights and places he'd come to enjoy over the past four years. The coffee shops with signs above announcing they were a *Soldatenkaffee*, but there were no soldiers inside drinking coffee now, the poster on the billboard near the Métro warning Parisians against the 'cancer of communist terrorism', the signs directing German soldiers to various hospitals and other points of interest. Despite the normality Halder was aware the streets were greyer, dirtier, and filled with thousands of leaflets tumbling around in the gutters.

Arriving at Rue Pierre Charron, Halder and his driver showed their identity cards to the SS guard; ignoring the piles of boxes in the foyer they walked up the stairs to the fourth floor. At Jean-Claude's office door Halder told his driver to wait and admit no one.

Halder walked into the outer lobby. The reception area was empty, the secretary absent. He was pleased. He didn't want Jean-Claude to anticipate his arrival. He pushed open the office door and, as expected, the banker was sitting at his desk. For over two years he'd spent countless hours investigating Jean-Claude, every detail of his life had been examined and re-examined. Now Halder knew the truth; that through his effortless charm Jean-Claude had seemingly co-operated with the SS as he financed a network that both spied on Germany and smuggled Allied pilots and prisoners of war out of France. Now the time had arrived for his arrest Halder was conflicted by emotions; Jean-Claude was a criminal who had worked against Germany, yet it was impossible not to like, even admire, him.

Jean-Claude looked up from his desk.

'I've come to arrest you,' Halder said.

Halder watched as the corners of Jean-Claude's lips pulled back making them flat, an expression of fear. Then, much to his admiration, Jean-Claude seemed to regain his composure.

'I see. But why now, when things are almost over, when you should be preparing to leave Paris, like your colleagues?' he asked.

'Because I have a duty to fulfil, that is to arrest you for working against the German Reich.'

Jean-Claude's hands moved below the desk, out of view. Halder pulled the Browning pistol out of his coat pocket. Jean-Claude raised his hands above the desk once more.

'You don't need to worry. I'm not armed; in fact I hate guns and the noise they make. Can I ask, are you going to shoot me now?' asked Jean-Claude.

'No, I'm not a murderer. You're coming with me to Gestapo headquarters.'

Chapter Twenty-Two

London, 19 August 1944

Philip found it easy to confide his emotions to Father Nicholas Gibbes.

'I never thought I would feel this wretched. I feel so lost without her. I know I need to be strong for the children but I haven't been and I don't know what to do...'

Philip and Sophie met the priest at a Russian exiles' meeting during the 1930s and their mutual connections to members of the Russian royal family made it inevitable that they would be friends. For more than ten years Sydney Gibbes had taught the English language to the heir to the Russian throne, the Tsarevich Alexis. By all accounts Gibbes became a trusted member of the imperial family's household. In turn he admired the royal family's kindness and Christian faith. So inspired was he that, after the martyrdom of the royal family and his return to his homeland, he converted to the Russian Orthodox Church, becoming a monk, then a deacon and finally a priest. People said he held a spiritual sensitivity and a genuine love for the imperial family, which resulted in tears streaming down his face whenever he conducted a service in their memory. After Sophie's funeral Philip invited him to stay a few days and he spent the time listening to Philip.

Father Gibbes placed a hand on Philip's shoulder. 'You and Sophie journeyed through this life, not on calm seas, but in storms that would have driven weaker couples onto the rocks. It's natural for you to feel emptiness like a heavy weight resting on your shoulders with nothing you can do to get out from underneath it. There are no magic words that I have that will take away your deep pain. However, there are two pathways with grief. You can allow it to crush you, like my grief for the imperial family, and allow it to rule and control everything you do for the rest of your life, or you can take the alternative pathway, which is to allow Sophie's love to radiate from inside you. True love is not a common gift – yet it's been given to you, so don't be selfish with it, be proud of it, and allow everyone, especially your children, to share in it. Can I make a suggestion?'

Philip nodded.

'The children love you very much. They see your grief and don't want to burden you further with theirs, but they're grieving too, in fact they're hurting very badly. But because you're not there they are trying to find their own solace, but they're young and don't know how. Then there's Juliette, she's lost her baby, is missing Michael desperately, and feels utterly alone in London; she also needs your comfort. If Sophie were here she would be embracing and comforting them all. She can't do that but you can; give them Sophie's love by being with them and allowing her love to come to them through you.'

A tear fell from Philip's eye. 'You're right. I'll speak to the children tonight and with Juliette. Thank you for being a good friend… to us all.'

****

When Parisians in the 19th arrondissement heard that the employees of the Paris Métro had gone on strike some felt brave enough to rise up and fight the Germans. When there were no reprisals from the Germans hundreds of men and women suddenly found the courage to defy their occupiers and put on armbands with the letters FFI, indicating they were part of the *Forces Françaises de l'Interieur*, and joined in. Michael had somehow expected a more disciplined start to the uprising but as he watched youths begin to tear down the German street signs, cut down trees, rip benches from the parks and even requisition a street urinal to build barricades across roads he thought it was chaotic and messy. With few weapons and even fewer bullets youths tore up cobblestones from the streets to stockpile as missiles that they planned to hurl at the Germans. Seeing what was happening on the streets the gendarmerie and police now joined the uprising. Michael thought the Paris population very forgiving; a few hours before they had been the same police that had helped the Germans with the round-up of resistants, but the police action was just in time to save their reputations and their skins.

When the first German casualties came the Germans took a brutal revenge. They rounded up some youths, executed them and dumped their bodies on the street. Jacques' unit came across them after they first smelt the putrid, sickly sweet scent of death that permeated the air. Despite the visceral sensation in their guts and the desire to vomit, Michael and the others couldn't take their eyes off the sight of the youths, half-sitting, half-laying on the pavement. Before they had been killed the young men had been tortured, their hands stripped of skin, their eyes gauged out and in their pain their bowels had been released. The Germans obviously hoped the spectacle would instil fear into the citizens of Paris but instead it stirred a yearning for a terrible revenge.

Two hours later Jacques' group ambushed a truck carrying a small group of German soldiers. One of Jacques' men approached from behind and threw a Molotov cocktail into the vehicle. As the petroleum ignited screams could be heard from inside, in their pain the wounded Germans pleaded to be put out of their agony, begging someone to throw a grenade into the vehicle and end their suffering. Ignoring their desperate screams Jacques' men turned away and as they walked up the road one of the younger members of the unit shouted to the others, 'Today's special: roast pork.'

****

Gestapo headquarters was empty of prisoners. Most had been shot and the remainder sent to prison camps in Germany. But Halder didn't intend to send Jean-Claude Moreau to a concentration camp; he'd invested too much time and effort to have some camp guard decide how the banker would die. Besides Halder had too many questions he wanted answering: how had Jean-Claude managed to finance the Resistance? How had he evaded suspicion while working in the same building as the SS? How had he run a resistance group under their very noses?

Halder needed the information but had already decided he would not torture the banker. His colleagues saw torture as a harsh necessity, but Halder knew torture didn't accomplish what its defenders said it did. Extreme temperature, starvation, thirst, sleep deprivation and immersion in freezing water were effective in forcing false confessions, but he wanted more than just a confession, he wanted the truth. He decided that he'd begin Jean-Claude's interrogation the following day. A night alone in the cells, contemplating the future would not be wasted on Jean-Claude Moreau.

Chapter Twenty-Three

London, the same evening

Philip Tagleva was sitting on Halinka's bed listening to his teenage daughter who was very angry.

'Father Gibbes said God called her home but she already had a home, it's here, and now she's not here, and it's not a home any longer. I hate God.' Halinka screamed before throwing her arms around his shoulders.

Philip held his daughter tight and whispered in her ear, 'Your mother's gone for now, but it's not forever, she's just out of reach.'

Halinka pulled herself from him and smiled through her tears. 'I'm sorry Daddy. I love you.' Philip wiped away the tears from her puffy eyes.

'I know and I love you too.'

Later that night, after Philip had spent time with each of his children and everyone was in bed, he walked into Sophie's dressing room and sat down at the dressing table. He looked at the array of brushes, combs and the empty silver topped perfume bottle, and smiled as he remembered Sophie had never complained at the deprivations of rationing. That was until cosmetics and face powder became unavailable. When a sad-looking cardboard box had been delivered with the wrong colour refill for her lipstick Sophie had thrust the printed apology into his hands, pointing out the man's signature at the bottom and accused him of using the war as an excuse for denying her the correct colour lipstick.

She told him, 'If one's lucky enough to buy powder it's always minus its puff. I'm not complaining for myself, it's for Britain... everyone knows Hitler abhors cosmetics, he thinks it un-Aryan. So it must be the patriotic duty for all British women to defy Hitler and look our best. Reason enough for cosmetics not to be rationed.'

He had managed to supress a chuckle as he explained, 'But war production is needed to produce tanks.'

'One less tank isn't going to make a difference to defeating Hitler,' Sophie had replied before looking at him and convulsing into uncontrollable laughter at the fragility of her argument.

The following day Philip sent a memo to the Ministry of Supply suggesting that makeup was as important to women as tobacco was to men. He pointed out to the ministry the unfairness of cosmetic companies that continued to advertise their wares, despite having none to sell, by reminding women that 'Beauty was a Duty', in the anticipation that once the war was over Britain's women would never have got used to not wearing makeup. Not surprisingly, the Ministry of Supply was deaf to Philip's pleadings and Sophie and the rest of women in Britain remained frustrated by the lack of proper makeup. That was until American GIs landed on England's shores with haversacks bulging with silk stockings, chewing gum, lipstick and face powders that included the puff.

Still smiling Philip opened a drawer. He looked at the paraphernalia of her life: old postcards, a broken necklace, some coins, a couple of old receipts and a few photographs. Then he saw an envelope, it was addressed to him. He picked it up and stared at it. *Why would Sophie have a letter addressed to me?* He carefully opened it.

My Darling Philip,

In case I'm ever deprived of the opportunity there are two things I want you to know.

Firstly, my darling, for many years after my brother Sergei was killed I punished myself because I'd never had a final chance to tell him how much I loved him. If anything were to happen to me I don't want you to punish yourself in the same way. When we met at the Hotel European in St. Petersburg, and you presented me with a white rose at dinner, you lit a fire inside me that has never been put out. You have been the only man I have ever loved. I know love bestows no rights and I knew I had no right to your heart, but was thrilled when you, so obviously and unconditionally, gave it to me.

My love, neither of us needs a final time to say to each other that we love one another. I knew it every day from the way you looked at me and from every tender word you spoke so often and you should know, in turn, I adored and loved you so very, very much in return.

Secondly, my love, I would ask that there should be a conclusion to the Tsar's jewels we brought out of Russia. We have kept them safely for the heirs of the imperial family. But it's obvious to me that there are no surviving heirs and I think we must consider the jewels should be restored to their rightful owners and I would ask that an appropriate time is found to do this.

Yours my darling Philip and for ever, your loving Sophie

XXX

Philip folded the letter, placed it back into the envelope and put it into his jacket pocket. He closed the drawer, stood up and as he did so was convinced he could smell Sophie's favourite perfume. He closed his eyes, took in a deep breath, and his mind flooded with warm memories.

Chapter Twenty-Four

Paris, 22 August 1944

After his arrest Jean-Claude had one dread: that he would be beaten with clubs and forced to endure the pain of torture in the same way that Luc had experienced, but to his surprise the opposite had been true. Since his arrival at Gestapo headquarters Halder had treated him with courtesy and the only discomfort he had suffered was the bright light, set into the high ceiling of his cell, had been left on all night. Even had the light not been on he would not have slept as his mind played out the next few hours inside his head. However, sitting in a comfortable chair with a glass of cognac on the desk in front of him as Halder politely presented the facts and the evidence against him in a nonchalant tone was not what he had imagined to be the usual style of interrogation.

'When the SS walked into Tagleva and announced they were occupying the building you must have been shocked, even angry. I must admit I have every sympathy with you, had the situation been reversed and Germany had been occupied by France, I would have felt the same.'

Halder paused, to see if Jean-Claude agreed with these conclusions, but his expression remained blank.

'The start of your resistance group probably began with you helping a couple of friends with money. Petty criminals who daubed V signs on walls, or perhaps you financed a black marketer who wanted to buy ration stamps. Am I right?'

Jean-Claude briefly looked away from the policeman's stare.

'Or maybe your crimes started in a more serious manner, possibly with the hiding of Jews. Which is it? Tell me, I'm interested,' enquired Halder softly.

Jean-Claude shook his head. 'It's neither. I'm not the banker you're looking for.'

Halder stood up and walked around Jean-Claude so that he was behind him. Placing his hand on Jean-Claude's shoulder he gently squeezed it.

'Oh come, come, you can confide in me now. Even if you confess I don't intend to shoot you. Paris will soon be liberated by the Allies and I'll have to rush back to Germany. The war in Paris is over and soon you'll be able to return to your comfortable life as managing director of the Tagleva bank. We could be friends and there's no reason for you to continue to protest your innocence, no need to protect the others in your resistance group. Even if I wanted to, I can't arrest any of the people you say are involved, I don't have the personnel or the resources any more. But as a policeman and a friend I've always hated loose ends and I'm interested in knowing if my suspicions are correct.'

'I keep telling you, I'm not the man you're looking for.'

Halder squeezed Jean-Claude's shoulder again before returning to his desk and sitting down.

'So tell me, why did you send Sébastien away? Was it to protect him from me in case you were arrested?'

'I told you before, we argued and Sébastien left. I don't know where he is,' replied Jean-Claude.

'Then perhaps I can tell you. My information is he's hiding somewhere near Villard-de-Lans. It's a commune in the Isère department of the Auvergne, but I'm sure you know that.'

Jean-Claude was shocked by the reference to Sébastien and wondered if Halder had some specific information. He desperately wanted to know the news, but in an effort not to betray the fact avoided looking at Halder.

'I guess that's where he is, because someone gave the police a description of a stranger in the area that matched Sébastien's. At least you know he's safe, but possibly not for much longer. I'm informed the Milice and the SS are about to launch an attack on the area, to punish attacks on our troops by the Resistance. Help me to help you. If you co-operate with me, I could protect Sébastien when he's captured. You know the Milice can be brutal; they're thugs, sadists, worse even than the SS. I don't want Sébastien to fall into their hands.'

At that moment Jean-Claude thought about telling Halder everything, anything to save Sébastien. Then he thought back to what Halder had said *someone gave the police a description of a stranger in the area that matched Sébastien's... I could protect Sébastien when he's captured.* It meant Halder wasn't entirely sure if Sébastien was there or not. *He was playing a game. Was it all a game?*

Before Jean-Claude could answer, Halder changed the direction of the questioning.

'Do you remember when you were outside Gestapo headquarters, the day the man leapt from the window and killed himself? He was a resistant. Did you know the man?'

'No.'

'I'm surprised. I was convinced you would know him. We found his photograph in a forger's workshop in a building owned by Tagleva.'

'That's just coincidence,' answered Jean-Claude.

'Is it? Are you sure you didn't know the man?'

'I'd never seen him before.'

'Then, tell me this, how is it that I found this in the man's apartment?'

Halder reached into his drawer, pulled out a leather bound book and passed it to him.

Jean-Claude took the book from Halder.

'Open it and read aloud the dedication inside.'

Jean-Claude didn't need to, he knew what he had written, but did as he'd been ordered.

'A Happy Birthday to a very dear friend. Best wishes Jean-Claude Moreau, 24 April 1939.'

'That is your dedication, is it not?' asked Halder.

At that moment Jean-Claude knew Halder had pieced together the jigsaw. He drew in a deep breath and gave Halder a burning stare of hatred for the murder of Luc.

From outside the building came the sound of gunfire.

As if to explain the noise Halder said, 'General Choltitz has received orders from Berlin to suppress any uprising by the citizens of Paris. I'm told the battle is to be conducted mercilessly.

It will be bloody; the Führer has ordered Choltitz to fight to the last man.'

'I trust the general will follow his orders to the letter,' replied Jean-Claude.

Halder chuckled. 'I've always admired your humour and intellect, even more now, considering the circumstances.'

****

Jacques' unit moved street by street towards the centre of the city and were now located on the third floor of a building. Jacques hoped that their elevated position would give them an indication of the location of fighting and where to move to next. As Michael and Jacques looked out of the window they saw a barricade being built at the far end of the street and the residents seemed to be having a party. As if they'd forgotten how to stand still everyone was dancing and children were running about as if it were the first day of the school holiday. The expression on their faces was a picture of excitement. They had won, the Germans were defeated and would soon be leaving the city and things were only going to get better from here on in.

Suddenly a deep rumble interrupted the jollity. The crowd stopped moving and went silent as they watched an eight-wheeled Schwerer Panzerspähwagen appear around the corner. The all-wheel-drive armoured vehicle was perfect for street fighting with two driver positions, one at the front and another at the rear, allowing the vehicle to be driven with maximum manoeuvrability in both a forward or reverse direction. It rumbled towards them. The open-topped turret had been covered with a wire mesh metal frame designed to protect the commander and gunner from cobblestones, grenades and other missiles. The vehicle came to a halt below the window. Michael watched as the barrel of the machine gun began to turn towards the barricade. Mothers pulled their children into the safety of the nearby apartment buildings, some men fled inside a café. A few crouched behind the barricade determined to confront the armoured vehicle. Michael saw that only one rifle was pointing towards the German vehicle from the barricade. With so little to defend themselves those who were determined to confront the Germans would lose their lives.

'Quick, pass me a Molotov cocktail,' Michael shouted.

Someone passed Michael a wine bottle half filled with petroleum and with a cloth wick protruding from the neck. Jacques struck a match and lit the petrol-soaked material; the flame took hold. Michael leaned out of the window and carefully tossed the bottle towards the turret of the German vehicle. As it flew through the air it spun, over and over, eventually smashing on the thin shell of wire mesh protecting the men inside. The gunner was sprayed with flaming petroleum and cried out more in surprise than pain. The German commander looked up to where the attack had come from just as his own jacket was set alight. Michael watched the two soldiers begin to beat their chests to extinguish the flames. A second wine bottle half full of petrol was handed to Michael and he tossed it out of the window. The glass smashed on one of the struts holding the protective mesh in place. To avoid further attacks the vehicle began to move down the street and a smell of burning petrol wafted up towards Michael. From within the armoured vehicle came a muffled explosion and it suddenly began to zigzag down the avenue before it slewed to the right and crashed into a building. One of the drivers staggered from the vehicle and took a few steps. A single shot came from the barricade. The soldier crumpled, falling face down onto the cobbles. A shout of triumph came from the barricade. The crowd's faces were lit up in triumph and a man rushed forward and began to dance around the burning vehicle, his arms raised in victory.

****

Despite the machine guns in their hands and grenades hanging from their belts the two teenage soldiers guarding the doors to Gestapo headquarters were terrified. Their thoughts were of their families in their farms in Westfalen and Thüringen, their fears… the Paris mob.

Inside Halder continued to question Jean-Claude.

'Tell me, you are the banker, aren't you?'

Jean-Claude sighed. He was exhausted by the endless questioning and the cognac Halder had encouraged him to drink was making his thoughts cloudy. His head was flooded with too many thoughts and 'what ifs'. As he looked at Halder the rifle fire seemed louder and closer than before. *What would it matter if I admitted to being the banker? The Germans are defeated. Halder could shoot me but those I care for and love are beyond his reach.*

Jean-Claude began to formulate an answer in his mind.

At the entrance to the building, the two young German guards lay dead as men with berets and FFI armbands stepped over them and rushed inside. Halder and Jean-Claude heard the heavy boots as they climbed the stairs and the doors along the corridor being kicked in.

Suddenly two men burst into the room. Halder and Jean-Claude stood up as the two Böhmische Waffenfabrik pistols, liberated from the two dead soldiers at the front of the building, were pointed at them.

Another man walked into the office and was obviously the leader of the group.

'Your identities,' he demanded.

'I'm Major der Polizeito Julius Halder.'

'And I'm Jean-Claude Moreau, managing director of the Tagleva bank.'

The leader spoke to Halder, 'You are now a prisoner of war.'

'And you, what are you doing here?' he asked Jean-Claude.

'I'm being questioned by this man.'

The leader looked at the two glasses and the half-empty bottle of cognac on the desk.

'An unusual interrogation, monsieur, not the style we have come to expect from the Gestapo.'

'I assure you that's what was happening,' replied Jean-Claude.

The man pulled out some papers from his jacket and looked down the list of names.

'Jean-Claude Moreau, you are on this list as a collaborator and a traitor, you are under arrest.'

Halder looked at Jean-Claude and began to laugh.

'What's so funny?' asked the leader with a snarl.

'Nothing, nothing at all, it's all too perfect,' replied Halder.

Two men walked over to Halder and began to lead him away.

'One moment,' said Halder and turned to Jean-Claude. 'You didn't answer my final question.'

'Your conclusions were correct and flawless,' answered Jean-Claude.

Halder smiled. 'I'm sorry that circumstances meant we were never able to be true friends. The irony is that I knew the answer all along. I could have saved myself and fled to Germany and left you to your fate at the hands of your countrymen. Anyhow, thank you for telling me the truth, I needed to know.'

Halder was led from the room.

Chapter Twenty-Five

London, 25 August 1944

Juliette was sitting in the living room trying to read a book with the radio playing softly in the corner of the room, but she couldn't concentrate on the words on the pages. All her mind could think about was the loss of her baby and when the radio played Dick Haymes' song, *You'll never know how much I miss you, you'll never know how much I care...* She put down the book to listen. A tear fell down her face. She had asked herself a thousand times if she could have done more to prevent her baby's death. She thought back to Sophie's death and how the family had found solace in the company of other mourners but, it seemed to her, the loss of her baby had brought with it a helplessness, hopelessness and bitterness that was an entirely private grief. When friends would ask, 'How are you?' in a conversational tone, Juliette wondered if they really wanted to know the blackness of her mood.

Suddenly the music stopped. *'We're interrupting this programme with an announcement. After four long years under German occupation, Paris is now free.'*

Juliette stood up, walked over to the radio and turned the volume up,

'...Last night, the French 2nd Armoured Division was the first Allied force to enter the city... The Free French wireless station has reported the German commander, General Dietrich von Choltitz, signed a surrender in the presence of General Leclerc... General Charles de Gaulle is to lead a liberation march down the Champs d'Élysées tomorrow.'

Suddenly all thoughts about her baby were gone and Juliette couldn't contain her excitement and rushed into the hallway shouting, *'Nous sommes libres! Nous sommes libres!'*

Without knocking she threw open Philip's study door.

'Have you heard the news?' she shouted.

Startled by the loud interruption Philip stood up from his desk. Juliette rushed to him, threw her arms around his neck and planted a large kiss on each cheek. Stepping back she looked at her father-in-law's startled face and seeing he hadn't understood the news shouted once more, *'Nous sommes libres!'*

Philip smiled back at her. 'Who's free?' he asked.

'Paris. Paris is free. It's just been announced on the radio. It's so exciting.'

'That's wonderful news.'

Her face fell as she thought she might have upset him by her embrace.

'I'm sorry. I've disturbed you, I forgot myself,' she said.

'Nonsense, I was deep in thought and didn't understand what you were so excited about. Despite everything it's a day we should all be happy. Your home's been liberated and we must find a way to celebrate... I know. I've got just the idea.'

Philip led Juliette upstairs to one of the spare bedrooms and opened up a Chinese camphor wood chest. From the bottom he pulled out an enormous French Tricolour that, before the war, had flown from the Tagleva bank in London to show the bank's connection with its headquarters in Paris.

'Let's hang this from the upstairs window above the front door,' he said.

They spent the next ten minutes hanging the flag from a window. Once done they walked out onto the street to admire their handiwork and both smiled at each other as the flag, now dominating the front of the house, began to gently flutter in the wind.

Philip turned to Juliette. 'I'm afraid I don't have any champagne for us to drink but how do you fancy celebrating with a beer at the York Minster?'

'The French pub? Oh what a wonderful idea,' Juliette exclaimed.

After telling the housekeeper they would be out for the rest of the afternoon Philip and Juliette walked the short distance from Mayfair to Soho. As they turned the corner from Shaftesbury Avenue into Dean Street the noise of the celebrations was deafening. It seemed every Frenchman and Frenchwoman in

London had heard the news and descended on the French pub. Their journey to the bar was a long one, squeezing past groups singing 'La Marseillaise', celebrants raising half-full glasses of beer into the air and at each step they had to exchange kisses on the cheeks of every stranger they bumped into. Breathless, they arrived at the bar just as someone produced a bottle of Ricard mixed with a little water. A thimbleful of the cloudy liquid was passed to each of them.

'God knows where they got this from, someone must have kept it hidden for the past four years,' shouted Philip into Juliette's ear.

They both took a sip. *'Vive la France,'* they shouted as they toasted each other. Next to them a chorus went up, *'Vivez la France libre'* and a group in the crowd began to sing the 'La Marseillaise' for the umpteenth time.

Philip bought two small glasses of beer that the French pub traditionally served and they squeezed themselves back towards the street, exchanging even more kisses with strangers along the way. Out of breath and with most of their beer spilled they arrived onto Dean Street and began to laugh at the effort it had taken.

Juliette looked at her father-in-law. It felt good to be able to smile broadly together. Philip shouted in her ear, 'Thank you for helping me and my family over the past weeks. My son's a very lucky man.'

Juliette smiled and they both joined in as someone began to sing:
Allons, enfants de la Patrie,
Le jour de gloire est arrivé!…

A couple of hours later Philip and Juliette walked back to the house and the door was opened by a maid.

'You have a visitor, sir. An army gentleman. He arrived a couple of minutes ago and I've put him in your study.'

Philip wondered who the visitor might be. He walked quickly to the study and opening the door saw the familiar figure of Colonel Tim Wilson, Michael's superior officer. For a brief, terrible moment, Philip feared it might be bad news but the look on the colonel's face suggested otherwise.

The two men shook hands. 'I'm sorry to disturb you at a time like this but I thought I'd come personally. Firstly, can I express my condolences on your wife's sad death?'

'Thank you, that's much appreciated,' replied Philip.

'I have news of Michael.'

'If it's bad news, then you can tell me alone, but if it's good then it would be only fair that his wife hears it first-hand.'

The colonel nodded. 'It's good news,' he said with a smile.

Relieved, Philip went to collect Juliette. A minute later they were both standing in front of the colonel waiting to hear what he had to say.

'Michael was in Paris when it was liberated. He's safe and well but he's had a hard time. I managed to get a message to him yesterday and ordered him home. It may not be for a few days but when he arrives he'll have two weeks' leave. I thought you'd both like to know. By the way, I haven't told him about his mother, I felt that would be best coming from his family.'

Philip walked the colonel to the front door and shaking Tim Wilson's hand said, 'Thank you for taking time to come and tell us this news personally, it's much appreciated.'

Walking back into his study Philip found Juliette in floods of tears. He could tell she was crying with relief at the news that Michael was coming home, but also because the homecoming would be a sad one, they would have to tell him about his mother and about the loss of their baby.

Chapter Twenty-Six

Paris, 27 August 1944

Jean-Claude had always planned to celebrate the liberation by opening the bottle of champagne he had kept carefully hidden in his apartment. Instead of sipping champagne with friends he was cold and thirsty, sitting on the floor of a room in the *Institut Dentaire* with his knees drawn up to his chest, a cut lip and his wrists bound with electric wire. Perhaps, Jean-Claude rationalised, within a short time sense would prevail, until then a period of chaos was inevitable. Parisians had lived through four long years of repressed anger and guilt over their country's defeat and now they wanted justice over those they thought had profited from the occupation. It seemed that they were prepared to do without judges and proper courts to obtain it and Jean-Claude reminded himself that it was not the first time. During the French Revolution and the period known as The Reign of Terror, the Paris mob had set up people's tribunals in cafés, on street corners and even in public gardens. Men and women were hauled before them to answer a charge of treason where a single fact, a rumour, sometimes personal jealousy and prejudice resulted in a guilty verdict and an appointment with Madame Guillotine. Jean-Claude sighed to himself, the French revolution and the liberation of the city from the Germans may be separated by a hundred and fifty-five years, but he knew the behaviour of the Paris mob was fuelled by the same misguided sense of revenge. This time the accused were those the mob believed had co-operated and benefited from the Nazi occupation, concierges who had scrubbed off anti-German graffiti from their buildings, café owners and women suspected of sleeping with Germans, the *collabos horizontales*. As he shifted his body on the hard floor in an effort to gain some more comfort Jean-Claude wondered if the mob had already set up the guillotine on the Place de la Concorde.

****

At the intersection of Boulevard Raspail and Rue de Sèvres Michael and Jacques were sitting in comfortable leather armchairs in the bar of the Hotel Lutetia. On the table in front of them was a bottle of Martell Cordon Bleu cognac, which, the day before, had been reserved for officers of the German Wehrmacht and had now been 'liberated'. Jacques and Michael each poured themselves a large glass of the golden liquid and as he savoured the bouquet Jacques resolved not to move from his seat until the bottle was quite empty.

'So when do you return to England?' enquired Jacques.

'As soon as transport can be arranged. It might take a few days but I hope to find space on an empty transport plane flying to England.'

'So, you have a few days to enjoy the highlights of Paris. I hear the Moulin Rouge is opening a new show, Edith Piaf is to sing with Yves Montand.' He paused. 'Or perhaps you'd prefer to find a nice girl to while away the time. If you like I could arrange it for you.'

'You forget Jacques, I'm married and my wife's expecting our first child.'

'You English are all stuffed shirts.' Jacques laughed and took a sip of the cognac.

'Besides, I can't spend my time on frivolities, I have things to do. I must visit the Tagleva bank and see my uncle Jean-Claude to make sure he's well. News of him and the bank will be the first thing my father will ask me when I return to London.'

Jacques looked at Michael. 'Remind me of this man's name.'

'Jean-Claude Moreau.'

Jacques slapped his knee. 'The man on the list. I'm sorry, I forgot with all the fighting and everything. One of the men told me last night he'd heard someone of that name had been arrested by the FTP.'

'When?'

'Yesterday, the day before, I don't know.'

'Oh my God,' said Michael. 'The FTP are communists.'

Jacques nodded. 'And they have a brutal reputation, and with good cause. The Nazis were never gentle with them.'

'Do you know where they've taken him?'

'I assume the Dental Institute. It's in the 13th arrondissement. The FTP are using it to hold their tribunals.'

Michael stood up. 'I must get there and quickly. How long will it take us to get to the Institute?'

'If we hurry, probably half an hour,' came Jacques reply but Michael hadn't heard him, he was halfway to the door. Jacques looked at Michael, looked at the bottle of cognac, sighed, drained his glass and followed him outside.

****

The FTP's membership was made up mostly of communists and controlled from Moscow. During the occupation it gained a reputation for being the most active and determined of the Resistance groups. When captured, being communists, they were brutally treated by the Germans and arrest usually resulted in deportation and death. With everything the group had suffered, denunciations against people for collaboration with the enemy flooded into the Dental Institute. In the past two days the tribunal had investigated the crimes of a dozen or more collaborators and the members of the FTP felt no contrition for mirroring the interrogation methods used by the Gestapo.

One journalist who'd worked for *Paris-Soir*, a man with a sharp anti-communist pen, had been investigated and while being questioned had been forced to skip. If he slowed down one of two men would poke his belly or buttocks with a bayonet. After two hours of skipping the journalist collapsed with exhaustion and was dragged to the back of the room. Then a woman was brought in and questioned about her husband's collaboration with the Germans. She explained to the tribunal that her husband was a dental surgeon and had been forced by the Germans to treat them and that she had acted as the dental nurse.

'What choice did we have when the Germans demanded treatment at the point of a pistol?' she said in her defence.

Her protestations of innocence were rejected by the three men acting as judges. After delivering the verdict on the woman, the head of the tribunal declared it to have been a good morning's work.

'Let's have lunch and then we'll deal with the banker Moreau.'

The woman was taken away and beaten with a rubber cylinder covered with electricity wire before being dragged to the courtyard and shot.

****

Michael and Jacques ran towards the Rue Notre Dame des Champs. The large numbers of people enjoying their newly found freedom crowded around the shops and cafés and slowed their progress to a walk; Michael stepped into the street to avoid the crowds and make faster progress. As he did so a cyclist swerved to avoid him. 'Stupid idiot, watch where you're going!'

'Careful, don't get yourself killed,' shouted Jacques.

Michael stopped and looked around him.

'What are you looking for?' asked Jacques.

'A taxi, a car, anything.'

'Fat chance! It'll be quicker to run.'

They began to weave between the crowds and, where space allowed, run down the street. After eight hundred metres Jacques turned right and into the wider Boulevard de Port Royal, a long avenue connecting the 5th, 13th and 14th arrondissements. The tree-lined boulevard was less crowded and they were able to run in the road without much difficulty. From deep within him, Michael knew he had to keep running; time was short.

****

Jean-Claude was hauled to his feet and almost dragged down the corridor to find himself in a lecture room looking up at three men on a dais, his judges. All three were dressed in dark brown shirts with a fawn, almost yellow, tie and on their left arms, an armband in the red, white and blue colours of France, and on the desk in front of each was a beret. Jean-Claude guessed their uniform, of sort, was to give some sense of being part of a legitimate army.

'Your name is Jean-Claude Moreau?'

'It is.'

'You're charged with having benefited financially from the occupation, co-operating with the SS and the Gestapo against France. Are you guilty or not guilty?'

'I'm, not guilty, in fact…'

'You will be quiet and only answer the questions put to you. Do you understand?'

A man stood next to him menacingly tapping a wooden chair leg into the palm of his hand and Jean-Claude anticipated that an incorrect answer or a protestation of innocence would be swiftly punished. Jean-Claude felt his mouth go dry.

'Throughout the occupation you acted as managing director of Tagleva bank.'

'Yes.'

'You didn't consider resigning when the SS took it over when France surrendered?'

'I had thought of resigning but stayed to protect the staff from the Germans. There was some benefit to me staying.'

'Benefit, to whom?' asked one of the inquisitors.

'I was able to protect the staff and make sure the money confiscated by the Germans and transferred out of France was properly recorded so that it could be recovered after the war.'

'So, you helped the occupiers with the confiscation of money from French citizens?'

'I was required to countersign documents the Germans put in front of me, but I made sure records were kept so the money could be recovered after the liberation.'

'You admit you signed papers for the occupiers to confiscate French property.'

'As I've said I was ordered to do it but always ensured records were kept. I can show you these at the Tagleva bank if you would let me.'

'We don't have time for such irrelevancies, besides there's other evidence that condemns you as a collaborator.'

'I am not a collaborator,' said Jean-Claude.

'So tell me why you were dining with a Gestapo officer at Tour Argent earlier last month. The waiter's given evidence that he heard you helping the Gestapo with their enquiries into members of the Resistance.'

Jean-Claude began to feel none of his answers was going to help his situation. *Their minds are made up.*

He felt the blow from the chair leg on his thigh. Pain seared through his body causing a light to blind him. He fell to his knees and clenched his teeth. He had obviously not answered the question in a timely manner.

'I will ask you again. You were seen dining with a Gestapo officer at Tour Argent. Why?'

'I was suspected of financing the Resistance, he hoped to trick me into confessing,' Jean-Claude cried out through the pain.

'You expect this tribunal to believe a Gestapo agent takes you to a restaurant to interrogate you, feeds you, even buying an expensive bottle of wine? Usually when the Gestapo arrested loyal French patriots they were tortured and shot not given a meal at one of the best restaurants in Paris.'

'It's true, I'm telling you the truth,' pleaded Jean-Claude.

'It says here your Gestapo host bought a fine bottle of burgundy for you to drink with your meal, a 1929 *Charmes-Chambertin* to be exact. An excellent choice for your meal monsieur, 1929 was a very hot summer with light rain in September resulting in a vintage with an elegant taste. The bottle cost a week's salary for a French patriot. I know; I'm a winemaker by trade. You seriously expect us to believe a German policeman bought you lunch because he had grown tired of torturing members of the Resistance?'

The man with the chair leg smiled menacingly.

'What I'm telling you is true, ask the Gestapo man,' answered Jean-Claude.

'We would but unfortunately for you he's been handed over to the Americans. He's a prisoner of war and not able to testify.'

Jean-Claude dropped his head towards the floor.

'When you were arrested at Gestapo headquarters, you were discovered in the same policeman's office relaxing over a cognac. I suppose you're going to tell us that that was another, cruel form of torture?'

The man with the chair leg gave out an audible chuckle and continued to tap the wood in his hand.

Jean-Claude pleaded. 'There are people in Paris that can confirm my story, people who were part of my network. It's called Liferaft. We helped pilots escape, hid Jews and other people on the run from the Germans.'

The inquisitor leaned forward. 'I've never heard of the Liferaft network. If it exists then you will be able to give me the names and the addresses of its members, people who can vouch for you.'

'I can't, when the Gestapo began to become suspicious I told my group to go into hiding... for their safety... I don't know where they are.'

Jean-Claude looked up at the three men behind the desk. They were whispering among themselves.

****

After Michael and Jacques reached the end of Boulevard de Port Royal they took a slight left into Boulevard Arago and then turned immediately right into the Avenue des Gobelins. Halfway up the avenue, opposite the entrance to the Le théâtre des Gobelins, Jacques stopped running to catch his breath.

Jacques spoke between breaths. 'It's not too far now... another six blocks... we arrive at the roundabout at Avenue d'Italie... take the first exit... into the Avenue de Choisy and three hundred metres further along turn left... into Rue George Eastman... and the Institute.'

****

The three men of the tribunal looked down at Jean-Claude.

'Jean-Claude Moreau, you have been unable to provide a believable explanation to the questions put to you, nor the names of anyone who can vouch for your innocence. This court martial finds you guilty of collaboration with the enemy. The sentence is that you are to be shot, sentence to be carried out immediately. There is no appeal.'

Jean-Claude was hauled out of the room. His legs moved but his mind was disembodied. He watched in a haze as his feet somehow moved, without any instruction from himself, one in front of the other, down a flight of stairs. He had never expected death to arrive, always assuming there would be a tomorrow and a day after that. Now the time had arrived he felt strange, there was no emotion, no heavy weight upon his shoulders, just a feeling of floating, as if in a dream. At the bottom of the staircase he was pushed through a door and into a courtyard. He squinted as the sun came out from behind a cloud. As his eyes became used to the brightness he began to take in the scene in front of him. In the centre of the courtyard a man was on his knees, his head was pushed slightly forward, behind him the executioner, a pistol was placed into the base of the neck and fired, the man slumped forward.

****

Michael and Jacques arrived at the door of the Dental Institute. It was guarded by a boy Jacques estimated to be around fifteen years of age proudly wearing the FTP armband on his left arm. The boy raised his rifle to bar their entrance.

'Unless you want to have your fucking arms broken you'll get out of my way,' growled Jacques.

Alarmed and deflated at being spoken to in such a gruff manner the boy took a step back. Jacques pushed him aside and with Michael rushed inside to be confronted by three more members of the FTP, each pointing a rifle at them. These men were older and battle hardened enough not to be intimidated by a shouted command; Jacques and Michael found their pathway blocked.

'What do you want here?' asked one of the men.

'You're holding a Jean-Claude Moreau. We've come to get him released. He's the leader of a Resistance unit called Liferaft. We're able to prove what we say,' replied Michael.

'Wait here,' said one of the men who turned and walked away as the other two men continued to point their rifles at Jacques and Michael.

A long couple of minutes passed before he returned in the company of a second man.

'You're enquiring about a man called Jean-Claude Moreau.'

'Is he here?' demanded Michael.

'He is, but he's been tried and condemned to be shot as a collaborator. But who are you?'

'I'm a British officer attached to the Special Intelligence Service. I parachuted into France before D-Day to work with the Resistance. Your prisoner, Jean-Claude Moreau, is not a collaborator, he's well known to London as the leader of a resistance group called Liferaft. It's helped hundreds of Allied aircrew escape capture. He's sent information to London that was useful to the Allies during the D-Day landings. If you don't believe me radio London yourselves, they will confirm it.'

The man rubbed his chin, as if to think.

****

With detached fascination Jean-Claude watched the scene in front of him as if he was merely an observer to a play being acted out. He watched as the man's body was hauled to the corner of the courtyard; another man was dragged to the execution spot and pushed to his knees. As before his head was pushed forward and the executioner pressed the barrel of the pistol into the base of the man's skull. He heard the shot and the man slumped forward.

Jean-Claude was hauled to his feet and dragged over to the spot; his turn had come. He was pushed towards the ground. Kneeling on the copper coloured gravel he saw in front of him the dark crimson stain. A hand pushed his head forward a few centimetres and exposed his neck. In that brief moment he wondered what Heaven would be like. Would St. Peter be waiting for him with outstretched arms as his mother had always promised and would there be gates to pass through? He felt the barrel of the pistol rub against the skin at the base of his skull. He was surprised, he'd expected the finger of death would be cold, but it was warm from the previous executions and he took some unexpected comfort from the warmth of the metal.

Jean-Claude couldn't understand the delay. He remained kneeling on the ground with his head bowed even after he felt the executioner was no longer behind him. Then he was pulled to his feet and felt confused sensing that Philip's son, Michael, was hugging him. Surely he was imagining it, such a thing was impossible, and then everything went black.

Chapter Twenty-Seven

Zurich, Switzerland, 27 August 1944

Bernstorff had been in Zurich for the past few days and had visited the larger financial institutions, such as Credit Suisse, rejecting them as being too big for his purposes, with too many employees and probably with links to Allied governments. So he had looked at some of the smaller banks and eventually selected, as the one that most suited his needs, a small bank in Zurich. It was owned and managed by one family and of a type the Swiss financial community referred to as a private banker and which he knew had already arranged a number of financial transactions for the SS during the war.

Bernstorff was listening to the banker, aged in his mid-thirties, conservatively dressed and with a confident and efficient manner explain how a Swiss bank account operated. The banker spoke in perfect German and Bernstorff assumed he would have been equally able to converse in any of Switzerland's three other major languages: French, Italian and Romansh, a language spoken predominantly in the Swiss canton of Graubünden, and quite probably he also spoke good English.

'Private banking was invented in Switzerland,' said the young Swiss banker smiling broadly. 'In an unstable world a Swiss bank is an island of stability and the place to keep your money safe. Since 1934 it's been a criminal offence for a Swiss bank to reveal the name of an account holder and that's not the same elsewhere. In London a banker is more than happy to share what he knows about a client, even with a complete stranger. In fact, I'm told that English bankers are so indiscreet they will talk about their clients' affairs at dinner parties.'

Carl Bernstorff half smiled back. In visiting the banks there were two things he had discovered. The first was that all Swiss bankers talked endlessly of their bank's secrecy and security;

never mentioning that the secrecy became a necessity after Adolf Hitler came to power when Germany pressed Swiss banks to divulge the names of Germans with bank deposits. When the Swiss refused, the Nazis declared that any German with a foreign bank account was an 'enemy of the state' and could be punished by death. To protect their Jewish clients the Swiss introduced their secrecy laws. Ironic, thought Bernstorff, those same secrecy rules designed to protect Jews from having their money confiscated by the Nazis would now serve his purposes in keeping Nazi money hidden from the Allies.

The second thing Bernstorff learned was that opening a numbered Swiss bank account is not a simple task; there are endless forms and questions. The young banker had already explained the bank's rules, including the requirement of a minimum deposit of one million Swiss francs and the annual fee of two thousand Swiss francs.

'Can I trouble you for your identification papers, please sir?'

Bernstorff passed over his passport and watched as the man leafed through the document and ticked the box on his form confirming it was in order.

The banker continued, 'Your account is a numbered bank account. To access the account you will be asked to identify yourself to the bank by means of the password you have supplied to us and the allocated number of the account. When making a deposit you need only give us the account number. However, if you can't attend the bank in person and instruct us to make a payment or an order for a third party to withdraw funds the password and the account number will be required. Without both we would be unable to comply with a request for a withdrawal. Do you understand?'

'I do,' Bernstorff confirmed.

'Then if everything is to your satisfaction could I ask for your signature to confirm that the minimum balance will be deposited within the next twenty-one days and that you accept the schedule of fees.'

Bernstorff didn't read the paper, he just signed.

'Can I enquire when we might expect the first deposit to be made?'

'Tomorrow afternoon. Ten million Swiss francs in gold bullion.'

Showing no surprise at the amount nor the manner of deposit the banker replied, 'Very good, sir,' and he passed over a small white card and a key on a chain.

'The key opens your personal safety deposit box that comes with the account. You will need the key if you wish to access your private box. Please keep the card safe – it's your account number. I suggest that once you have memorised the number you destroy the card.'

Bernstorff looked at the twelve-digit number on the card and placed it into his pocket. Ten minutes later he left the building.

Chapter Twenty-Eight

Paris, 30 August 1944

Michael walked into the living room with a tray of hot steaming coffee. After Jean-Claude had been released, with few apologies from the FTP, Michael and Jacques took him to his apartment in Rue le Tasse and, after attending to his cut lip and the large bruise on his thigh, put him to bed. Twenty-four hours later Jean-Claude woke, took a hot bath and was now sitting on one of the sofas dressed in a long duck-egg blue dressing gown.

'Another second and we'd have been too late,' said Jacques.

'When I first entered the courtyard and saw you kneeling in front of a man pointing a pistol at your head I just screamed,' said Michael.

'Even after the executioner put his pistol in its holster and stepped back, you remained kneeling on the ground with your head bowed,' added Jacques.

Jean-Claude nodded. 'I had expected to die. It was like a dream, not at all real. I was confused by the noise and by being lifted up. It was when Michael hugged me that everything went black and guess that was when I fainted.'

Michael passed around the cups of coffee.

'The FTP were reluctant to let you go free. Before they would release you the head of the so-called tribunal insisted a radio message be sent to London. It took a threat from London saying he would be arrested if you were harmed, for the FTP to be convinced of your innocence,' said Jacques.

'So what now?' asked Michael.

'I've instructed the bank to close for a couple of days. The staff can have time to celebrate the liberation of Paris. Then there are a few things I must do. Alain will be hurting over Luc's death and I want to see him and the other members of Liferaft and help them, if I can. Besides, I need to allow my leg to recover, it's painful and I walk with a limp. After that there are things at the bank that need sorting out.'

'Like what?' asked Michael.

'When the SS left Paris they did so in a hurry. There were papers and files everywhere all stacked up in piles. It'll all need to be sorted out. So many of Tagleva's clients had money and property confiscated and we must do our best to discover where it is and restore it to the rightful owners. And then there are the works of art stolen from the Tagleva Foundation, they too must be recovered.'

'I'm sure you can expect my father to come to Paris and help you as soon as he's allowed to travel by the Allies.'

'It will be so good to see him. I've missed your father very much. When do you go back to London?' asked Jean-Claude.

'I fly home tomorrow. I've been given two weeks' leave and I can't wait to see Juliette. After paying a fortune for a bottle of her favourite perfume, Mais Oui by Bourgeois, yesterday I expect a warm welcome, and I can guarantee a big kiss from my mother when I give her a bottle of Chanel N°5, it's her favourite.'

Jean-Claude smiled. 'I know you don't need to bribe your family to give you hugs and kisses. But I have a favour to ask you. It's been ten days since Paris was liberated and there's still no telephone connection with London; I'm told letters will take weeks to be delivered. I want you to take a letter to your father, if you would. I'll write it today.'

'It'll be my pleasure,' said Michael.

The following morning, Jean-Claude said farewell to Michael. Then, despite the pain in his leg and with the aid of a walking stick, he left Rue le Tasse; half an hour later he arrived at an apartment and knocked on the door. It was half opened, as if in preparation to slam it shut again, a familiar face peered around the door. The man looked back at him with a dazed expression, sore eyes, days of stubble on his chin, unkempt hair and a deep vertical crease at the top of his nose.

'Hello my friend,' Jean-Claude said to Alain.

The door was thrown open and the two friends hugged each other for the longest time without saying a word.

****

Michael's plane landed at RAF Northolt in west London. As soon as the wheels of the plane hit the tarmac he felt an excitement, within a few hours he would be reunited with his family. He had a good feeling and nothing that felt this right could possibly go wrong, it just couldn't. Despite his excitement Michael decided to delay going home to make a detour to Fortnum & Mason and browse the special Officers' Department and the luxury items, stocked exclusively for officers, for a gift for his father. Finding nothing his father didn't already own, Michael chose a box of Cuban cigars. As Fortnum's didn't cater for children, he decided he would take Dorothy to the cinema one afternoon and watch the comedy, *The Miracle of Morgan's Creek* starring Betty Hutton.

Carrying his gifts he walked from Fortnum and Mason to the house in Mayfair and, because he'd not dared take his house keys to France, rang the bell. There was some delay but half a minute later it was opened by a maid just as Dorothy was passing in the hallway.

'Michael,' cried out Dorothy and she ran and gave him a hug.

'I'm so pleased you're safe,' she said wrapping her arms around his waist.

Then letting go of him she ran back inside and into Philip's study. Michael walked into his home. Everything looked the same, but he had a strange feeling there was something very wrong. He turned to look at the maid for some indication of what it might be; she averted her eyes. As he gently put down the gifts onto the hall table the door to his father's study opened. Michael looked at his father framed in the doorway and at Dorothy standing behind him, biting her lip. His father was smiling but his eyes were tired. Michael knew his father was not given to emotion so when a tear ran down his father's cheek he knew it couldn't be relief at his safe homecoming. There was something else, something terrible.

'Is it Juliette?' whispered Michael.

His father shook his head and as Michael was looking into his father's face he guessed the awful news. He walked to his father and hugged him.

'Oh Dad,' he said and closed his eyes. 'How?'

'A doodlebug. Your mother was in the East End,' his father whispered back.

Michael felt a soft hand on his shoulder; he looked to his left. There was Juliette struggling to hold back her own tears. She kissed Michael on the cheek. The twins, still home from school, appeared at the top of the stairs and slowly walked down to join the family.

Philip looked into Michael's pale face. 'Let's all go and have a talk.'

The Tagleva family walked towards the living room. Halfway across the hallway Michael threaded his hand into Juliette's. The maid walked over and gently closed the drawing room door and returned to the kitchen to arrange for tea to be prepared.

An hour later Michael and Juliette were in their own bedroom, her arms squeezed him tightly and he felt her body shake. Michael held her head gently, kissing her cheeks that tasted of salty tears.

'I'm sorry,' she said.

'My mother's death wasn't your fault.'

'Of course I'm sorry about your mother, but it's not what I meant. No, I'm sorry about the baby.'

'What about the baby?'

'The same day as your mother died, I was helping her and was caught up in the same blast… I'm so sorry. I lost it.'

Michael felt icy tentacles wrap themselves around him.

He stepped back from Juliette. 'We'll have more children,' he said comfortingly and hugged her; she couldn't see that he'd clenched a fist, screwed up his face and let out a silent howl of anguish.

A little while later Michael left Juliette to dab her puffy eyes with cool water and brush her hair back in place. At the bottom of the stairs in the hallway, he looked at the gifts on the table, scooped them up, opened a drawer and hid them away. Walking to his father's study he knocked gently on the door and opened it. His father was sitting in his favourite leather armchair in front of the fireplace. Seeing Michael he stood up.

'Forgive me, in all the emotion over your mother I haven't told you how sorry I am about your baby.'

'Thank you, Father. I haven't had much time to think about it. Juliette's healthy and we're both young, I'm sure we'll be able to have more children.'

'She's been a very brave girl and a huge help to me after your mother's passing. You're so lucky to have each other. If there's anything I can do, just ask.'

'Thank you, but you need to look after yourself,' replied Michael.

'My boy, I'll never get over your mother's death, but I'm comforted by having had almost thirty years of perfect marriage. I know that one day we'll be reunited and I intend to devote the rest of my time to my children and their families.'

The following afternoon Michael carefully placed flowers in front of the white Russian Orthodox cross marking his mother's grave. As he bent down he noticed the morning dew had stuck strands of freshly cut grass to his shoes. Looking at the mound of fresh earth he recalled how, when he was still in the nursery, his mother told him all people, no exceptions, were full of love and kindness. As he looked at her cold grave, not for the first time in this war, he found himself questioning his mother's words. *How could your belief be true when a few hundred people peddle their toxic soup of hate to the masses, frightening millions into identifying whole races as parasites?* He felt a demon growing inside him feeding on his compassion and its hunger would only be satisfied by a savage and brutal revenge. He turned and walked away.

That afternoon Michael was sitting in his father's study.

'Colonel Tim Wilson came to the house and told me you were in France before the liberation.'

'Yes Father.'

'Do you want to tell me about it, or is it secret?'

'No it's not secret, though I guess I can't tell you much more than you will have read in the papers. I thought you'd prefer to have news of Uncle Jean-Claude and Tagleva.'

Philip listened as Michael recounted how Jean-Claude led the Liferaft organisation, his arrest by the Gestapo and rescue from the FTP. On hearing the news Philip's grief was momentarily suspended and replaced with pride over his friend's wartime adventures and a relief that Jean-Claude was safe.

'At the start of the war your mother and I wondered if he was involved in something he wasn't telling us. He had a youthful excitement and energy about him, but I never expected he would end up leading a resistance group,' said Philip.

'Before I left France he gave me a letter with news about Tagleva and his plans for the next few months. He hopes you can get over to Paris; you may feel, in the circumstances you don't want to leave London, but I think he needs your help.'

Michael passed his father a brown envelope.

'Thank you. While I read this I suggest that you go and spend time with Juliette.'

Michael got up and smiled. Before closing the study door he glanced back at his father who had his spectacles on and had already begun to read Jean-Claude's report.

Chapter Twenty-Nine

Somewhere in southern Germany, 12 September 1944

As Bernstorff studied the map of Europe he knew the war wasn't going well for Germany. In the west the Allies had liberated much of France, in the south they were halfway up the boot of Italy, in the east a massive Soviet attack had smashed into a thinly held German line trapping a hundred thousand troops. In his mind Germany would soon be defeated.

He knew that his final battle would be won through planning and as he pored over the map he was replicating the planning of the ancient generals he most admired, Alexander the Great, Julius Caesar and Frederick the Great. They had all prepared for battle by studying the terrain; using reconnaissance to decide how best to deploy their forces, employing the rivers, valleys and choke points to their best advantage when planning an attack, and identifying the best places to create obstacles and defences against an attack by the enemy. Bernstorff knew the task given to him by Himmler wouldn't involve the movement of infantry, tanks and guns. The terrain for his task would not be mountains and rivers but the political chaos brought about by the end of the war. Even before D-Day the nations that made up the Allies had a new enemy… themselves. The Americans and the British were distrustful of the Soviet Union, in turn the Soviet Union distrusted the Americans and the British; the British and the Americans distrusted the French, and the French distrusted everyone. For the choke points he would use the disbanded armies, prisoners of war and the millions of displaced civilians moving this way and that way, over the continent of Europe in their frantic effort to go home. In all the confusion he would spirit away the leaders that would form a Nazi government-in-exile, and the six hundred civil servants, military experts, business advisors and economists needed to support the government.

A thought distracted him, *would Hitler escape to lead the government-in-exile or would he choose to heroically die in Berlin, and if the Führer chose death, then who would lead the government... Himmler... and if not Himmler... then who?* He smiled to himself, even imagining the Führer's death was treason.

Bernstorff looked at Italy and jabbed a finger onto Rome. He turned away from the map and picked up a file containing the lists of names of people and organisations that could provide support and opened it.

The relationship between the Vatican and Nazi party:

The treaty guaranteeing the rights of the Roman Catholic Church in Germany, the Reichskonkordat, was signed in July 1933. All German bishops are required to take an oath of loyalty to the Führer (Article 16) and the Reich's leadership consider the treaty gives a moral legitimacy to the Nazi regime.

However, care must be taken in assuming the Vatican as a whole supports the Nazi cause. It's known that several senior members of the Vatican's Curia, cardinals, bishops and priests have been working, on the Pope's direct instructions, to rescue Jews and escaping Allied prisoners of war... It is believed that hundreds, possibly thousands, of Jews have been hidden in the Vatican City State and at the Pope's summer residence of Castel Gandolfo.

There followed a list of senior priests within the Vatican known to be sympathetic to the Nazi cause. Bernstorff finished reading the list and turned the page.

Passports and documents issued by the Vatican:

Identity documents issued by the Vatican Refugee Organisation (Commissione Pontificia d'Assistenza) are not full passports and, in themselves, are not enough to gain passage overseas. However, information provided to the SS suggests they could be used to obtain a passport from the International Committee of the Red Cross (ICRC), which in turn could be used to apply for visas to sympathetic countries. In theory the ICRC should perform background checks on all passport applicants but, in practice, it's considered that the word of a priest, particularly a bishop, would suffice to obtain one.

His thoughts returned to the file Himmler had given him that identified South America as a likely destination for a new beginning. Both the leaders of Argentina and Paraguay were sympathetic to the Nazi regime. A further advantage was that both countries had large populations of Volksdeutsche, people who defined themselves as culturally and ethnically German.

Bernstorff put down the file, got up and walked to the sideboard. He picked up a glass tumbler and filled it with Petsovka vodka, the drink flavoured with honey and pepper he'd become attached to when fighting in Russia. He drank the golden liquid, feeling it burn the back of his throat, and then placed the glass against his temple. The coldness relieved the throbbing in his head, just a little. However, the vodka would not be enough, he would soon have to go to his bedroom and inject himself with a phial of morphine. Though dreading the period of constipation the morphine brought on, it was the only way he gained complete relief from the pain in his leg and it would provide him with a period of intense relaxation. As he poured himself another glass of the vodka he looked at his fingernails and the tell-tale tint of blue that was the mark of a morphine addict.

Chapter Thirty

London, 12 October 1944

Each morning in the space between sleeping and waking Philip was reminded that Sophie was gone by her absence from their bed. But, despite the reminder, throughout the day he strongly felt her presence in the house. Whenever a door opened he expected, hoped, she might walk in. So when there was a gentle knock on the study door and instead a maid entered with a tray Philip smiled trying not to let his disappointment show.

'Sorry to disturb you, sir. Cook thought you might like a tray of tea and biscuits.'

The tray was placed on his desk and the maid departed. Philip returned to his thoughts and back to May 1944 when Winston Churchill had instructed him to attend a conference to discuss proposals on *creating a financial order in a post-war world*. He'd made many useful contacts at the conference and now it was time to use them. Picking up the phone he asked the operator to connect him to the American embassy. Twenty minutes later a seat had been found for him on an American transport plane flying to Paris.

****

The first instruction Jean-Claude gave on his return to the bank was to collect all the pictures and portraits of Adolf Hitler. Together with a couple of German flags they were piled up in the centre of Rue Pierre Charron and, watched by every employee, publicly burned.

Now, for the first time since the start of the German occupation, those at the Tagleva bank in Paris were working with an enthusiasm and purpose. The masses of paper left behind by the SS were carefully gathered up and moved to the fifth floor where a group of staff were tasked with putting them into some sort of order. On the second and third floors client accounts were updated and in the basement locksmiths were busy repairing the safe deposit boxes.

Halfway through the morning Jean-Claude's secretary informed him he was wanted on the fifth floor. Walking up the stairs he was met at the door by the head of the department, Katherine du Bois.

'We've found something I think you should see.'

She handed him a file. He smiled at the hole on the front where, a few days before, an eagle and swastika would have been. He opened it up and inside found three sheets of paper authorising transfers of gold to Switzerland.

'Do we know which bank received the money?' asked Jean-Claude.

Katherine shook her head. 'Not so far, but we're looking for any other papers mentioning either gold or Switzerland. However, if you look at the dates at the top of the pages it proves that just after D-Day the SS began transferring substantial amounts of gold to Switzerland.'

'Thank you, see what else you can find and keep me informed.'

At the end of a long day Jean-Claude arrived home and stared out of his sitting room window. He watched as the golden orb of the sun disappeared behind the Eiffel Tower. Threads of light lingered in the sky and mingled with the rolling cumulus clouds, dyeing the heavens first a blood orange and finally deep amethyst. It was the first day in four years that he'd felt free, really free. Suddenly he was disturbed by a knock on the door. Jean-Claude sighed; the interruption was not welcome. He was looking forward to an evening alone, being able to relax and do nothing. He ignored the knocking, hoping that it would go away, but it was persistent. Reluctantly he walked to the front door and pulled it open. Before he could draw a breath Sébastien stepped from the shadows, entered the apartment, kicked the door shut with his heel and enfolded him in a strong embrace. Jean-Claude felt the firm, muscular body Sébastien had developed by hiking around the Central Massif and melted into his arms. With a calloused finger Sébastien wiped away the tear that had begun to run down Jean-Claude's cheek.

Jean-Claude croaked, 'I'll never send you away again, I promise.'

'A good thing too because I won't go,' Sébastien replied.

Before Sébastien knocked on the door he had planned to recount his adventures in the Central Massif, how he'd managed to escape arrest and joined the Maquis, now he was inside and holding Jean-Claude in his arms as if he was part of an almost forgotten dream, all he could think of was taking Jean-Claude to the bedroom.

Chapter Thirty-One

28 October 1944

Philip's seat on the transport plane to Paris was scheduled for the following morning and he was in his study packing his briefcase with the papers he thought he might need. There was a gentle knock on the door and Juliette walked in.

'Sorry to disturb you. I was hoping to have a word.'

Philip stopped packing, waved her to one of the leather chairs and sat opposite her.

'How are things with you now that Michael's home?'

Juliette smiled. 'I'm pleased he's home but his mother's death and the loss of our baby has hit him very hard. He's distracted.'

'We've had time to digest the news but for Michael it's still raw and he's hurting. He was very close to his mother, give him time, I'm sure he'll begin to be his old self in a short while and if there's anything I can do to help in the meantime just ask,' said Philip.

'You're right I guess. Michael's safe homecoming has been a blessing. But that's not what I wanted to talk to you about. It's more of a favour to me. Michael's leave is over and from tomorrow he'll be at work all day, you're off to Paris, the twins and Dorothy are preparing to go back to school and I'm dreading being stuck at home, all on my own, with nothing to do and my thoughts over the loss of our baby.'

Philip looked into Juliette's eyes and saw a sparkle. It seemed to him that she'd had an idea and was about to share it, but her face betrayed an uncertainty, as if she was unsure how to proceed. Philip remained quiet and waited for her to collect her thoughts.

'The war's coming to an end but the work for Sophie's Foundation doesn't stop. Since Sophie's… the people at the

Foundation have been contacting me, asking what to do next. Some have asked me to ask if you would agree to—'

'Yes,' interrupted Philip.

Juliette looked at him quizzically.

'Yes,' he repeated.

'I don't understand... you don't know what I'm about to ask.'

'Just before Sophie was killed she told me how much help you were to her, your excellent administration skills and how everyone at the Foundation liked you.'

'Oh, that was nice of her. But I'm not sure I understand... you see, now that the war's almost over a new refugee registration desk is needed and I've come to ask if funds could be given to the Foundation, to hire some staff to work with the British Red Cross. Sophie had planned to tell you about her plan the day she...'

Philip smiled. 'I must apologise, we've been talking at cross purposes. Of course the Foundation can have funds for a refugee registration desk. I'll sign the authorisation before I leave for Paris.'

'Thank you, I'll tell the managers. They'll be delighted.' Juliette got up to leave.

'However, it still leaves me with a problem.'

Juliette sat back down wondering what the problem might be.

'A few weeks before Sophie was killed she told me that she intended to retire from the Foundation when the war ended. She felt she couldn't before because there was no one to take over. But the solution had become clear to her. You should become the new head and, if you were, you wouldn't need my permission to allocate funds for a refugee reception desk, you could arrange it yourself.'

Philip looked at his daughter-in-law and savoured a delicious moment as Juliette's face washed blank with confusion. Her brain couldn't turn fast enough to take in what he'd just said and it took a second or two for her hand to go to her mouth as if to stop a word.

'Well?' he asked.

'I couldn't do it. It's too big; Sophie *was* the Foundation. She started it, built it, I—'

'You'd be perfect. Sophie always spoke so highly of you, she admired your energy and enthusiasm. If she were here, she'd be telling you there would be no one who could do the job better. What do you say?'

Juliette smiled. 'I don't know, I suppose I could give it a try… I'll try not to let you and Sophie down.'

'I have no fear of that.'

Philip and Juliette stood up.

'Anything I can do to help you, please feel free to ask me,' he said.

'Thank you, I will.'

Philip then went to his desk and picked up some envelopes.

'Now I can post these to the trustees informing them you've agreed to lead the Foundation and confirming the appointment.'

'Then… you had already decided!' exclaimed Juliette.

'Days ago. I had intended to speak to you before I went to Paris, but now your appointment's agreed we can make it official. The only other question is when can you start?'

'Would today be too early?' beamed Juliette.

Over the days that followed Juliette met with the Foundation's managers, the Royal Voluntary Service, the Order of St. John, Salvation Army and British Red Cross Society. Over endless cups of tea she assured them that the purpose and direction Sophie had created for the Foundation would not alter. At the end of the week she was utterly exhausted.

If there was one concern Juliette had, it was for Michael. Ever since he'd arrived back from France the laughter seemed to have evaporated from his eyes, the warmth she had thought as a natural part of his being had gone. His focus was far away and whenever she stole a look at his face it seemed to be creased with a smouldering rage burning inside him. She had wanted some comfort but whenever she tried to embrace him, or snuggle up to him in bed he seemed distracted and uninterested. Juliette prayed that time would heal his wounds, for her own sake if not his.

Chapter Thirty-Two

Paris, 8 November 1944

Orly Airport, in the southern suburbs of Paris, had been partially repaired by US air force engineers after D-Day and was now the French base for the US Ninth Air Force and referred to as tactical airfield A-47. Philip's plane landed at eleven thirty and when he met Jean-Claude outside the perimeter fence they hugged and shook each other's hands, squeezing them tightly for the longest time. On the way into Paris by car Jean-Claude shed a tear on hearing of Sophie's death and that night, over a bottle of wine, they exchanged their stories of the past four years, and it was not until the following morning, still with a slight hangover, that they went to the bank.

Jean-Claude took Philip on a tour of the building; after four years of occupation the building looked tired. They noted where the paint was flaking off the walls, the silk on the salon chairs was threadbare and the many gaps in the walls and mantlepieces where there had once been works of art. Philip was particularly upset that the Italian Murano glass chandelier, made by the family firm of Barovier & Toso, Sophie had chosen to hang in the lobby, had been removed and sent to Germany at the start of the war.

'The whole building will need to be repainted and redecorated,' said Philip.

'I agree but let's start with the lobby and the rooms used by the staff. The director's rooms should be the last to be made good. Our staff and customers will feel better about things if done in that order.'

Back in Jean-Claude's office their attention turned to the serious topic of banking.

'Even though the war's not yet over we need to talk about Europe's recovery and the part Tagleva should play.'

'The problem is there's so much devastation – where does the world begin?' asked Jean-Claude.

Philip smiled. 'It's already begun. The Belgian, Dutch and Luxembourg governments have signed the London Customs Convention. It lays the foundations for a political and economic union in Europe and, if it's a success, I can see it expanding to include France and the other European countries.'

Jean-Claude sighed. 'Some economists in the US are saying that when the war finishes the world will sink into a deep depression. They believe the demobilisation of ten million men from the army will flood the labour market. That unless wartime controls are extended there will be long periods of unemployment and the greatest industrial dislocation the world has ever faced.'

Philip smiled and waited for Jean-Claude to continue.

'That, of course, reflects the pessimistic view that when a government stops employing soldiers and buying armaments the factory profits will evaporate sending the economy into a downward spiral.'

'Do you believe that?' enquired Philip.

'No, in my opinion, the opposite will actually happen. American economists fail to appreciate that every European city has been reduced to rubble and everyone wants to get back to the normality they knew before the war. Roads, bridges and houses need to be rebuilt or repaired and that will fuel demand for building and consumer goods. As governments stop buying bullets and bombs the factories will change production to make toasters and cars. I believe the next twenty, possibly thirty, years are likely to be a time of financial boom.'

'So where should we be investing our clients' money?' Philip asked.

'I'm recommending building and construction firms, telephone and communication companies.'

'And I agree,' said Philip.

Jean-Claude changed the topic of conversation. 'There's one other thing I want to discuss. Katherine de Bois and her team have been making a list of the property the Germans stole from

Tagleva clients, mostly Jews. We need to try to recover that property for our clients.'

'I also agree to that,' said Philip.

'She's found a few scraps of paper containing information about money and gold being transferred to a Swiss bank. Some of that money belongs to Tagleva clients.'

'Do we know how much?'

'Hundreds of thousands of dollars, and that's just the Tagleva bank. Banks all over Europe must be in the same position. The total must amount to millions of dollars.'

Philip sighed. 'Knowing the Swiss, getting it back will be God's own problem. However, that doesn't mean we shouldn't try. You wouldn't mind if I took copies of those papers back to London with me?'

'I'll ask someone in Katherine's department to make up a copy of the file for you. But one very interesting scrap of paper relating to gold transfers was discovered… It was part burned, but a couple of sentences were visible which talked about a *new Reich government* and a few words, *Operation Red House, Bernst and Collegio Teutonico'*.

Philip rubbed his chin. 'New Reich government could mean anything. Bernst could refer to the Swiss city of Bern… I don't know what Collegio Teutonico means… it's probably nothing.'

While they would talk animatedly about the Tagleva bank, whenever Philip asked Jean-Claude about the Liferaft network and his war experiences Jean-Claude seemed reluctant to talk about it.

'All that's over, we have to move forward and rebuild,' he would say.

Philip didn't know whether his friend's reluctance to talk about the war came from modesty or because he was trying to put the memories of the four years of occupation out of his mind. Whichever the reason Philip stopped enquiring. It was only when, on Michael's recommendation, Philip visited Jacques' restaurant and enjoyed a delicious meal of sautéed pigeon in Muscat that he learned the full extent of Jean-Claude's

Resistance network and the details of Michael's exploits in Paris. As he walked back to his hotel it seemed to Philip that the war had created so many heroes; those that fought on the battlefield, others by helping strangers in danger, and millions that had shown perseverance in the face of bombing. Most of those heroes had a reluctance to shout about their own exploits wanting only to move forward.

****

As the Soviet armies fought their way towards Berlin and the end of the war drew ever closer Michael's days in London were filled by poring over maps, moving chequered tiles over paper cities, mountains and rivers and reading countless intelligence reports; the time seemed to flow like cement. He felt it was all so pointless, being cooped up in his office when he could be fighting, and his thoughts often drifted into an unpleasant daydream that allowed his inner demon to gorge itself on feelings of revenge. He knew the demon was wrong, he didn't care that it wanted to kill Germans, lots of Germans, and if he could he would be content to let it destroy the whole damned lot of them. His thoughts were disturbed by the phone shrilling. He picked up the receiver. 'Major Tagleva.'

Ten minutes later he walked into Tim Wilson's office.

'Afternoon, old man,' the colonel said as he motioned Michael to a chair.

'Have you heard of Trent Park?'

'No, should I have?' replied Michael.

'Probably not, it's a stately home in north London we use as a prisoner of war camp. It holds around eighty captured German generals and staff officers. The difference between it and other POW camps is that the prisoners are treated with great hospitality, which they believe is our acceptance of their important status. They're given special rations of food, excellent whisky and even allowed to play billiards and take unsupervised walks in the grounds. What the German generals don't know is their accommodation, the lampshades, plant pots, billiards table and even the trees in the grounds are all bugged by MI5. Throughout the war the hidden microphones have given us a huge amount of useful information, including the existence and location of the German rockets at Peenemünde, as well as a clear picture of the Resistance within the German High Command that led to the attempt to assassinate Hitler.'

'Have the generals really been that indiscreet?' asked Michael.

'I know. It's amazing how much a general will reveal after a couple of whiskies. But to get to the point, ever since D-Day the Americans have been telling us about rumours of a German guerrilla army. We British have always dismissed the idea as unlikely. Anyhow, a week ago the fears the Americans have seemed to be confirmed when two generals, one a new prisoner, started mentioning a guerrilla army is being recruited by the Nazis.'

'Do the Americans know about Trent Park?'

'They do, but we try to keep them at a safe distance, despite being our closest ally, many of the top brass think the Americans can't keep secrets, and if they knew too much about Trent Park they'd only want to interfere.'

'You said we dismissed the idea of a guerrilla army, has that changed?' asked Michael.

'Last week, quite by chance, an underground hideout was discovered in eastern France by a Canadian soldier. It was cleverly camouflaged on the slope of a hill densely covered with fir trees. So well constructed, in fact, it hadn't destroyed the living trees around it. Had the Canadian soldier not put his foot through the entrance and fallen into it, it wouldn't have been discovered.'

Tim Wilson paused and passed some photographs to Michael.

'You can see the entrance is a hole approximately two feet in diameter. Inside it extends horizontally to a length of about eight to ten feet with a wooden floor and a drainage ditch and has a capacity for three men. Inside we found a mortar, machine guns, rifles and food consisting of canned meat and vegetables, biscuits, crackers and chocolate sufficient to last three or four months.'

Michael studied the photographs as Tim Wilson continued.

'The Americans are convinced the intention is to hide a guerrilla army that will harass our troops and destroy gasoline and oil supplies behind our front lines. They think the Germans might have constructed hundreds, possibly thousands, of these dugouts.'

'It would make sense. In Britain we planned a top secret "stay-behind" resistance organisation which would have been activated in the event of a German invasion. It's what the Resistance did in France, and with great effect,' replied Michael.

'I agree but there was another interesting and possibly connected bit of information. Two newly captured generals in Trent Park were recorded arguing. One said to the other...'

Tim Wilson picked up a piece of paper from his desk and read aloud...

'The Third Reich is finished. We won't make the same mistakes next time.'

'Sounds like bravado, no one likes to think of their country being defeated,' said Michael.

'True but a heated argument ensued where one general blurted out "Project Red House will be the birth of a new Reich". He was then told very firmly to shut-up, that the meeting at the Maison Rouge Hotel in Strasbourg was a state secret.'

With a growing sense of excitement Michael asked, 'So what are my orders?'

'You're to find out all you can about these dugouts and particularly anything about this Project Red House. To help I'm attaching a Captain Peter Maclean to you. He's a tough Scot and a good man to have at your side. When you're ready you and Captain Maclean will be flown to France.'

Tim Wilson handed him a brown folder marked MI5: SF52-4-16 TOP SECRET.

'Inside this file you'll find the transcripts of the conversations from Trent Park that might refer to any plans the Nazis have for after the war.'

Back in his office Michael sat down to read the MI5 file.

INDICATIONS OF POST-WAR PLANS FOR CONTINUED GERMAN ACTIVITY.

After D-Day reports were received by the Americans and passed onto London that the SS and German Intelligence Service were making plans for continued activity after the end of the war, under the code name Wehrwolf. Heinrich Himmler is reported to have initiated Operation Werewolf in late summer or early autumn of 1944, and ordered an SS Obergruppenführer, named Hans Prützmann, to begin training elite groups of volunteer forces to operate secretly behind enemy lines. It's expected the main tactics of the guerrilla army will include sniping attacks, arson, sabotage and assassination.

Experts consulted by MI5 indicate the name 'Wehrwolf' may come from the title of Hermann Löns' novel 'Der Wehrwolf', published in 1910, covering a similar scenario set in the Lower Saxony region during the Thirty Years War. The protagonist is a peasant named Harm Wulf whose family are killed by marauding soldiers. Wulf organises his villagers into a militia to pursue the soldiers and execute any they capture. The author Löns was not himself a Nazi. He died in 1914, but his work is very popular with the Nazi elite...

Michael read through a couple of the transcripts of the recorded conversations at Trent Park. One particular line caught Michael's attention.

Conversations between Nazi generals prove that Nazi Germany's defeat has been long anticipated and some are already looking towards a time when a German rebirth could be achieved... a Germany that would dominate Europe politically and economically.

Michael's sense of boredom left him.

After reading the file, Michael returned home. He looked at Juliette as they dressed for dinner. He had told her that he'd been ordered to go back to France.

'I'll be in an office based in Paris, and won't be part of any fighting,' he'd lied, 'so you don't need to worry,' and hated himself for the deceit.

That night, after dinner, Michael and Juliette climbed the stairs to their bedroom. Before the door had even closed Michael wrapped his arms around Juliette from behind. His right hand dropped to her thigh. Michael turned her around and pushed her onto the bed, his eyes bore into hers. She couldn't move even if she'd wanted to. He kissed her and she tried to kiss him back but as his hands moved over her body Juliette felt a momentary paralysis as his mouth moved to her left ear and he whispered what he wanted. Michael's lovemaking was rough and climax came quickly, and after he walked to the bathroom. On his return he slipped into the bed. While the sex was not altogether disagreeable, Juliette would have wished for something more loving during the few nights that they had left together before he was to return to France. She wanted to hold him gently, to comfort him and in turn to be comforted by him but, it seemed that's not what he wanted.

'Sorry, I was tired.'

'It's OK,' said Juliette and she leaned over and kissed him on the forehead but Michael was already asleep. Juliette rolled over to her side of the bed; a tear fell from her cheek staining the bedsheet.

The following morning Michael was up early and after giving Juliette a peck on the cheek and eating a quick breakfast left for his office where he began to pack his kit bag. Picking up the Welrod pistol, he weighed it in his hands. Michael liked the magazine-fed assassin's pistol with its bolt action. It was reliable and the suppressor at the end of the 12-inch barrel made it an almost silent weapon and had proved to be the perfect killing tool in Paris when he had silently killed an unsuspecting German sentry at point-blank range. After removing the grip that acted as the eight-round magazine he placed the weapon into his kit bag.

Chapter Thirty-Three

Rome, 30 November 1944

Despite the early hour it was already light when Bishop Hudal left his office in the Collegio Tuetonico and began to walk in the direction of the Vatican. Arriving at Castel Sant'Angelo, the fortress with a tunnel connecting it to the Vatican so that popes could scurry to safety in times of crisis, he looked down the Via della Conciliazione and took a deep breath of the crisp morning air. It pleased him that the early hour meant the boulevard was almost empty. It would allow him to walk the five hundred strides down the grand boulevard that obscures the majority of the Vatican and appreciate how the magnificence of St. Peter's Basilica, its forecourt, the tall colonnades topped by statues of the first-century apostles is only revealed when one finally arrives at the Piazza San Pietro. He was halfway as he passed a group of nuns returning to their convent from morning Mass, they acknowledged him by bowing their heads, he ignored them. Arriving at the piazza the bishop walked towards the left of the basilica and the entrance to the Vatican's administration offices. As the bishop passed through the archway the Swiss guard, dressed in his Renaissance uniform of blue, red, orange and yellow, high ruff collar and black beret, came to attention and saluted.

Hudal made his way through the corridors to the Secretariat of State, the oldest department in the Vatican and the body through which the Pope conducts the affairs of the universal Catholic Church. The secretariat is divided into two sections: the first being for the general affairs of the Church and the second for its relations with other countries. Until three months previously both sections had been headed by Cardinal Luigi Maglione, a man with whom Bishop Hudal had always had a very satisfactory working relationship. Unfortunately the cardinal had died the previous August; even more unfortunate was that His Holiness the Pope had appointed two under-secretaries to each run one section of the Secretariat. Hudal's meeting was with one of the two newly appointed undersecretaries, Domenico Tardini, a mere priest he had nothing but disdain for.

On entering Tardini's office Hudal extended his hand. Instead of genuflecting and kissing his episcopal ring in acknowledgement of his elevated status, Domenico Tardini looked at the bishop's hand and simply smiled.

'Good morning, Your Excellency, what am I able to do for you?' Tardini asked.

Hudal withdrew his hand. The offence was not lost on the bishop and, without being asked, he sat in one of the leather chairs in front of Tardini's desk, an action he would never have precipitated when meeting Cardinal Maglione but which he felt able to do so in the presence of a priest. If protocol was restored and properly observed the priest would remain standing until he had given him permission to sit, Hudal felt a glow of satisfaction when the priest continued to stand.

'I'll come straight to the point. The war is quickly coming to an end and as the Austrian bishop I feel it's my duty to provide some ministry to the many German and Austrian prisoners of war in the Allied POW camps.'

'Your Excellency, are you requesting permission to leave Rome?'

'No, not for myself. I'm aware His Holiness restricts my ministry by commanding me to remain in Rome,' replied Hudal.

The bishop knew Tardini disliked him and vocally disapproved of the book he had written, *The Foundations of National Socialism*, an enthusiastic endorsement of Hitler. Hudal also suspected that Tardini believed the gossip that Hitler had sent him a Golden Nazi Party membership badge in appreciation. As a result Hudal anticipated Tardini would take pleasure in declining his request.

Tardini replied, 'I'm not sure the Holy Father *restricts* your movements or *commands* you to remain. It would be more accurate to say he considers your work in Rome too valuable to lose at this time.'

Hudal bowed his head slightly. 'His Holiness is most gracious. No, I will be staying in Rome but I'm hoping the Holy Father will give me permission to send some of my priests to take Christ's comfort to our German flock, so many are in need of such comfort at this difficult time.'

He looked at Tardini, the priest's expression betrayed that he didn't believe, for one second, the bishop's request was motiveless but could see no practical or religious reason to oppose it.

After some seconds the priest spoke, 'As long as you yourself remain in Rome I see no reason why your request would be denied.'

'Should I wait for His Holiness's official notification?' asked Hudal.

'That won't be necessary. I will inform the Holy Father of our agreement when I have my audience with him later this morning.'

Hudal rose from the chair and Tardini bowed his head, very slightly, as the bishop left his office.

Arriving back at the Collegio Teutonico Hudal picked up the phone and dialled. A few seconds later it was answered.

'Please inform His Eminence the Cardinal that permission has been granted.'

Hudal replaced the receiver in its cradle.

****

Captain Peter Maclean and Michael had been watching the mound of earth a couple of hundred feet in front of them for two days. Despite lying in the same position for many hours they were remarkably comfortable as they lay hidden in complete silence, necessary because they both knew sound can carry over a very long distance in the right terrain.

After meeting the farmer's son from Dundee and over more than a few beers in the bar at the St. Ermin's Hotel Michael had quickly come to like Peter. He listened attentively as Peter told him, 'I was the third son and, being much younger than my two brothers, was probably an afterthought. I grew up always feeling I was considered more of a drain on the family's finances and was desperate to justify my existence to my dad. At four year's old I would follow him around the farm wanting to learn how to manage pasture, wean sheep, when to turn out the ewes and lambs onto wet ground...'

Michael listened with increasing fascination.

'My brothers used to tease me a lot and when I was a youngster, they always ganged up on me in a fight. As a wee ten year old I decided to build my strength and began to build myself up by throwing bales of hay about in the barn. Each year the family would attend the Strathardle Highland Gathering in August and when I was seventeen I surprised them all by entering my name for some of the games. After beating both my brothers at the wrestling, caber competition and the Highland dance, they niver bullied me again.'

Michael smiled at the vision of Peter, dressed in a kilt, dancing the Highland Fling and the Swords. Peter saw Michael was amused at the thought of him dancing and added, 'The Swords be victory dances. When th' Scots won a battle they danced over their enemies' weapons and armour because they were happy the battle was over and could go home tae their farms and wives. There's a great deal of skill and discipline needed to perform the Highland dances and it allows men to demonstrate their strength, stamina and agility. An' in the past clan chiefs used the Highland Games as a method to choose their best men at arms.'

When out for a few beers after work Michael noticed, with some amusement, that women were drawn to Peter's six foot, lean and muscular frame, blonde and ginger hair that, in sunlight, made it look as if he wore a helmet of shining gold. They flirted with him outrageously and he flirted outrageously back in return though it never seemed to advance more than that. Michael heard from fellow officers that Peter could look after himself. A reputation gained from an incident at Les Ambassadeurs, the club in Hanover Square in Mayfair known as 'Les A'. Rumour had it that Peter had taken a girl to the club and, while he was busy at the bar buying drinks, an American GI sat down at Peter's table.

'Hey sugar, you rationed?' the GI asked Peter's date.

'Rationed?' she asked confused by the strange language and the thick New York accent.

'Taken, spoken for.'

'Oh. Yes, I am,' she replied.

The GI placed his hand over hers.

'Well baby-doll he's a knucklehead for leaving such a pretty gal alone.'

Peter's date tried to pull her hand away but the GI grabbed it again just as Peter was arriving with two beers.

'Is this man annoying ye?' Peter asked.

'Hey bufflehead, you left her on the shelf so do yourself a favour and say goodbye,' said the GI.

Two other uniformed GIs took up positions of support behind their friend. There followed a few more verbal exchanges until one of the Americans threw a punch at Peter. The fight lasted a matter of seconds and when it was over, all three Americans were out cold on the floor; not a single chair had been upturned and not a drop of beer spilled.

Picking up the girl's shawl Peter turned and asked her, 'Shall we go somewhere quieter?'

Minutes later the Military Police arrived and hauled away the dazed Americans for being drunk.

Michael noticed the light of the day was beginning to fade. He reached into his pocket and pulled out the Vampir night vision device he'd liberated from a German earlier that week and looked through it towards the mound. Since taking possession of it both agreed the German infrared night sight was superior to the Snooperscope issued by the US army. After a few minutes Michael put down the device to give his eyes some rest. Peter silently indicated there was movement ahead. Michael looked through the night vision device once more. A small hole had opened up on the grassy mound and a figure dressed in German infantry uniform emerged; two riles were passed out and a second man appeared. The grass door was carefully replaced and the Germans crept away.

Michael and Peter waited for the men to move into the undergrowth before they began their pursuit. The attack would be a classic 'bulls horn' manoeuvre. Michael would come from one side and take out one German, at the same time Peter would strike from the other side and take out the second man, their quarry wouldn't realise what was happening until it was too late. Taking advantage of the undergrowth Michael silently worked his way ahead of the two Germans and took cover. He felt little emotion at the thought of killing the soldier in cold blood, *everyone has to die sometime and a commando knife plunged into the heart or pulled across the throat is a good way to go, no illness, no drawn-out goodbyes. Alive one second, dead the next,* and in Michael's mind, his quarry was already dead. Michael waited until his man was three inches past him. He rose up, placed a hand underneath the man's chin and yanked the head backwards. The razor-sharp pointed knife was thrust into the man's arched back between the ribs and into his heart. The German stiffened and then went limp. It was brutal, callous and part of the score that had to be settled for the deaths of his mother and unborn baby and less trouble than peeling a banana.

At the same time as Michael's blade entered the German's back, Peter rose from the undergrowth and placed his hand under the second German's chin. He thrust his own dagger towards the man's back but it became entangled in the soldier's rifle strap and was twisted from Peter's grip. The dagger tumbled to the ground. With no weapon Peter had no option but to wrestle the man to the ground. As they fell Peter heard the German cry out, it was a strange cry, soft, like that of a child. Ignoring every part of his training Peter hesitated in delivering a punch to the German's throat that would rupture the external carotid artery and instantly, and silently, kill him. In that split second of hesitation the German turned his head and Peter saw the face of a boy no older than thirteen.

Seeing Peter struggle with the German, Michael rushed over and raised his knife. The blade was travelling through the air when Peter deflected Michael's arm from delivering the fatal blow. The blade sank up to the hilt into the soft dewy earth half an inch from the boy's throat.

Peter hauled the boy to his feet and Michael stared at the brown haired youth in his ill-fitting uniform with a skin so pale it had a waxy appearance, his eyes wide with terror.

'*Wie alt sind sie?*' whispered Michael into his ear.

'*Vierzehn.*'

'What did he say?' asked Peter as he began tying the youth's hands behind his back.

'He says he's fourteen years of age.'

Michael looked at Peter. 'You take him back to the Dingo and I'll go and search the dugout.'

'Tell him I'll slit his throat if he's any trouble,' said Peter.

Michael translated.

'*Ich lüge nicht,*' came the panicked boy's reply.

'I understand that all right,' laughed Peter as he began to haul the child by the shirt collar in the direction of the well-hidden Daimler Scout Car they had parked a few hundred feet from the mound.

Pulling the Welrod pistol from his jacket Michael moved to the dugout entrance. He waited to see if he could hear any sound inside. With his free hand he carefully pulled open the grass entrance, just a crack, and rolled away in case someone should fire from inside. No one did. Shining a flashlight he pointed the beam into the dugout, it was empty and Michael crawled inside.

Six days later Michael and Peter were in London reporting what they had found out to Tim Wilson.

Michael began. 'The boy had been recruited into the Werewolf brigade a month ago. He told us he was among two hundred volunteers. The oldest volunteer in his group was aged seventeen, the youngest twelve. The instructors told them the object of Werewolf was to create confusion and relay useful intelligence to a central armed forces unit, located in un-occupied territory. Their orders were to operate behind

Allied lines as guerrillas, sabotage vehicles, communication facilities, poison wells and food supplies, for which they were told they would be given large quantities of arsenic. Their training began early in October in rudimentary use of small-arms, demolitions skills, and radio-communication and survival skills given by instructors from the Wehrmacht.'

Tim Wilson sighed. 'We train our commandos for thirty weeks and after fewer than four the Germans are sending children to fight. They *are* desperate.'

Michael continued his report. 'It gets better. The recruits were told they would be led by an older, battle-experienced and hand-picked man from the German army or Waffen-SS. The reality was very different. The man with him was a member of the Volkssturm, the German equivalent of our Home Guard. When he arrived at his dugout there was very little food so the man showed the kid how to shoot rabbits to get enough to eat. The boy said he was a kind old man, reminded him of his grandfather and was genuinely upset at his death.'

'So, if these dugouts are all the same we'll have very little to worry about,' said Tim Wilson.

'I guess so, but there may be a few that are fully equipped, so we shouldn't ignore them entirely,' chipped in Peter.

'Thank you gentlemen, I'll pass on your report,' said Tim Wilson.

Outside Tim Wilson's office Michael turned to Peter. 'If you've no plans for this evening how do you fancy coming to my place for dinner? It'll be pot luck I'm afraid but there's always a few beers available and you could stay the night if you liked.'

'I'd like that. I was going back to my billet with only my book for company.'

Forty minutes later Peter was being introduced to Michael's father, who'd returned to London from Paris a few days before, and then to Juliette and Dorothy, the twins were absent having returned to school in Wales.

On meeting Dorothy Peter was asked, 'Where do you come from?'

'A place called Stirling. That's in Scotland,' he answered.

'You sound strange, does everyone speak like you in Scotland.'

'Don't be rude, Dorothy,' scolded her nanny.

'Aye, we do. An' do all wee gals speak lik' ye in London?' replied Peter exaggerating his accent.

Dorothy giggled and with a broad smile mimicked a posh London lady and replied, 'Yes, we girls do.'

Peter pushed back his head and roared with laughter.

Walking into dinner Dorothy insisted Peter sit next to her.

They were each served a small bowl of parsnip soup made with water. It was almost tasteless but hot. There followed plates of what looked like a mound of grated carrot on top of which lay two tinned sardines. The family looked down at the food in front of them and then at each other.

Seeing everyone's surprised expression Dorothy announced, by way of explanation, 'It's the recipe of the week! Cook heard it on the radio programme *The Kitchen Front*. Marguerite Patten said on the radio, "Every woman who values a good complexion should eat this salad".' Dorothy adopted the pose of a model advertising cosmetics she'd seen in *Woman's Weekly* and giggled loudly as she exaggeratedly stroked her cheek with her fingers.

'What's in it?' asked Michael, more used to eating in the officer's mess where the rations were more substantial.

As if imparting a secret Dorothy said, 'I watched cook make it. At the bottom of the bowl are two lettuce leaves, then cook boiled potatoes in their skins and mashed them, covered them in some oil, or something, and piled them on top of the lettuce. It's topped with grated carrots.'

Dorothy looked at Peter and with a serious expression announced, 'Cook says the sardines are a special treat because we have a guest.'

Michael said to Peter, 'Well, I guess we all have you to thank for our two sardines.'

The whole table dissolved into laughter.

After the sardine salad they were served a small bowl of bread and prune pudding for dessert.

As the supper came to an end Juliette announced, 'The blackout ends tonight. They're turning on the lights in Piccadilly, the Strand and Fleet Street. Shall we walk up to see them?'

'That would be fun, it's been years since Piccadilly was lit up,' said Michael.

'An' will ye be comin' too?' Peter asked Dorothy.

'Yes please,' squealed Dorothy, looking towards Philip for permission.

'Just this once, but don't be too late, you have school tomorrow,' said Philip with a broad smile, pleased the family would have some fun at last.

Half an hour later Michael, Juliette, Dorothy and Peter walked up the street towards Piccadilly past bollards painted with white visibility stripes and a policeman wearing his white coat and carrying a flashing red torch as he enforced the 20 m.p.h. speed limit.

Arriving at Piccadilly Circus there was a general sense of excitement among the crowds of Londoners, all come to see a sight not seen for five years.

'So ye can see more easily would ye like to ride on my shoulders?' Peter asked Dorothy.

Dorothy held her chin with her right hand and looked down at the pavement… after a full five seconds she looked up at Peter and smiled. 'That would be nice.'

Peter bent down, picked Dorothy up and placed her on his shoulders.

Dorothy whispered into his ear, 'I like your golden hair, it reminds me of my Mummy's, but she's dead now.'

'Hold on tight now,' Peter told Dorothy.

As the time came for the lights to be switched on the crowds began to count down the seconds not quite getting the timing right. Dorothy's face was a picture of pure excitement, and when the lights went on she joined in the 'Ooooh!' from the crowd. Then everyone wandered the streets, as if they'd forgotten how to stand still, looking into shop windows, also lit up for the first time. Juliette smiled at Michael, threaded her arm into his, the smile was returned, but it seemed to her that it was a little forced and despite the crowds she felt very alone.

When the party returned home Dorothy said goodnight and ran upstairs to bed. Michael took Peter into the living room and handed him a large glass of whisky.

'I hope you're not too tired. You carried Dorothy on your shoulders for two hours.'

'No, I'm not tired. She's a nice kid and anyway she's much lighter than a full kit bag.'

Michael smiled. 'Will you stay in the army after the war?'

'No, I intend to go home and work on the farm and the lass I've been sweet on since I was at school.'

'So, none of the girls you've dated in London are of interest?'

Peter smiled. 'I never considered I was dating them and never gave them any encouragement to think otherwise, my heart belongs to my girl in Stirling. The real reason I took them out is that I love dancing and it's nae something you can do on your own. They were dance partners, nothing more.'

'Will you marry this girl in Stirling?'

'As soon as the war's over, I already have the engagement ring; bought it in Hatton Garden a few months ago.'

Michael sighed. 'There will be so many broken hearts in London when you go home to Stirling.' He laughed as Peter blushed a little.

The following morning at breakfast Dorothy regaled Philip with the excitement of the previous night. When it was time for Dorothy to go to school she walked around the table and held out her hand to Peter.

'I'm off to school now, but thank you for giving me a ride on your shoulders last night. It was fun.'

With a slight bow of his head he replied, 'My pleasure, Dorothy. It was fun for me too.'

Peter then shook Dorothy's small hand for the briefest of moments.

Dorothy looked at Peter for a couple of seconds, smiled broadly and then ran towards the hallway and without a backwards glance mimicked his Scottish accent as she shouted, 'Bye then, hope we meet agin soon.'

Peter roared with laughter.

Once Dorothy had left the room Peter turned to Philip. 'She's a bright little girl.'

'Oh yes she is, and good at school too, she tells me that she wants to work in the Tagleva bank, which obviously pleases me, but she's young and may yet change her mind.'

'So, talking about the bank, how were things in Paris?' Michael asked.

'The bank's being redecorated but I'm afraid the SS left our house in a mess.'

Turning to Peter, Philip explained. 'Before the war, as the chairman of the Tagleva bank, I used to spend half my time in this house in London and the rest in a house in Paris. During the war an SS officer occupied the Paris house and when he returned to Berlin his wife or mistress, I don't know which, decided she couldn't live without the curtains, rugs and most of the paintings. They even tore the nineteenth-century gilt bronze wall lights off the walls. It was wanton destruction and I doubt we'll see any of the furniture again, or the wall lights.'

Turning to Michael Philip said. 'Your mother would be quite angry. She bought those wall lights at her favourite antique shop on the Rue du Faubourg Saint-Honoré.'

'So how's Uncle Jean-Claude?' Michael asked changing the subject.

'Now Sébastien's safely back home he's feeling much better and, as usual, he's working very hard. He's been trying to trace money the Nazis stole and moved to Swiss banks; he's determined to get it back. The strange thing is the Tagleva staff keep coming across papers that mention gold and linking it to a Project Red House. He doesn't know what it's about, and it's annoying him.'

Michael glanced at Peter.

'Does he say which banks in Switzerland?' Michael casually asked his father.

'No, the details are in code, but the world of banking is small and he's working on it.'

Just then the maid entered the room and spoke to Juliette.

'Madame, we've had a telephone call. A V2 rocket has landed in Holborn, the wardens say there are some dead and possibly a few hundred wounded. They are asking if you and some of your people could go there and help with the wounded and their families.'

Juliette stood up. 'I must go, please excuse me,' she said and left the room.

Ten minutes later Juliette was travelling towards High Holborn, and Michael and Peter were walking towards their office in the Strand.

'I think we need to pass that nugget of information on to the colonel, don't you?' said Michael to Peter.

'The one about Project Red House?'

'Precisely.'

Chapter Thirty-Four

Vienna, 16 December 1944

When Bishop Hudal instructed Father Marius to go to Austria and take God's comfort to the needy he had instructed that, while he was there, he was to visit the Argentinian embassy in Vienna. As Father Marius sat in the reception room he noticed the time he'd been given to see the Argentinian ambassador had passed twenty minutes earlier. He pulled a rosary from his jacket pocket and holding the crucifix began to recite quietly, *In the Name of the Father and of the Son and of the Holy Spirit.* His fingers moved onto the single bead just above the cross… *Our Father who art in Heaven…* Once the Lord's Prayer had been completed his fingers effortlessly moved to the first cluster of three beads and he began three Hail Mary's while, at the same time, meditating on the divine virtues of faith, hope and love… He hadn't finished the second Hail Mary when he was distracted by someone approaching him.

'Father Marius. I'm sorry to have kept you waiting. For security reasons, could I trouble you for your passport?'

Marius put away the rosary, reached into his jacket pocket and pulled out the leather covered passport and handed it over. The Argentinian had never seen a diplomatic passport from the Vatican and looked at the gold leaf stamp of the papal coronet and cross keys of St. Peter on the front. It was reverently opened and the paper inside unfolded. The information on the parchment confirmed Father Marius was in the service of the Holy See. After studying the details the Argentinian carefully folded the paper back into its holder and returned it.

'Thank you, Father. Would you follow me please?'

A minute later the priest was shaking the hand of the ambassador.

'How can I help you?' he was asked.

'I've been sent by Bishop Hudal to request the delivery of two letters. The first is to your President Edelmiro Farrell and the second to Vice-President Perón.'

The ambassador smiled. 'Out of curiosity, can I ask why these letters aren't being sent via the Argentine ambassador at the Vatican?'

'It's a sensitive matter. My bishop considers that the contents of letters sent via the Vatican's post office become known to those who are not as supportive of our mutual benefits.'

'I see, and which mutual benefits might your bishop be referring to?'

'Both letters contain fraternal greetings from the head of the Austrian-German congregation of Santa Maria dell'Anima in Rome. The bishop talks of the devastation in Europe brought about by the war and makes enquiries if the Argentine nation might offer places of safety to prominent members of his congregation.'

'I see,' said the ambassador. 'He is, no doubt, aware that Argentina is soon to declare war on Germany.'

'He is, but the bishop also appreciates that, at this late stage, Argentina's decision to declare war on Germany is driven more by diplomatic pressure from the United States as opposed to any real antipathy towards the Third Reich... After all, a great many of the Argentine population trace their families to German descent.'

The ambassador smiled. 'Your bishop is well informed on these matters. I will pass these letters on to the president and vice-president. However, I should warn you that, while Argentina welcomes people with expertise, it is itself a poor country. The vice-president would be reluctant to grant people seeking, how shall I put it... refugee status... without some assurance that there would be no financial disadvantages of such charity... to Argentina.'

'Such a position is fully appreciated, ambassador. My bishop is at pains to assure the vice-president that the country would not find itself out of pocket, in fact everyone would benefit from the arrangement.'

The ambassador smiled broadly. 'I understand the bishop completely.'

Chapter Thirty-Five

Somewhere in Germany, 21 April 1945

Even as Soviet forces under Georgiy Zhukov began their final assault on Berlin large parts of Germany were still under Nazi control. If one had access to a car or a small plane it was possible to move around much of the country. So when Carl Bernstorff received orders to meet with SS Reichsführer Himmler at a farmhouse outside Schwerin, a picturesque town located just over sixty miles east of Hamburg, he made the necessary arrangements. Even so, the only plane with a pilot Bernstorff was able to commandeer was a single-engine Arado Ar 96, the Luftwaffe's standard trainer for advanced night- and instrument-flying. As the two-seat plane flew to its destination Bernstorff guessed the location for the meeting with Himmler had been chosen because Schwerin is surrounded by seven lakes, was of no military significance and had escaped Allied bombing. As a result the journey was made without incident.

Bernstorff arrived at the farmhouse to find a disconnected group of people clinging together for protection and recognised, as they evaded looking him in the eye, the faces of defeated soldiers. There was SS General Walter Schellenberg, head of the Reich Foreign Intelligence Department, Werner Grothmann, Himmler's personal aide-de-camp, Himmler's doctor, a masseur whose nails had been bitten down to the quick, and a group of ten other SS men Bernstorff didn't recognise. What did connect them were the tight, fixed smiles as they contemplated the end of the Reich after only twelve years, not the thousand Adolf Hitler had promised.

As Bernstorff waited to be shown into Himmler's presence he noticed a man talking to Werner Grothmann in an unnatural high-pitched, stuttering voice. The man seemed to be recounting a story and when they laughed together Bernstorff guessed it was probably the type filled with gallows humour and false confidence that soldiers recount to each other the night before a battle.

Bernstorff didn't have to wait long before being ushered into Himmler's presence. On entering the room he looked at the Reichsführer; gone was the splendid uniform and insignia of his rank, replaced by the uniform of a lowly NCO of the *Geheime Feldpolizei*. It was obvious Himmler intended to vanish by joining the thousands of German troops that had given up the fight and were walking away from the Russians and towards the British and Americans in order to surrender. The Reichsführer put down the paper he was reading.

'Come in, Bernstorff. I am looking at the Führer's horoscope on the day he became Chancellor of Germany in 1933. Its accuracy is quite amazing. It predicts the outbreak of the war, Germany's victories at the start, the reversals, even that we would be defeated. But did you know it also predicts Germany will be reborn, phoenix like, out of the ashes of defeat and the rebirth will start in 1948. What have you to say to that Bernstorff?'

Bernstorff looked at Himmler's smiling face – it had an expression as if something good were about to happen. In a flash Himmler's smile disappeared.

'What news have you about your mission?'

'Since you gave me the orders in Berlin last April I've organised a network of safe houses that will be used to hide those we need to evade the Allies. Contact has been made with the governments of Argentina and Paraguay and both are willing to take in… the refugees. Gold to finance the operation has been moved to a bank in Switzerland. It will be converted into bearer bonds which can be more easily transported and cashed anywhere in the world. Some of the money will be used for the living expenses of those in exile and the remainder to establish the new Reich and government.'

'Very good, you've done well. I know this is a short meeting and I appreciate you coming across Germany to meet with me; it was important that I knew what progress you had made, but now I have other things I must do,' said Himmler.

'Can I ask, what plans you have for yourself?' asked Bernstorff.

'My group and I plan to cross the Oste River. We aim to walk through the sparsely inhabited countryside around the town of Bremervörde and reach the coast where a U Boat is waiting to take us to safety.'

'Then can I wish the Reichsführer luck?' said Bernstorff.

'Thank you Sturmbannführer,' replied Himmler.

Bernstorff saluted *Heil Hitler*, and departed for the airstrip.

While in the Arado Ar 96 flying back to the airstrip where he could safely slip into Switzerland, Bernstorff was thankful it would be the last time the Reichsführer could order him to fly across Germany for a two-minute meeting for no other reason than to assure him that he would have money available for his exile.

Ten days later, on 1 May, Bernstorff was sitting in his hotel in Zurich listening to the German radio station when the announcer interrupted the martial music that had been playing for hours.

'The German wireless broadcast has important news for the German people,' said the announcer and there followed three drum rolls.

'It's reported from the Führer's headquarters that our beloved Führer, Adolf Hitler, fighting to his last breath against Bolshevism, fell for Germany today in his headquarters in the Reich Chancellery. The Führer had appointed Grand Admiral Doenitz his successor and the Grand Admiral now speaks to the German people.'

There came a new voice over the radio and Bernstorff recognised the clipped manner Doenitz adopted when speaking to subordinates, *'Men, women and soldiers of the armed forces. Our glorious Führer, Adolf Hitler, has fallen… His life was one of single service for Germany and his hero's death, fighting against Bolshevism, must concern the entire civilized world. The Führer has appointed me to be his successor…'*

Bernstorff got up from his chair, turned off the radio, and walked out of the room. Now Hitler was dead and he had things to organise.

****

Six days later Michael listened to the BBC news reporting that, in a schoolhouse at Reims, General Jodl had signed the unconditional surrender of all German forces to the Allies.

The following day in Paris, Brussels, New York, Moscow and Montreal people celebrated the end of hostilities. In London more than one million people congregated in Trafalgar Square, the Strand and up the Mall to the gates of Buckingham Palace. Later that day King George VI and Queen Elizabeth, accompanied by Prime Minister Winston Churchill, appeared on the balcony and waved to the cheering crowds. In Paris Jean-Claude, Sébastien and Alain opened the bottle of champagne that had been saved especially for the occasion. Within days the largest movement of people in human history began as millions of civilians, prisoners of war and soldiers started their long walk home.

Chapter Thirty-Six

Switzerland, 30 May 1945

To avoid the suspicion of being identified as German, Bernstorff and Otto, his second in command, registered in the comfortable Zurich hotel as businessmen from Limburg in Holland, where German is spoken by a large part of the population. The three other men of his unit were billeted in a hotel two minutes' walk away.

Bernstorff ignored the waiter at the far end of the dining room who was clearing away the cereals, breads, cheeses from the breakfast buffet table. Bernstorff poured himself another coffee from the silver-plated pot in front of him and looked out of the window towards the shores of Lake Zurich.

Otto walked into the dining room and sat in the chair opposite. There was none of the nonsense of past formality, no *Heil Hitler* salute, no clicking of heels and Bernstorff didn't miss it. Otto passed an English newspaper to Bernstorff, who looked at the picture on the front page. Even without the distinctive moustache and uniform he recognised the unmistakable face of Heinrich Himmler. He read the article:

Gestapo Chief Heinrich Himmler, defiant to the last, killed himself by cyanide capsule at a British military prison in Lüneburg on Wednesday… The dishevelled figure was arrested by British soldiers at the Bremervörde bridge in northern Germany. Disguised with a patch over his left eye, Himmler claimed to be Sergeant Heinrich Hitzinger in the 'field police'… Himmler was detained and taken to an internment camp. It was while he was at the internment camp that it became obvious that Hitzinger was, in fact, Heinrich Himmler. An army doctor was about to give Himmler a thorough examination when Himmler bit on a cyanide capsule embedded in one of his teeth.

Bernstorff folded the newspaper, leaned back in his chair and thought for a moment. The Führer and Himmler were dead, Göring, Dönitz, Hess, Ribbentrop and the other leaders of the Nazi party were under arrest, to suffer the indignity of the victor's revenge: a trial at Nuremburg for crimes against humanity. The result was that there was no Nazi leader remaining and Bernstorff felt released from the oath of allegiance made to the Führer all those years ago.

'Are we ready?' asked Bernstorff.

'Everything is as you ordered,' came Otto's reply.

****

In France petrol was still strictly rationed so Jean-Claude was travelling by bus towards Alain's apartment for his weekly visit to his friend. The bus stopped to allow some people to alight and to pick up others. Jean-Claude noticed the passengers opposite seemed to be looking towards the back of the bus and he turned to see what was of interest. The vision was quite unbelievable, even shocking and the bus became strangely quiet as more passengers watched the spectacle. The man that had climbed on board was shuffling, as opposed to walking, along the bus; his clothes swallowed him in folds of material and Jean-Claude looked away, then back to see if he was still there, he was. Everyone was trying to determine the man's age but it was difficult, his head was completely shaved, cheekbones protruded from out of his face, hollow eyes looked into the middle distance. The man seemed completely exhausted by the effort he was making and while some of the passengers looked away others couldn't help themselves and stared. Prompted by his mother, the schoolboy opposite Jean-Claude rose from his seat to let the man sit. Gratefully the man slumped into the vacant space and as the bus began to move Jean-Claude looked down to the floor to avoid the man's gaze but his eyes seemed to focus on Jean-Claude.

'*C'est moi,*' the man whispered.

Jean-Claude looked up, *He recognises me, but I don't recognise this man*. Yet, as Jean-Claude stared at the skeleton, there was a familiarity, not a memory, but an echo of a past life.

'*C'est moi,*' the man whispered again.

As the other passengers looked on, Jean-Claude's hand went to his mouth; tears welled up in his eyes making him forget where he was. Before Jean-Claude knew it he was hugging Samuel's slight frame as his thin arms encircled Jean-Claude, but with no strength to the embrace. Most of the other passengers could only stare at the reunion; the only noise coming from a couple of women who'd begun to cry knowing there could be no similar reunion with their loved ones.

Samuel was moved out of the hotel, the temporary accommodation for concentration camp victims, and into Jean-Claude's apartment in Rue le Tasse where Jean-Claude and Sébastien set about bringing Samuel back to health. A nurse was hired and a doctor consulted who told Samuel that he must eat something, no matter how small, six times a day. Food was purchased from the black market and a tray with a small appetising meal was presented to Samuel at breakfast, mid-morning, lunch, mid-afternoon, evening and at bedtime. Over the days and weeks that followed Samuel slowly put on weight and while his body recovered it was obvious his experiences at the hands of the Germans haunted him. There were times he would sit for hours staring into the distance deep in his own thoughts, then at other times he'd spend hours recounting parts of his story.

'After our arrest my family and I were sent to Sachsenhausen concentration camp. There were twelve hundred people in our transport. Although I didn't know it then my wife and children were sent to the gas chamber within an hour of arriving at the camp. The following day I was one of only a hundred and fifty people still alive from the transport. The German humiliation towards those they allowed to live was total. Everything had been taken away from me except for my glasses and a belt, and within hours, I'd been reduced to a bald, shaven, rag-clad soul identified only by a number. From that moment on my life was one of hunger, cold, and the constant threat of the gas chamber… The SS had allowed me to live a little longer because they knew I was a printer and a forger…'

On another occasion Samuel talked about the work.

'In many ways I was lucky. They knew I was a forger and I was allocated to a group forced to produce foreign currency for the Nazis; it saved my life. It meant I wasn't required to spend the whole day labouring outside in the cold winter and the Germans gave us extra food rations. In early 1945 the unit was moved to the Mauthausen camp in Austria. Then later we moved again to Redl-Zipf and finally to Ebensee concentration camp. I'd only been at Ebensee a few days when it was liberated by the Americans.'

'What type of currency were you forging?' asked Jean-Claude.

'Mainly British five-pound notes and we did a good job.'

Samuel smiled at Jean-Claude with a little of the same pride he'd shown when making forged identity papers for Liferaft.

'We managed to produce a near-perfect engraving block of the British five-pound note even creating the alpha-numeric serial code, the system that numbers each note differently. When the war ended we had perfected the artwork for US dollars, although the paper and serial numbers weren't quite good enough to fool people.'

'Do you know what the Germans wanted the notes for?'

'At the time I didn't care. I… the work kept me alive, that's all I cared about, but I suppose it was to ruin the British economy.'

One day Samuel felt strong enough to take a short walk and Jean-Claude accompanied him. After a few minutes Samuel became tired and they stopped at a café and ordered two coffees and two pastries. When the pastries arrived Samuel looked down at his plate as if it were something alien.

'It was after I was moved to Mauthausen concentration camp they stopped the special rations and I began to know how terrible hunger can be. It starts with a dry mouth and I wanted to urinate all the time as my body lost its fluid. It's then you notice how rapidly your weight falls off. I'll never forget the yearning for food. At night I would dream about matzoh soup, flaky borekas and would even wake from a dream convinced I could smell challah bread being baked. To look at these pastries now brings tears to my eyes.'

Jean-Claude didn't know what to say and watched Samuel as he made no attempt to eat his pastry.

Eventually Samuel began to speak again.

'After a while of having so little food you would think the cravings would become more intense, but it's strange, they don't. The craving becomes less urgent and it's replaced by apathy and a general feeling of weakness. In the end I looked no different to the other inmates, a youthful old man with pale, papery, scaly skin and brown blotches covering my body. Eventually I was so weak I became slow and clumsy, a skeleton tripping over my own feet, and I had a hoarse voice and could only groan. When the Americans liberated the camp I was so weak and consumed with fever I couldn't walk and was lying on a wooden bunk. The Americans gave me food but my weakened bowels couldn't cope with it and I vomited it up again... it only increased my exhaustion. All I wanted to do was to sleep but I told myself *if I fall asleep now, I won't wake up* and it was at that point I decided I couldn't allow myself to die, that I must live, to bear witness to what happened to my wife and children.'

Samuel went silent for a few seconds and then looked up at Jean-Claude, smiled and whispered, '*Hakarat ha'tov.*'

'What does that mean?' asked Jean-Claude softly.

'It's Hebrew. It literally means "recognising the good". Like so many, I' have lost my wife and my beautiful children, but I'm alive and here, with a kind friend, a little food and in that very small way, it's good.'

Chapter Thirty-Seven

London, late May 1945

Since their return from France Michael and Peter had been stuck in an office in London reduced to mere observers to the collapse of Nazi Germany. Over the past weeks the BBC had reported that the Italian war had effectively ended, Berlin was encircled by the Russian Red Army, Soviet and American troops had made contact at the river Elbe and the Royal Air Force had flown its last significant mission of the war, bombing Hitler's retreat at Berchtesgaden. Instead of passively listening to the BBC they would both have preferred to be in the thick of the fighting.

Michael glanced at the clock for the umpteenth time, it was still not even ten, and the only sound was the click clack of the keyboard of Peter's typewriter. Michael went to get his third cup of coffee. As he poured the lukewarm liquid from the thermos into a cup he heard a familiar voice.

'I'll have one of those, old man, if you're offering.'

Michael poured a mug for Tim Wilson, added the usual four teaspoons of sugar, and passed it over.

'I have news for you two,' said the colonel.

Guessing their days of being paper-pushers were over Michael couldn't contain his smile as he followed the colonel into the office.

'As you chaps know, we've been listening in on our German prisoners of war at Trent Park, particularly for any mention of Project Red House. The top brass now believe Project Red House is an SS initiative to create a new Nazi government.'

'I thought our people had dismissed the idea as impossible,' said Michael.

Tim Wilson smiled. 'It's true that our top brass had dismissed the idea as absurd, but then the prime minister got to hear about it. Churchill believes that if there is even the slightest chance that such a plan exists it must be stopped.'

'I don't see how Germany can go on fighting,' said Peter.

'In a traditional way they won't, but it's thought the Nazis have made plans to finance a government-in-exile somewhere, and wait until conditions are right for a resurgent Germany to re-emerge and dominate Europe.'

'So why not arrest and imprison the people who would form such a government?' asked Peter.

'We would, if we knew who they were, but we don't. All the top Nazis are either dead or in custody. So you two are being ordered to investigate who might lead a Nazi government-in-exile and how it will be financed.'

Michael and Peter looked at each other.

'I guess you're wondering how you do that on your own?' said Tim Wilson.

'That small detail had crossed my mind,' replied Michael.

Tim Wilson handed Michael a file. 'Inside this you'll find the details of three men I'm attaching to you.'

'Three men – hardly the brigade of guards,' Peter laughed.

'Better than nothing and besides, it's all that can be spared at the moment,' answered Tim Wilson with a smile.

'So what are our orders?'

'Find the leaders of this new Nazi government.'

'An' when we've done that?' asked Peter.

'You're ordered to kill them.'

Two days later Michael and Peter were interviewing three men. The first man marched into Michael's office and saluted. 'Sergeant John Evans. Coldstream Guards, sir. Age twenty-five, sir. I've served in North Africa during 1942, Morocco and Algeria during Operation Torch, Sicily in 1943. Was first attached to SOE 1944.'

Michael looked at the thick-set man that wouldn't be out of place on a rugby field and then at the notes from his file:

This soldier is resourceful and highly intelligent. Previous career: Cambridge University studying Mathematics.

Half an hour later Private Nigel Begg, 1st Canadian Division walked in. He was lean, with an olive tan that Michael guessed was natural and not sun induced.

'Age twenty-three. I was born in England, my family left for Canada when I was a child. I left school with no qualifications, bummed around with a street gang and, when this show kicked off, joined the army to save myself getting into trouble with police. Served in France 1940, Italy in 1943 as part of Operation Baytown... in the Moro River Campaign... and at the Battle of Ortona. Joined SOE in 1944 and I'm an expert in the use of the crossbow.'

'I've read from your file you've been mentioned in dispatches,' said Michael.

'Yes sir, during a battle in France and I neutralised a German machine-gun post using a bayonet as a knife, after my rifle jammed.'

'That was brave,' said Michael.

'My sergeant major would disagree with you sir, he said it showed a distinct lack of imagination,' replied the Canadian, smiling.

Peter supressed a chuckle.

The last man walked into Michael's office.

'Private Edward Daniels, Royal Northumberland Fusiliers. Served in North Africa and Italy.'

'Your file tells me you're an intelligent soldier with a tendency towards insubordination,' said Michael.

'I guess that's about right. When the war started I was studying at The London School of Economics and my studies were interrupted when I was conscripted. I don't much like army life.'

'What don't you like about it?' asked Peter.

'People giving me bloody dangerous and stupid things to do,' came Edward's answer.

Peter managed to suppress another smile.

'Sounds like a useful trio of men,' said Peter to Michael once they were alone.

'I suspect you're right.'

Chapter Thirty-Eight

Rome, Mid-June 1945

Bishop Hudal smiled as he walked into the room and held out his hand in greeting. 'You must be Carl Bernstorff. I've been expecting you, my son, you are most welcome.'

Bernstorff bent down and kissed the ring on the bishop's hand; he was waved to a chair by the bishop who settled himself behind his desk and indicated that Bernstorff was free to talk.

'Your Excellency, your secretary and I have agreed on the special donation of a hundred and twenty million dollars for the expenses attached to our project.'

'Yes, he told me of your generosity. You can be assured the money will be used to great benefit.'

Bernstorff pulled an envelope from his jacket and passed it over the desk towards the bishop.

'The envelope contains the first part of that contribution towards your work.'

The bishop's smile faded a little as if he was uncomfortable at having an envelope containing money on his desk. He slipped it off the desk and into the top drawer. As the drawer closed the bishop's smile returned.

Placing the fingertips of both hands together, as if in prayer, the bishop leaned back in his chair and began to speak, 'After I received the messages from the late Reichsfüehrer Himmler I drafted a letter to Juan Perón in Argentina, requesting five thousand visas for German and Austrian citizens who were fighters against communism and whose wartime sacrifice saved Europe from Soviet domination.'

'Have you had a reply from Perón?'

'I have, my son. I'm delighted to tell you my request for the visas has been granted.'

'That is excellent. How will the arrangements be made?' asked Bernstorff.

'I've sent priests to Germany and Austria and they are already making contact with those in hiding. When it's safe for them to do so, they'll be helped to travel into Italy. They will be found lodgings in safe houses, here at the Collegio Teutonico, at the Croatian College of di San Girolamo and in other religious institutions. The Franciscan order is being particularly generous in allowing us to use some of their monasteries for accommodation. Once everything is in order they will travel to Genoa and board ships leaving for South America.'

'Can I ask what Argentina and Vice-President Perón hopes to gain in return for offering sanctuary to our people?'

'That's easy to answer. Before the war in Europe Argentina was concerned there might be war with Brazil and purchased the weapons it needed from Germany. Perón feels a war with Brazil is still likely and wants his army properly trained in German battle techniques. He's also very interested in the rocket technology that was developed by Germany.'

'I see. Such help will be easy to deliver once our people arrive in Argentina,' said Bernstorff.

The bishop continued. 'That's not the only interest for Perón. With the end of the war, relations between the Allies and Russia have become frosty and he believes a third world war will soon erupt, this time between the United States and the Soviet Union. In such circumstances Perón intends that Argentina will be a neutral country and become an honest broker between the ideologies of capitalism and communism. Perón feels it would give him significant political influence in the world.'

'Is there anything else?' asked Bernstorff.

'Yes, one final thing. I'm informed Perón expects a personal donation of five thousand dollars for each refugee. It's to offset, he says, his personal expenses.'

Bernstorff nodded, 'I will arrange for twenty-five million dollars in bearer bonds to be delivered to you. That will be the *personal* amount Perón is asking for. I would be grateful if you could arrange for it to be forwarded on to him. The money for the living expenses of those who travel to Argentina will be delivered after they have arrived in the country.'

'I will make all the arrangement, my son,' answered the bishop.

A few minutes later Bernstorff and his lieutenant walked away from the Collegio Teutonico to travel back to Zurich.

****

Two days after Michael told Tim Wilson that the Tagleva bank in Paris had evidence that gold had been transferred by the Germans to Switzerland, Michael and Peter were sitting in Jean-Claude's office in Rue Pierre Charron and listening attentively.

'The first thing the Germans did after invading a country was to strip the central banks of all gold and transfer it to the German central bank in Berlin. When the SS took control of the Tagleva bank I instructed secret records to be made of any money transfers. Naturally our records only include what was happening to our account holders, but I would expect similar looting to have occurred in the banks in Poland, Romania and the Netherlands… in fact all the countries the Germans occupied.'

Jean-Claude opened a paper file on his desk.

'Since the Nazis left Paris we've been sorting through every piece of paper they failed to destroy. From the information we've gained, much of the gold initially confiscated by the Germans was spent on the German war effort. But as the war progressed increasing amounts were moved to salt mines in Germany or to neutral countries, very little was sent to Switzerland. However, after D-Day that changed and transfers of gold to Switzerland turned into a flood… and gold was only part of it. Paper money, works of art and jewellery have also been secretly transferred to Switzerland.'

Jean-Claude paused to take a sip of his coffee.

'How much could we be talking about?' asked Michael.

'That figure possibly runs into hundreds of millions of dollars.'

'So why don't we ask the Swiss to hand it back?' asked Peter.

'Because much of it has already disappeared. Even before the end of the war the Nazis had begun turning significant amounts of the gold into other assets such as life insurance policies and company shares. The result is that Nazi money is to be found in companies and investment funds in New York, Chicago, Vancouver, even London, and linking it to the Nazis is difficult, if not impossible.'

'So what'll happen to this money, and particularly the money in Switzerland?'

'In time it'll be absorbed into the world's banking system and will eventually be lost. The Swiss, however, will hide behind their secrecy laws and refuse to disclose money being held, even from the children of Jews murdered in the gas chambers, and eventually it too will disappear into the world's banking system. Those children may never see their family's money again.'

'But, that's immoral,' said Peter.

'Quite, but as Maynard Keynes said about the economic consequences of war, "By this means the government may secretly and unobserved, confiscate the wealth of people, and not one man in a million will detect the theft."'

Michael became silent before shrugging his shoulders. 'So, if the Swiss won't help us locate the money we may never find out who's leading the organisation that's planning to form a government-in-exile until it's too late.'

'Well not quite,' said Jean-Claude.

Michael and Peter leaned forward.

'The SS that occupied Tagleva used a specific, and small, Swiss private bank. For some reason the SS preferred this one bank above the others. Large amounts of gold and money seem to have been transferred to it, particularly towards the end of the war. I wonder if that could be your starting point. All the information you might need is in this file, including letters with some names of Swiss bankers at the bottom.'

Jean-Claude passed over a file. Michael opened it and Peter leaned over to read the information.

After a few minutes Michael looked up. 'Can I keep this file?'
'Of course.'

****

In London Philip Tagleva had just finished his coffee when Dorothy walked into the room. He looked at her as she sat down, screwed up her face and looked into the distance.

'Anything wrong?' asked Philip.

'I was wondering about something.'

Philip leaned back into the chair and waited for Dorothy to tell him what was on her mind. He didn't have long to wait.

'I know the family is in banking, and banks look after people's money. But I've been thinking… I don't know as much as I should about the family business. At ten years of age it's time I should know more, don't you think?'

Philip chuckled. 'I think that's an excellent idea, and no time like the present. I'm off to the bank this afternoon. As there's no school today would you like to come with me?'

Dorothy pursed her lips, and replied in her most precocious manner, 'That would be most convenient. I'll go and tell nanny I'll be out for the afternoon.'

Philip watched Dorothy leave the room and once the door was safely closed began to shake with laughter, tinged with more than a little pride in his adopted daughter.

That afternoon Dorothy was shown around the London branch of the Tagleva bank, and she bombarded the staff with questions.

'Where does money comes from? How is money made? Who makes it? If people's money is kept in one lump how do you know which bit belongs to who? What type of things do people borrow money for? Where's the money kept?'

After a couple of hours of Dorothy's endless questions Philip asked if she'd like to see the vault.

'What's the vault?' she asked.

'It's where the bank stores its most valuable things.'

'Yes please,' said Dorothy, her eyes sparkling.

A minute later they descended the stairs to the vault. Dorothy looked at the door of the twenty-four-bolt Diebold vault with its polished steel door proudly displaying the bank's crest on the front.

'It's the biggest piggy bank I've ever seen,' said Dorothy.

The vault manager and his assistant punched the codes into the combination mechanism. The door slowly swung open on its ball-bearing hinges and they both smiled as Dorothy's eyes widened in anticipation. When the door was open Philip led Dorothy into the vault and she looked all around as if it were magical.

'I'm going to show you something very special,' said Philip.

Philip pulled down a leather box from one of the shelves. He laid out a velvet cloth on a table. Opening the box he extracted two diamond and ruby bracelets and laid them on the cloth. There followed four diamond and sapphire necklaces and a platinum chain set with a huge emerald and studded with diamonds.

'These are some of the things Mummy and I brought out of Russia a long time ago. They belong to the Russian royal family.'

'They're beautiful but why are they here, don't the royal family like them?'

'We were asked to look after them, but the family were killed and the Tagleva bank is keeping these things safe until the rightful owners can be found.'

'When will that be?'

'One day soon I hope,' replied Philip as he put the jewels back into the box.

On the way home Dorothy said, 'Thank you, it's all been so much fun. I think I'd like to be a banker, looking after people's money is an important job.'

****

Pedestrians walking the streets around Paradeplatz in the financial district of Zurich know the buildings stand on the most valuable piece of real estate in Switzerland, but as they pass UBS, Credit Suisse and a number of smaller banks, few realise that in the vaults a few metres below their feet is a sea of gold.

In the centre of this financial district is the fabled Hotel Savoy Baur en Ville, a grand style hotel with lofted ceilings, tastefully furnished bedrooms and an excellent restaurant, which serves the banking community and the bank's wealthier clients.

Michael hadn't been able to sample the delights of the famed Orsini restaurant in the hotel. Instead, for the past three days, he and Peter had been sitting in a bedroom watching the entrance to the small family-owned private bank opposite the hotel. Whenever Matteo Keller appeared Michael signalled to one of his team to follow him. Matteo's signature was on one of the letters given to Michael by Jean-Claude that confirmed the SS deposits of gold to the bank; he was their only lead.

Over three days Michael's team investigated Matteo and discovered he'd excelled at school, obtained a first-class degree from the University of Bern and had worked for his current employer for the past eight years. Promotion had come quickly after he married the daughter of one of the bank's directors and he lived with his wife in a modest house on the outskirts of Zurich. Within a year of their marriage they had a baby daughter. Matteo was punctilious, didn't drink or smoke and was an active member of the Swiss Reformed Church.

On the third day Peter said to Michael, 'He lives a perfectly boring existence. He kisses his wife and baby goodbye, goes to work until lunchtime when he leaves the bank and walks up the road to the same café, looks at the menu but always orders a cheese sandwich, and exactly thirty-five minutes later returns to work. At the end of the day he leaves the bank at exactly six and takes the bus home, goes to bed at ten and each Sunday goes to church. He's boring.'

Michael looked at Peter. 'What about his wife?'

'His wife is from the Canton of Ticino in Switzerland. She's quite plain looking, doesn't use much makeup, is frugal with the housekeeping and is no cook. We've been through the refuse bins – she's made saffron risotto with sausage twice this week. It's a common dish of the Ticino district... risotto rice, saffron and cheese with a few slices of sausage thrown in, it's an easy dinner to make. He's a boring banker with a boring life and an equally boring wife.'

'Let's spend another day watching him and if nothing's changed decide what to do,' came Michael's reply as he settled down to watch the bank's entrance once more.

Chapter Thirty-Nine

Zurich, June 1945

The following day over a breakfast of coffee and croissant that room service had delivered Michael and Peter were discussing the Swiss banker.

'We could threaten to harm his wife to get the information we need,' said Peter.

'I know you're not serious. Besides, if it went wrong, it might result in the Swiss police being involved and would warn the Germans we're onto them. They'd change their plans and we'd be no better off. No, we'll watch him for another day or two and if we don't have any ideas by the end of Friday we'll have to think of something else.'

Halfway through the afternoon the telephone rang. Michael walked over to the bedside table and picked up the receiver, he immediately recognised Edward's voice.

'His wife's left the house with the baby and was carrying an overnight bag. I risked helping her onto the bus with the child's pram and casually asked her where she was going. She told me she spends every Thursday night at her parents' house. They like to spend time with their daughter and grandchild.'

'You might as well come back to the hotel. No point in watching an empty house,' said Michael.

At the end of the working day Matteo Keller left the bank, but instead of turning left to walk to the bus stop that would take him home, he turned right. Michael watched through binoculars as Nigel began to follow at a discreet distance.

Three hours later Nigel was back in the hotel reporting what happened after the banker left work.

'Instead of walking to the bus stop he walked over the bridge to the old town. It's an area with cobbled streets, lots of shops, restaurants and bars. I thought our banker might have been looking for somewhere good to eat, to make a change from the sausage risotto he gets at home, but he stopped at a florist and bought some flowers and a few shops further on purchased a small box of chocolates. Ten minutes later he arrived at Niederdorfstrasse. It's a road in the middle of the red light district. Every Thursday when his wife spends the night at her parents' house, our boring Swiss banker takes the opportunity of having a good fuck with a whore. I managed to speak to one of the other working girls who told me he's been seeing the same girl, Elena, every Thursday for about a year. Much to the amusement of the other tarts, he's become quite stricken by this Elena. As well as the flowers and chocolates he's recently bought her some expensive jewellery.'

Michael smiled, 'The naughty boy.'

A week later, on the following Friday, Matteo was distraught. Up until lunchtime the simple and uncomplicated life he'd created for himself was perfect, now it was close to collapse. He remembered being irritated when the stranger sat opposite him at lunch, how he'd become increasingly angry with the man's inane attempts to make conversation and had toyed with the idea of moving to another table when the stranger suddenly asked him about *his Elena*. Hearing her name so shocked him that his sandwich hovered halfway between his plate and his mouth. When the stranger passed him a photograph, as if sharing a holiday memory, showing him arriving at Elena's apartment he felt a cold clammy sweat break out. When he was shown the second photograph, taken through the half-open curtains from the building opposite Elena's bedroom, he felt sick. It clearly showed him naked, on his knees and looking up at Elena, dressed in the black lace lingerie he'd bought her, with her large, exposed breasts inches from his open mouth. He was firmly told there were other photos, even more compromising. There was no time to recover from the shock of the photograph before the stranger's demands began. He listened with growing dread. At the end, was told that he could probably say goodbye to his wife, his child and his career if he didn't comply. Then the stranger passed him a box of the same chocolate truffles he always gave to Elena and suggested he take them home to his wife.

Back at the bank Matteo told his secretary he had a headache and not to disturb him. He sat down at his desk hoping to plan how he might escape the nightmare. The twenty minutes with the stranger played in his mind, like a movie, over and over again. He thought back to when his wife asked if she could spend time with her parents every week, he had encouraged it. Soon afterwards he'd met his lovely Elena who provided him with the sex he never got at home. The demands the stranger ordered him to reveal horrified him. If he complied and was discovered it could earn him a long prison sentence. He thought of confessing all to his father-in-law and the other directors of the bank, he could justify his infidelity by telling them that prostitution had been legal in Switzerland since 1942, but in his mind he knew that it was not the legality of the situation he feared most but his wife's anger. He pictured himself confessing all to her, saying how he regretted the things he'd done, that he didn't deserve her, that in his heart he'd always only loved her, that he would give up Elena... but knew he was not brave enough. He couldn't face the tears, the endless rows, the condemnation, the lifetime of mistrust and a stalled career. By the end of the day he was worn down with the mental conflict and knew he would comply with the stranger's demands.

Nigel's substantial payment to Elena to leave the bedroom curtains open when Matteo visited next had more than delivered the results Michael hoped for. By the following Monday Michael was reading a full breakdown of the account the bank held on behalf of the Nazis. He knew the exact amount of gold that had been deposited by the SS, how much had been sold and converted into bearer bonds, even the identification numbers of each bond.

Peter said, 'Now we have all that information why don't we order Keller to give us the list of account numbers and password then HM treasury could empty the account. With all that money the prime minister would promote us to the rank of field marshal in gratitude.'

Michael laughed. 'That would be too easy. Anyway as Matteo explained, for security reasons, the account passwords are kept separate from the account manager. He doesn't have access to the information.'

'Shame,' sighed Peter.

Michael looked at him. 'However, we do know the name of the account holder. His name's Carl Bernstorff, I contacted London and they've sent me some details. He was a member of the Waffen-SS attached to the elite tank division of the 2nd SS Panzer Division… fought in Russia and France and with distinction… awarded the Knight's Cross, one of Germany's highest military honours. London's even managed to attach a blurred picture taken before the war.'

He passed the photograph to Peter who studied the face.

Michael continued. 'Since that picture was taken he's been badly wounded. He now has scars to his face, lost his left arm and apparently walks with a limp, all from when he was in Russia.'

'Then he shouldn't be too difficult to identify. When do we liquidate him?'

'Liquidating Bernstorff might be more difficult than we think. I suspect he's protected by members of his old panzer unit. Our Swiss banker says that whenever he visits the bank he's always accompanied by a second, very fit looking man. It would seem logical. His old unit are battle-hardened members of the SS with a gruesome reputation in Russia. So I asked London to send over a photograph of his unit and this arrived this morning. The photograph was taken in Russia; Bernstorff's sitting in the middle. I suggest we all study those faces. It may save our lives if we're able to instantly recognise them.'

Peter looked at the photograph. 'I'll pass it round to the others. So where do we start?'

'The key to all of this is the money. If we follow the money trail it should eventually lead us to the men who'll be setting up the new Nazi government-in-exile. There's an interesting piece of information our Swiss banker told me. One of the bearer bonds has been cashed by a seminary in Rome that trains Germans for the priesthood. Not the sort of organisation we would expect to be in possession of a Nazi bearer bond. I suspect the answers we're looking for can be found in Rome.'

'I've never been to Rome,' said Peter.

'And I'm afraid you still won't. Someone needs to stay in Zurich to keep an eye on Matteo in case he can give us more information if the Germans make contact with him again.'

'Oh well, never mind. I'll slum it at the Hotel Savoy while you lot enjoy yourselves sightseeing in Italy.'

They both laughed.

Chapter Forty

Florence, Italy, June 1945

Nestling in the midst of Turkey oak woods, about eighteen miles north-east of Florence, is a small Franciscan monastery originally built in the twelfth century. The noble family who built the monastery donated it, for the good of their souls, to the Franciscan order and because the Franciscans are a mendicant order the monastery remained a small, impoverished building until the Medici family bought the land three hundred years later. To reflect their importance in the region the Medici's set about enlarging the property, adding a refectory, bell tower, cloisters, sacristy and loggia. As the friars prepare for their daily prayers they are reminded of the generosity of their medieval benefactors whenever they look up at the sixteenth-century wooden panel above the door of the sacristy displaying the Medici coat of arms.

Near the cloisters a man was shown into an office.

Sitting on a seat in front of a large desk he said, 'Thank you for allowing me your sanctuary, Prior.'

'You are most welcome, my son, but my correct title is Guardian. St. Francis never used the word prior, which means first or superior. He preferred the title Guardian, meaning one who cares for and looks after another.'

The Guardian looked at the man in front of his desk and tried to estimate his age but, with such people, it was hard. He was skinny, his hair hung as a tangled mop of messy curls and his unkempt appearance was exaggerated because his clothes, once high end, hung loosely where they shouldn't, no doubt made worse by having been slept in for a couple of nights. Despite having had a bath and a shave, the man's skin was grey giving the impression his face was covered in grime. In the past months the monastery had given sanctuary to more than a few young men fleeing from the crimes the world now heaped upon them. As the Guardian looked at him the man averted his gaze. There had been many times over the past weeks the Guardian had observed the fear of capture that had taught such men to stay isolated and as invisible as possible as even a stray glance could mean trouble they'd best avoid.

The Guardian spoke. 'What was your job during the war?'

'I was a police commander in Paris.'

'Gestapo?'

'Yes,' came a mumbled reply.

'You were lucky to remain hidden in the POW camp until one of our priests managed to get you released.'

'Yes, I was lucky. I disguised myself using a dead private soldier's uniform. The British soldiers running the camp weren't interested in low ranking soldiers of the Wehrmacht.'

The Guardian said, 'I'm informed the French and British authorities are after you. They say you were responsible for the round-up of civilians as hostages and for the execution of members of the French Resistance and four British SOE agents.'

The man looked at the floor and mumbled, 'You must understand I had no choice, I was ordered to do it... believe me when I say that I was simply doing my duty, following orders. The SOE men were spies, responsible for the deaths of many of our soldiers...'

The Guardian smiled comfortingly. 'It's not for me to pass judgement on you, my son, only God has that privilege, so let's not dwell on those matters.'

The man looked up and seemed to take some comfort from the words.

'I've been informed that within a few days you'll receive new identity documents. Your papers will be issued by the *Commissione Pontificia d'Assistenza*, the Vatican Refugee Organisation, and your name will be changed from Julius Halder to Julius Schafer, a builder from Innsbruck in Austria. The Vatican papers will allow you to obtain a passport from the International Committee of the Red Cross; it will be the Red Cross document which will be used to apply for your visa to live in Argentina. While you wait for your Red Cross passport you're to be passed from one monastery to another until you arrive in

Rome. There you will be put up in a safe house until all your papers are in order. The day you depart for South America you will be given funds for six months. These are for your living expenses and later you will receive money to establish a business in South America.'

'I'm most grateful,' said Halder.

In the background a bell began to toll.

'The bell tells me it's time for the friars to meet in the chapter room for our daily discussion and for the Divine Office of Compline, the night prayer. We will meet again tomorrow. So I will allow you to return to your monk's cell and wish you a goodnight.'

Julius Halder got up from his chair and left the room closing the door quietly behind him. Before joining the other friars to lead the evening prayers, the Guardian offered up his own prayer for the man's soul.

'O my Jesus, forgive us our sins, save us from the fires of hell: lead all souls to Heaven especially those who are most in need of your mercy.'

Chapter Forty-One

25 July 1945

Once Michael and the rest of the team had left for Rome, Peter decided he would enjoy his time at the hotel in Zurich while maintaining the, not so difficult, task of keeping an eye on the Swiss banker. If Matteo Keller had any news about the German's bank account he had been ordered to leave a note with the concierge; to ensure his compliance Matteo had been given another photograph as a reminder of the consequences of any failure.

The waiter placed a plate of cheese crêpes in front of Peter. He looked with relish at the pancakes filled with fluffy curd cheese, raisins, vanilla sugar and a hint of lemon zest. Then, out of the corner of his eye, he noticed the concierge approaching. The concierge handed him a note, Peter gave him an overly generous twenty-franc tip and read the information. He sighed, looked at the crêpes sitting temptingly on his plate, picked up a fork, cut a large mouthful and stuffed it into his mouth. The delicate flavours of the dish burst around his taste buds and he cursed under his breath as he pushed his chair back and left the dining room.

As there wasn't a cloud in the sky, Zurich was bathed in a brightness that would make fresh snow look grey. Peter put on his sunglasses but still had to squint from the glare as he walked to the café where he was to meet the Swiss banker. Sitting down opposite Matteo Keller, Peter noticed the banker's lips were tightly compressed and he was contorting his hands together.

'You look nervous,' said Peter.

'Not at all,' said the banker unravelling his hands and pushing his cheek with an index finger.

Peter smiled, 'You have some information for me?'

'Yes. The account holder has made an appointment with me for today.'

'What time?'

'Four, this afternoon.'

'What's the purpose of the meeting?'

'He's arranged for a withdrawal of coupon bonds from his bank account.'

'Coupon bonds?' enquired Peter.

'It's a technical term. Bearer bonds are called coupon bonds because the certificates have coupons attached to them so that they can be detached and redeemed by an authorised agent bank. The activity is commonly referred to as clipping coupons.'

'What's the value of the bonds your client's asked for?'

The banker looked around him to ensure that no one was listening.

'One hundred and fifty million dollars,' the banker whispered.

Peter pursed his lips in a silent whistle. 'Won't that amount be bulky?'

'Not really, it amounts to only one hundred pieces of paper. Each is worth one and a half million.'

'What do these coupons look like?' enquired Peter.

'Similar to share certificates, the only difference to a share certificate is that there's no registered owner's name printed on the face.'

'If there's no name on the certificates what happens if they get lost or stolen?'

'As there is no registration there's virtually no way to prove who the rightful beneficiary is. If they're lost or stolen it creates a great risk for the legitimate owner as anyone holding a bearer bond need only submit the certificate to a bank or broker to anonymously cash it for the amount of the coupon.'

'All right, that's enough for now.'

As the banker rose from his chair Peter grasped his wrist.

'Don't forget to keep in touch, remember we still have those photographs.'

'I won't forget,' the banker spat back.

After leaving the café Peter went to the offices of the British vice-consulate in Zurich and arranged for a message to be sent to Tim Wilson in London, it would be forwarded on to Michael in Rome. A circuitous route for such a message, but Peter knew Michael would have the information about the banker's appointment with the German before Bernstorff walked into the bank later in the afternoon.

For the remainder of the day Peter watched the bank's entrance from the hotel bedroom, only leaving his post to follow Matteo Keller when he went for lunch. The banker spoke to no one and returned to work thirty-five minutes later.

At exactly four in the afternoon, as the sun spread shadows across the street, a two-door Mercedes-Benz 170 V easily identifiable from the external spare wheel on the car's rear panel, drew up at the entrance of the bank. A man with scars on his face and a slight limp got out. He was carrying a light tan briefcase as he walked into the building. Peter left the hotel and positioned himself in the darkness of an office entrance where he had a clear view of the bank. A policeman approached the parked Mercedes and ordered the driver to move the vehicle as it was obstructing other traffic. Peter watched as the driver remonstrated with the policeman who shook his head firmly; the car was driven away.

Twenty minutes later Bernstorff reappeared still carrying the tan briefcase. He looked up and down the road for his car, saw it parked on Bahnhofstrasse, a main street off the square, and began walking towards it. Peter left the shadows of the office entrance and followed at a short distance. It was not an easy task, Bernstorff's limp made his progress slow and Peter was conscious that, unlike the other pedestrians, he was not hurrying past Bernstorff and any trained observer would guess he must be following him. Peter crossed the road and was twenty feet behind when Bernstorff arrived at the Mercedes and put the briefcase down on the pavement to open the passenger's door with his one free hand. As the door opened Peter ran forward. The car door was now fully open and Bernstorff bent down to retrieve the briefcase. His hand hadn't taken hold of the handle when Peter barged into him. Surprised by the assault Bernstorff cried out as he lost his balance, crashed against the car door falling awkwardly onto the pavement and knocking the briefcase over. His legs and an arm thrashed about as he tried to grab hold of it. Seizing his opportunity Peter reached down, wrapped his hand around the handle of the briefcase and began to run down the tree-lined street. Peter was fifteen yards down the street before Bernstorff managed to pick himself up, jump into the car and pull the door shut. Before it had closed the driver pressed his foot down on the accelerator to give chase.

Peter knew if he could outrun his pursuers and reach the gardens, only a few hundred feet away, he could disappear among the crowds of shoppers and coffee bars, and the Mercedes would be forced to drive on. He twisted round to look behind him. The sun shone into his face but despite the glare he could see the car was catching up fast. At that moment something bumped into him. Peter stopped running and wondered what was happening; it felt like a slap on the back, followed by a kind of numbness, a sense of something being wrong, akin to an electrical jolt and his brain told him *yes, that's pain*. Peter felt himself supported and dragged into a doorway. The passing pedestrians assumed the two men had been in too much of a hurry and had bumped into each other and ignored them. Without warning, the knife in Peter's back was twisted and roughly pulled out, causing more internal damage. Peter gave out a guttural choke and dropped the briefcase. As he sank to his knees he felt himself positioned so he was sitting against a wall. The assailant expertly returned the knife to its hidden sheath, picked up the briefcase and walked away. Peter became conscious of having no energy, being lightheaded and unable even to speak more than a whisper, he looked down to see his life source spreading across the marble entrance to the office. Leaning his head back against the tiles he closed his eyes.

As the car turned the corner of Bahnhofstrasse the assassin said to Bernstorff, 'Stupid to have a man with shiny golden hair follow you, made things too easy.'

Chapter Forty-Two

Rome, 27 July 1945

It was late afternoon when Michael received two messages from London. The first was from Peter informing him that Bernstorff was to collect bearer bonds from the bank. The second, received a couple of hours later, was from the British embassy in Switzerland saying Peter was dead. Details were scarce but the Swiss police were saying Peter's death was the result of a failed robbery on the street. Michael scrunched up the second message in his fist, stood up and told Edward he was going out.

Michael didn't know how long he walked, but it must have been many hours until he found himself on the edge of the ancient Roman forum, leaning against a pillar in the stadium of Domitian, watching the sun going down behind one of Rome's seven hills. He opened his fist to see the paper message informing him of Peter's death. He unfolded it, ironed out the creases by wiping the paper on his knee and read it again. His thoughts became tormentors, *as leader I shouldn't have left Peter on his own in Zurich; Peter's death was my fault.*

Leaning against the ancient Roman pillar in the fading light Michael thought back to the anger he felt at the deaths of his mother and unborn child. That anger was one that boils blood, consumes a person leaving a man enraged, desperate for vengeance and a danger to others. Since reading the note Michael was no longer thinking irrationally. The desire for vengeance was the same but his thoughts had become crystal clear; he felt an increase in stamina and a clear head. Peter's death had turned Michael's anger as cold as ice.

The following morning Michael was briefing Edward, Nigel and John.

'Peter's death means we have to assume Bernstorff and his men know we're after them. They'll most likely have left Zurich to avoid the Swiss police. The only lead we have is the bearer bond cashed here in Rome. How easy will it be to have the Collegio Teutonico watched?'

John answered, 'I had a look at the place yesterday. It's not going to be easy. The college is surrounded by a high wall and it's not possible to get a good view of the inside from the surrounding buildings. The main entrance to the church is on a narrow road, not wide enough for two cars to pass, so anyone hanging about watching the entrance would be easily spotted.'

'Could one of us sit inside the church?' suggested Nigel.

Michael scratched his head. 'It's not on the average sightseer's list. One person sitting in the church for hours at a time watching who comes and goes is bound to raise suspicion.'

Michael paused and came to a decision. 'I'll send a message to London, ask them if they're able to help.'

Three hours later a message from London confirmed Michael's appointment with Britain's Envoy Extraordinary and Minister Plenipotentiary to the Holy See, the grand title given to the British ambassador.

Michael arrived at the British ambassador's offices in the San Giovanni area of Rome. He was met by a secretary who immediately ushered him into the presence of Sir D'Arcy Osborne. Michael found himself facing a spry, trim and bespectacled sixty year old who warmly welcomed him in the manner of English courtliness associated with the country-house party of long ago. In this respect Michael was reminded of his father, who shared the same unruffled poise, and yet he found it impossible to behave towards Sir D'Arcy with anything but the strictest formality.

'It's very kind of you to afford me the time to meet with you,' said Michael as they shook hands. He was waved towards one of the comfortable leather armchairs.

Sir D'Arcy smiled. 'I've ordered tea, I hope that's all right.'

'Perfectly,' answered Michael.

'While we're waiting for it to arrive I wonder if I might give a very short history of Britain's diplomatic relations between the Vatican and England. As you are no doubt aware, they have not always been good. But understanding it might help you with your work in Rome.'

Anticipating there would be a purpose to the history lesson Michael nodded.

'Since medieval times the papacy has been recognised as a sovereign entity by almost every country in Europe. In the eleventh century popes used to send a papal representative to every European monarch. It wasn't until the fifteenth century it became customary for European countries to have resident ambassador to the Pope based here in Rome. In 1534 our King Henry VIII declared himself "the only Supreme Head in Earth of the Church of England", quite naturally, this upset the Pope and relations were severed with England. They have remained severed, on and off, mostly off, ever since. However, at the start of the Great War in 1914 the United Kingdom formally re-established diplomatic relations with the Vatican and an ambassador has been at the papal court ever since. In terms of importance, however, the British government considers the British envoy to the Vatican as being of value to Britain's prestige and a quiet place to put a not very distinguished diplomat. I'm the current holder of the post.'

Sir D'Arcy chuckled at his own joke and continued. 'I tell you this, not to bore you with a history lesson, but to demonstrate the fragile state of Britain's relationship with the Vatican. If there were a scandal or any unfortunate accidents while you and your team are in Rome, which could be linked to members of the SOE, it could have all sorts of political ramifications.'

'I do understand, sir. You can rely on my own, and my men's, utmost discretion.'

'Excellent, I knew you would understand.'

The tea arrived and Sir D'Arcy poured two cups, threw a slice of lemon into the liquid and passed the cup to Michael.

'I'm told by London that you and your team are on the track of Germans who hope to escape Europe and set up a Nazi government-in-exile. I suspect you'll have great difficulty preventing it.'

'Why so?' enquired Michael.

'All priests, bishops and even cardinals see it as their Christian duty to help those in need. During the war there were clerics, such as the Irish priest Monsignor Hugh O'Flaherty, who concealed some four thousand Jews and escaped Allied soldiers from the Nazis both within the Vatican and around Rome. Now the war is over there are different priests who consider it's their duty to devote similar charitable work to persecuted National Socialists and Italian fascists and especially towards those the Allies claim to be war criminals.'

'Are these fugitives here in the Vatican?' asked Michael.

'The Vatican is a world in miniature; packed into it is everything a state needs, only smaller. Its frontiers are well guarded, its bank is housed inside an old fortress, it has a small cinema, the fire engines are tiny and there is even a jail. Because it's populated by priests who are known to maintain the confidentiality of the confessional, a library containing countless secrets that outsiders are prevented from entering, most people's perception is that the Vatican is shrouded in secrecy. However, this perception is wrong. Among the cardinals, bishops and the Curia there's more gossip than in any city on earth and, the reality is that it's almost impossible to keep a secret in the Vatican. For example, the group led by Monsignor Hugh O'Flaherty that helped Jews during the German occupation was an open secret among the diplomatic community. Even the head of the SS and Gestapo in Rome, Herbert Kappler, knew what O'Flaherty was doing and openly referred to him as The Pimpernel of the Vatican. To answer your question, there are Nazis being hidden within the Vatican.'

'I see, can you tell me the names of the priests who are helping them?' asked Michael.

'The information I have is that there are two main institutions involved. The first is the Instituto Teutonico headed by Bishop Hudal. But I know you are aware of him. The second group is led by a Franciscan priest centred on the San Girolamo

Seminary, also in Rome. What I can't tell you is the extent that these groups are co-operating.'

'Can the groups be closed down somehow?'

'You can't just barge in and destroy them. Both groups are supported by some of the most powerful people within the Vatican. The Girolamo group, for instance, is led by a Father Dominik Mandic who happens to be the treasurer of the Franciscan order. The Franciscans are, despite their vows of poverty, one of the wealthiest and most influential orders in the Catholic Church. Both Bishop Hudal and Father Mandic are protected by senior members of the Catholic clergy, among them Archbishop Antonio Caggiano who is soon to be elevated to a cardinal by His Holiness the Pope.'

'So what do you advise?' asked Michael.

'The point I'm making is that you and your group are pitted against an organisation which resembles the Hydra, the many-headed serpent in Greek mythology. Cut off one head and another will grow in its place. And remember if Britain were identified as the instigator of the murder of a cardinal, a bishop or even some priests the Roman Catholic world would consider it as great a crime as any committed by the Nazis. Your name and the names of your men would be damned for ever.'

Sir D'Arcy paused and took a sip of tea.

'Are you suggesting my mission is pointless and I should take my unit home to England?'

Sir D'Arcy looked hard at Michael and smiled.

'During the war Monsignor O'Flaherty often told me, "Overcoming evil with good, Romans 12:21, is one of the most profound statements ever uttered". Like so much of Jesus' teaching, it stimulates something deep within us that we find peculiarly attractive and yet, often, it's dismissed as too difficult to succeed.'

Another sip of tea was taken as the ambassador looked over the tea cup at Michael.

'I suspect you're telling me that my task should not be considered too difficult. If that's the case then what I really need is information,' said Michael.

Sir D'Arcy put down the tea cup and smiled broadly. 'Ahh now information *is* something I can help you with. What would you find most useful to know?'

Michael passed him the photograph of Bernstorff and his unit.

'I'd like to know if and when any of these men are seen in Rome and, if so, where.'

'I can probably have the information you need within a day or two,' beamed the ambassador.

Chapter Forty-Three

28 July 1945

Napoleon Bonaparte was not the first general to visualise the military importance of the Simplon Pass through the Alps. It was why he included the passage in plans for his invasion of Italy and built the Simplon Road to transport artillery pieces through the pass between the Rhône valley and Italy. One hundred years later passenger trains were running through the world's longest tunnel connecting Brig in Switzerland and Domodossola in northern Italy.

In the comfort of the first-class carriage Carl Bernstorff, accompanied by five members of his unit, was thankful the German army had been thwarted by Italian partisans in blowing up the tunnel as part of its withdrawal from Italy. Had the tunnel been destroyed the journey from Zurich to Rome would have been inconvenient, taking many days, instead of nine hours.

In the darkness of the tunnel Bernstorff looked at his reflection mirrored in the window and thought back to the events over the previous few days. The realisation the British knew about Project Red House could have been predicted, what had made him angry was learning how much the Swiss banker had revealed to the British about the bank account and the details of the bearer bonds. Bernstorff sighed, so much for Swiss banking secrecy laws and confidentiality. Proper investigation of the banker should have uncovered that he used the services of prostitutes. His death was unfortunate but an inevitable consequence of his betrayal and necessary to prevent the British gaining any further information. It was fortunate the Zurich police had been easily convinced by the suicide note in his jacket pocket explaining that he was overburdened by guilt for betraying his wife and family by visiting prostitutes. A more serious situation had been created by Boris killing the British agent; it alerted them to the fact that Project Red House was a reality.

The train emerged from the tunnel and Bernstorff squinted as bright sunshine flooded the compartment. After his eyes adjusted he continued to look through the window, pondering his plans, without noticing any of the beautiful Italian countryside.

If the British knew of the bearer bonds… did they know of the escape network? How large was the British team set against me? He guessed not many, *four, possibly five… It would be unlikely to be more… The British and American intelligence agencies were fully occupied with the deteriorating trust between themselves and the Soviet Union.*

Bernstorff smiled to himself. As he had predicted it hadn't taken long after the war ended for the Russians to mistrust the Americans' threat of nuclear weapons, the Americans to mistrust the spread of communism, the British to fear the loss of their empire and the French, as usual, to mistrust everyone. The lack of trust would continue to divert the Allies' attention away from his plans.

The train rattled over some points. Bernstorff's thoughts turned to the oath he'd made all those years ago: 'I vow to you, Adolf Hitler, as Führer and chancellor of the German Reich, loyalty and bravery and to the leaders you set before me, absolute allegiance until death. So help me God'. *What relevance was the oath now? Hitler and Himmler were dead and those other leaders set above him were in prison awaiting trial for crimes against humanity.*

As the train rumbled along the tracks Bernstorff considered the future. He was in control of four hundred million Reich marks deposited in a Swiss bank. He was the only person who knew the complete list of those waiting to be spirited away, the names of the companies that would be financed to create Germany's revival and only he had the resources capable of financing a new German Reich. It meant he was Adolf Hitler's successor, the new Führer, and the man to lead Germany to a phoenix-like rebirth. Unlike Hitler's Third Reich his new order would not tread the well-worn path of the old – it would not repeat the same mistakes. Instead of tanks invading parts of Europe his Germany would use political and economic leverage to dominate a united Europe. His plan was that the major European countries should sign a treaty to co-operatively manage their heavy industries – coal and steel. In time those countries would be dominated by Germany and would be forced to follow Germany's pathway.

When Bernstorff and his men arrived at the Ostiense railway station in Rome, unusually for the time of year, the sky above the city was dominated by the dark greys and silver of rainclouds and a soft drizzle began to fall. In ones and twos Bernstorff's unit transferred to a safe house on the Via dei Salumi in the Trastevere area of the city. The owner of the building, Mario Boano, had once been an enthusiastic supporter of the *Partito Nazionale Fascista*, the political party created and led by Benito Mussolini, and had fully supported the fascist's aim of expanding Italy's territories.

'If Italy is to assert its superiority and strength and avoid succumbing to decay Mussolini needs to be supported,' he told friends in the local trattoria before the war.

Now that Italy's new constitution had banned the Fascist Party, Mario had become an equally enthusiastic supporter of the Christian Democrat Party and would inform those same friends, 'It's right that Catholic social teaching and ideology guides Italy on a path to democracy,' adding that he'd made, 'a modest financial contribution to party funds.'

When approached by a party worker asking if he would rent his beautifully decorated house to a group of visiting businessmen Mario was anxious to oblige and arranged a short holiday, for two months, with his sister in her comfortable apartment overlooking the bay of Naples.

Bernstorff was delighted with the accommodation. It was in the centre of a working-class district with crumbling buildings, faded paintwork and washing strung across the streets. It attracted few sightseers and the cobblestoned side streets were crisscrossed by a warren of alleyways affording any number of routes of escape in a crisis. It was also conveniently located within easy walking distance of the Vatican and the other places he and his team needed to visit.

The unit began their occupation by searching for hidden microphones. Wires that seemed not to go anywhere were pulled off the walls and the light fixtures exposed and inspected. After a full hour they were satisfied there were no listening devices in the house. Despite having no expectations the house would be attacked, their experiences in Russia had proved time and again that preparations for an attack saved lives and Bernstorff's men prepared for such an eventuality. A hole was cut in the wall of the upstairs bedroom overlooking the staircase large enough to be used as a firing point onto unwelcome visitors entering through the front door. Then the house was stripped of all unnecessary clutter, which was thrown into one corner of the back yard and quickly soaked by the rain. Even the dozen valuable antique books of poems, called *Cantari*, that Mario had spent a lifetime collecting, were pulled from their shelves and thrown onto the pile of possessions in the yard. Once the house was cleared of clutter a deep drawer in the kitchen was identified that would accommodate a change in depth, a change which wouldn't be obvious to a cursory search. A wooden slat from underneath one of the beds was removed and cut to fit the drawer and rested on wood strips hot-glued to the drawer sides to create a false bottom. A piece of kitchen equipment, not out of place in the drawer, was then hot-glued to act as a handle allowing the false bottom to be easily lifted to reveal the hiding place of the bearer bonds. It was then Bernstorff's men unpacked their own luggage.

That evening two Italians delivered a couple of suitcases to the house. The first contained black cassocks, the ankle-length garment traditionally worn by priests, and derived historically from the tunic the ancient Romans wore underneath the toga. Within two sheets of tissue paper was found two black fascias, the cloth worn by Catholic clergy between the waist and the breastbone with ends that hang down on the left side of the body. Made from watered silk the fascia signified the wearer was attached to the papal household and was thus the key that would open almost any door in the city.

The second case contained some civilian clothes, maps of the city, three Browning Hi-Power pistols and a luger. At the bottom of the briefcase was a fourth pistol, a Walther PPK. Its small size made it easily concealable and was Bernstorff's weapon of choice.

****

The Café Greco on Via dei Condotti in Rome is the second oldest bar in Italy, only the Café Florian in Venice is older. As expected, for the time of day, it was packed with people when the Italian dressed in dark blue slacks and fawn jacket walked in. Unable to find a vacant table he waited next to the huge wooden carving of Pan, the half-man half-goat god that dominates one of the café's rooms. Just as a table became vacant the man he was waiting for appeared, he took possession of the table and one of Bernstorff's men slipped into the seat next to him.

'Do you have a progress report?' asked the German.

'There are twenty men hidden in various monasteries with travel papers and visas ready to enter Argentina. Within a few days we will be ready to begin moving them out of Italy.'

'That's good.'

'There is one thing,' the man whispered to the German, 'my bishop is wondering when the remainder of the money you promised will be delivered.'

The German looked irritated.

'The money will be delivered as agreed. However, there's a complication. One of the bearer bonds has been cashed before the agreed time. As a result the British have become aware of the operation and of the Collegio Teutonico's involvement. We think there may be a group of British agents in Rome. They may cause trouble.'

'Yes, my bishop regrets that oversight. But remember the Collegio is protected by the sanctity of the Vatican. What can the British do? They have no way to cause problems for us.'

'Nevertheless you should be on your guard. We don't want any problems.'

'The British can't interfere in Vatican business and no one is going to harm a bishop in Rome. They wouldn't dare.'

'My commander asks that you are careful. Tell your bishop not to cash any more bonds, not until everything has been agreed.'

'I will inform the bishop of your instructions.'

'Very good,' said the German.

The priest rose and left the bar to walk back to the Collegio Teutonico, and the German ordered a large glass of Moretti beer from a passing waiter.

Chapter Forty-Four

The following day

The following morning one of Sir D'Arcy's staff called on Michael.

'We've had a small group of priests keeping watch on the Collegio Teutonico. Early last night the bishop's secretary was seen leaving the building and was not wearing his collar.'

'His collar?'

'Oh, I'm sorry, not being a Catholic, you wouldn't understand the significance of such an action. 'The collar is worn in place of a tie and identifies a priest. It's a sign of consecration to the Lord much like the wedding ring distinguishes a husband and wife. It serves a practical purpose. The collar sends a clear message to everyone that a priest visiting a private house in Christ's name has come to minister to the sick and needy. It prevents idle speculation that might be triggered by a strange man visiting a widow's house for instance.'

'You're telling me the collar restrains gossip and inappropriate behaviour?' said Michael.

'Yes, quite so.'

Michael smiled broadly. 'I see, go on.'

'As I was saying, last night the bishop's secretary left the Institute and went to a popular bar near the Spanish Steps. He only stayed a few minutes and didn't order a drink, but he did meet one of the men in the photograph you left with Sir D'Arcy.'

'Do we know what was said?'

'I'm afraid not. Our man couldn't get close enough and the noise from the bar was too loud to hear anything.'

'A shame. After he left the bar where did the man go?'

'We don't know. Our watcher was alone and had to make a choice of who to follow. He followed the bishop's secretary back to the Collegio.'

'Damn it. However, if one of Bernstorff's team is in Rome, it's probable the rest of his unit is too. Is it possible my men can join the group watching the Collegio?' asked Michael.

'I'm sure that can be arranged.'

Within a few hours Edward and John were in a building opposite the church of Santa Maria dell'Anima. Looking out of the third-storey window Edward had a clear view of the three entrances of the church. Above the central door, larger than the two on either side, was a triangular pediment containing a statue of Mary with the child Jesus flanked by two souls in purgatory. He looked at the inscription carved into the stone – *Speciosa facta est* – and, using his schoolboy Latin, translated it as 'you were made beautiful'. He smiled to himself.

They were given a commentary on the comings and goings of the various visitors by Armando, a young priest who worked at the British consulate. Edward and John were surprised how many people visited the building.

'It's not so remarkable,' said Armando. 'The church attracts visitors and worshipers as it acts as an entrance to the seminary and the church also houses the funeral monument of Pope Adrian VI. The altarpiece has an amazing fresco painted by Giulio Romano in 1522 depicting the Holy Family and the masterpiece attracts art lovers to visit the church.'

At dusk Michael and Nigel arrived to relieve them.

'Anything happened?' asked Michael.

'Apart from visitors to the church, nothing interesting,' replied John.

'Go back to the hotel and get some sleep. If we need you we'll telephone, so don't go out on the town,' said Michael.

Edward tutted. 'And I'd arranged to go to a Roman orgy tonight!' Noticing Armando's collar he added, 'Oh, sorry Father.'

Armando smiled. 'That's OK my son, but I'm disappointed. Hearing your confession in the morning would have been more interesting than the usual ones I hear.'

Everyone in the room smiled.

As the daylight softened and the evening closed in so the atmosphere in the street changed. Pedestrians who had previously rushed around doing their daily business were replaced by couples and family groups, some talking quietly of serious matters and others about nothing at all, but all enjoying the cool of the evening and the most enduring tradition of Italian life: the *Passeggiata*, the evening promenade.

Just after seven, when the street was at its busiest, Michael noticed two priests walking along the road. One was holding a small tan briefcase; the other had a limp and an empty sleeve of his cassock was tucked into the fascia. Arriving at the main entrance to the church they rang the bell. The door opened and before both men stepped inside the man carrying the briefcase turned his head towards the street, as if he was checking they weren't being followed. Once they had disappeared inside Michael reached for the phone, when it was answered he said down the receiver, 'Our man's arrived, get over here.'

Fifteen minutes later John and Edward walked into the room.

'What's happened?' asked John.

'Bernstorff and one of his men are inside. When they come out I want you two to follow them. Don't be seen and don't get involved, but with luck you should be able to discover where they're holed up. Then come back and tell me.'

Michael had only just finished giving the instruction when one of the smaller side doors opened and the two Germans, still dressed as priests, re-emerged.

'Quickly, they're coming out,' said Nigel.

John and Edward rushed down the stairs and joined the crowds in the street.

As Michael watched them disappear into the crowds Nigel asked, 'So, what next?'

'Somehow I have to get inside the Collegio, find out what's happening,' replied Michael.

'And how are you going to do that?'

There came a soft cough from the other side of the room.

'Perhaps I can be of some help,' said Armando.

John and Edward found it easy to follow the two priests, even at a distance. Their black cassocks stood out from the other pedestrians dressed in their more colourful evening wear. John guessed that, as they couldn't be observed disrobing in the street, they would wear their disguise until they arrived at their destination. They followed the two men south towards the Trastevere area. As they approached the working-class district, leaving the bars and restaurants behind them, the numbers of pedestrians promenading the streets began to thin out. To avoid being seen John and Edward were forced to drop back. The two priests crossed the Garibaldi bridge and eventually turned into the Via dei Salumi. John and Edward arrived at the corner and peeped down the street, the men were nowhere to be seen.

'We've lost them,' whispered John.

'Perhaps,' whispered Edward back. 'Let's wait here for a minute.'

Halfway up the street a light was illuminated above a door, seconds later a second light went on upstairs. A window opened and a man dressed in black leaned forward, looked up and down before pulling the wooden shutters closed.

Edward whispered, 'You wait here, I'm going to walk past the house. I'll meet you back here.'

John watched as Edward casually strolled up the street. At the house with the light above the door he stopped, took out a cigarette and lit it. A cloud of smoke rose into the air and John watched as Edward continued to walk on down the road. Two minutes later John felt Edward approach him from behind.

'Well?' Even in the gloom of the night John could see Edward was smiling.

'That's the place. As I lit my cigarette I clearly heard German being spoken through the shutters. To get the best of the evening's cool air the window hadn't been closed.'

'Let's go back and tell Michael,' said John.

'Are we going to raid the house?' Edward asked after they'd told Michael the location of the house.

'Not yet. First I want to have a look around the Collegio and Armando's going to help me.'

Michael removed his jacket and began to take off his shirt. A few minutes later he stood before them dressed in a dark jacket, black shirt and wearing a priest's collar.

'He makes a good priest, does he not?' Armando said to the others.

'Not really, Father. You don't know what we know,' replied Edward with a smile.

Armando laughed.

It was late, the restaurants were closed and the streets were almost empty, when Michael stood to one side of the door of the church as Armando rang the doorbell. After a couple of minutes it was opened and a young priest popped his head around the door.

'What can I do for you, Father?' he said to Armando.

'I'm sorry to disturb you but I was called to a house to see a sick parishioner to find that, quite unexpectedly, she's taken a turn for the worse. I hadn't expected to have to administer the *Viaticum* and I need a wafer and holy water.'

'Wait here Father; I'll bring you what you need.'

The priest disappeared to collect the items needed for the preparation of the dying person's soul: the absolution of sins and the final Eucharist. Armando promised God he would confess his lie when he next said confession.

Armando gently pushed the door open and, at his signal, Michael slipped into the gloom of the church. Moving away from the entrance Michael hid in the shadows of the memorial to Cardinal Andrea d'Austria. A couple of minutes later the young priest arrived back at the door and passed Armando a small box.

'Everything you need is in here. Please Father, return it in the morning and God be with you.'

'Thank you, I will, and may God also be with you.'

Michael watched as the door of the church was closed and locked again. The priest disappeared into one of the side chapels. Michael waited in the shadows of the memorial for everything to go silent and for his eyes to adjust to the soft lighting from the few candles that flickered on the high altar. The interior of the church was larger than he had expected partly, he guessed, because the aisles were the same height as the central arch of the church. Armando had given him an idea of the church's layout and where to find the entrance to the seminary. Michael crept, as quietly as he could, towards the door at the far side of the church though it seemed that every step echoed. Finding the door Armando had described, Michael carefully turned the brass handle. It silently slid open and he slipped inside, finding himself in a long corridor with a wooden staircase to one side. Armando had told him that the Collegio had only two floors, the third was false, designed to complement the architecture of the church, the bishop's study would be found on the landing of the second floor. To avoid the chance of any noise Michael carefully climbed the stairs using the sides of the step closest to the wall. Stepping onto the third stair there began a creak; he took his foot off and stepped onto the one above it. Arriving at the landing he saw three doors with light escaping from under the middle door. Armando had told him that Bishop Hudal was known to work late into the night and so he guessed that it would be the door to the bishop's office. Michael checked the Welrod pistol was safely tucked into his trousers so that he could get a hold of it quickly, and crept forward and reached for the door handle.

Chapter Forty-Five

29 June 1945

Bernstorff poured himself a second glass of red wine and began working through, in his mind, the finance of operation Red House. Earlier that evening he'd delivered twelve and a half million Swiss francs that would be shared among the five thousand Germans helped to escape. The two thousand five hundred Swiss francs they would each receive were for their immediate living expenses and would be just enough to have a frugal existence for a few months. Additional finance would be dependent on their loyalty and unquestioned obedience to their new Führer. Twenty-five million Swiss francs each had been given to Bishop Hudal and Juan Perón in Argentina for their 'personal expenses'. A further two hundred million dollars in bearer bonds to refinance the new German Reich, hidden in the kitchen drawer, would be with him on board the ship when he sailed to Argentina. The remaining ninety-eight million Swiss francs, still deposited in the bank in Zurich, would finance the new Nazi party when, as the new Führer, he returned to Germany. In all it amounted to three hundred and fifty million Swiss francs.

Bernstorff allowed his mind to picture the five-bedroom house he would buy when he arrived in Buenos Aires. He felt it should be appropriate to his status, one of the grand houses near the Plaza de Mayo Columbus, where he could walk the wide boulevard to the opera house and listen to the world's greatest orchestras and singers.

****

On the landing of the Collegio Teutonico Michael's every sense was heightened and his heart pounded inside his chest as if it was desperate to escape the confinement of his ribcage. With his hand on the door handle he tried to listen and detect any conversation coming from within the room but heard nothing. He slowly pushed the door open. Inside was a study with a large desk in front of a window; chairs and bookshelves lined the walls. Standing in one corner of the room in front of a wall-safe, with his back towards Michael, was a priest wearing a black cassock. Detecting some movement the priest turned his head. Michael watched as the priest's face washed blank with confusion before a frown crept over his face.

'Who are you? What are you doing here?' he said in German.

'Who I am doesn't matter. But who you are does,' replied Michael.

Hearing Michael reply in his native German the priest seemed to relax a little.

'I'm the bishop's secretary. You shouldn't be in here. What is it you want? Who are you?' he said, gently pushing the safe door closed as if he were a little boy trying to hide something.

'I want to know what Bernstorff wanted here.'

'Who?'

'The German SS officer called Bernstorff,' repeated Michael.

Without turning around the priest replied, 'I don't know who you're talking about.'

'He was here earlier this evening. Disguised as one of two priests and carrying a briefcase. Forty minutes later he left without it. I want to know what was inside.'

'I don't know this Bernstorff or anything about a briefcase.'

'That's surprising because it was exactly like the briefcase on the side table over there,' said Michael motioning to a table on the opposite side of the room.

The secretary turned to look at the table. It seemed to take a second or two for him to understand his lie had been exposed. Recovering some of his composure the priest turned back to the safe, pulled the door open and reached inside. Facing Michael he extended his arm and pointed a pistol at Michael's chest.

'I don't know who you are but don't move. I'll shoot if I have to.'

The priest moved to the desk and reached down to pick up the telephone.

Michael raised the Welrod bolt-action pistol. A dull *click, click*, not loud enough to have been heard outside the room, came as the trigger was pulled twice. The priest had no idea he'd been shot – his expression didn't change, he didn't cry out, he didn't fly backwards, he just slumped to the floor. Michael was grateful the suppressor had dampened any noise and the only sound had been the bolt action of the firing pin hitting the primer.

Michael walked over to the man, bent down and placed his index and middle finger over the artery in his neck to check there was no pulse. Michael felt no emotion at killing the priest; the man's spirituality had been lost when he had picked up the pistol and threatened to shoot him. Michael stood up and looked inside the safe. He riffled through some papers. Then his hand felt a thick package. Lifting it out, he tore open one corner of the brown paper wrapping and saw the unmistakable decoration of the bearer bonds. He checked the rest of the safe but found nothing more of interest. Stuffing the package into the waistband of his trousers he stepped over the priest, turned off the desk light and waited for his eyes to adjust to the gloom. Still holding the Welrod he moved silently to the door. Opening it a couple of inches he listened to see if anyone had been disturbed by the noise. There was silence. Slipping onto the landing he made his way back to the church. At the bottom of the staircase Michael pressed the release button inside the Welrod trigger ring and detached the barrel of the pistol from the handgrip. He stuffed each of the two parts into a different jacket pocket. All of a sudden a light came on the landing above him and he heard someone moving about upstairs. Michael gently opened the door and slipped back into the church closing the door behind him.

'Hello, Father,' said a voice.

Michael whipped around. It was the priest who had collected the Eucharist box for Armando earlier in the evening.

'Err, hello' said Michael.

'I'm sorry, Father, did I startle you? Do you want to leave?' enquired the priest.

'Yes, please, I'm on an errand for the bishop.'

'The bishop often keeps people busy late into the night.'

As they strolled towards the door their footsteps seemed to echo a hundred times around the church.

'I've not seen you before. Are you new?'

'Yes,' muttered Michael, 'I arrived from Essen yesterday.'

'There was terrible bombing of Essen by the Allies during the war. Were you there?'

'No,' Michael said willing the priest to stop talking and walk faster. He half expected that any second people would burst into the church shouting that there had been a murder. Arriving at the church door the priest pulled back the bolt. The sound echoed like a thunderclap.

Before the priest opened the door he turned to Michael.

'Nice to meet with you and I'll see you at Mass tomorrow, no doubt.'

The door was finally opened and Michael gratefully stepped into the street and rushed away.

Chapter Forty-Six

Vatican City, the following morning

After officiating at the seven o'clock Mass the cardinal had been waylaid by a minor official wanting to talk about some unimportant issue and he arrived back at his apartment later than he had wished. He pushed the catch that allowed him entry into the four hundred square feet of his apartment, allocated to him as a member of the Roman Curia. The luxurious lifestyle he enjoyed within the Vatican had long ago caused him to forget the humility of a simple parish priest. In fact, since becoming a cardinal, and dealing with the politics of the Church, he found himself moving away from God and, at times, even questioned His existence. He strode to his bedroom unbuttoning the mozzetta, the short elbow length cape with twelve buttons each representing the twelve apostles, as he did so. In the bedroom he threw it onto the large double bed. The other vestments were added to the growing pile and when naked he went to the bathroom. The shower washed away the sticky sweat caused by the layers of thick wool, silk and embroidered lace he was required to wear when celebrating Mass. On the way out of the bathroom he paused to look at his reflection in the long mirror. *Not bad for sixty-three* he said to himself pulling in his stomach.

Twenty minutes later, dressed in the cooler black cassock with scarlet buttons and the scarlet sash around his lower chest, he walked through the secret door that connected the bedroom to his study.

'Good morning, Your Eminence,' said his personal assistant. 'Bishop Hudal is in the anteroom, he says he must see you on a matter of the gravest importance. He's been waiting for fifteen minutes.'

'By his patient endurance, he might gain his soul,' the cardinal muttered.

The priest smiled at the cardinal's modification of Luke 21:19.

'However,' said the cardinal, 'patience has its limits, even for Bishop Hudal. I'll see him now.'

Still smiling, the priest chuckled to himself and went to collect the bishop.

Bishop Hudal entered the study and was waved to a chair.

'What can I do for you?' asked the cardinal thinking the bishop's face was more than usually pale and drawn, as if his belief in the heavenly host had been challenged by a bad dream during the night.

'Your Eminence, I should have come to you before now. Last night Bernstorff handed me the living expenses for those we will be helping to travel to South America. I put the package in the safe in my office... It's been stolen... And that's not all, my secretary has been murdered.'

Settling himself into his chair for what he suspected would be a long morning the cardinal said, 'Perhaps you should start at the beginning.'

Half an hour later the cardinal, deep in thought, was rubbing the gold ring presented to him by the Pope when he had been elevated. Bishop Hudal nervously removed his glasses and gave them a polish as he waited.

Eventually the cardinal spoke. 'The first thing we must arrange is for the burial of your secretary. It's to take place this afternoon. You are to say he died of a heart attack in the night. Since his death was on Vatican property there's no need for an autopsy. I will sign the authorisation exempting the autopsy myself... As he was German, you can arrange for the burial to be in the Collegio's cemetery. As for the bonds stolen from your safe last night, they were to cover the living expenses for our friends going to live in Argentina, or wherever they were going. You'll have to tell them there's no money.'

'It's not what they are expecting.'

'Then tell them to be thankful for God's small mercy, they are being given passports and travel papers to escape their accusers in Europe.'

'They won't be happy,' said the bishop.

The cardinal looked irritated. 'Then I suggest you give them a copy of the *The Imitation of Christ* and instruct them to pay particular attention to book one, *Helpful Counsels of the Spiritual Life*. It should be easy enough for them to understand, it's been printed in German since the fifteenth century.'

The meeting was obviously at an end. Bishop Hudal stood up and left.

****

That afternoon Michael began briefing Nigel, John and Edward.

'The priest's death at the Collegio last night has not been made public and there's been no police involvement. That's good, now we know where Bernstorff and his unit are we're able to neutralise them. However, it's still important we avoid any involvement by the Italian authorities. So we'll not be carrying any documentation that can identify us as British.'

When it was dark, each of them took a different route to the Trastevere area. Michael had his Welrod pistol in his coat, Edward and John had a Webley & Scott pistol each and Nigel his weapon of choice, a crossbow. Unlike a traditional crossbow the weapon was roughly the size of a large handgun with a rigid triangular frame and a number of strong elastic rubber bands providing the propulsion mechanism. It was highly effective up to two hundred yards and had the benefit of being completely silent.

At the agreed time they were in position. Michael, Edward and Nigel in Via dei Salumi from where they had a clear view of the front of the building while John had taken up a position at the back to thwart any escape from the rear.

As Michael looked down the street he let out a silent curse. The light above the front door illuminated the street, making any approach to the front of the building without being seen impossible. The door opened and a man stepped out into the street. Michael and the others pressed themselves into the shadows. The man wandered a few feet up the road and then back again, obviously checking to see if anyone was about. Satisfied that all was quiet he returned to the house. Again Michael cursed under his breath, the patrol meant Bernstorff's men were on their guard. Any element of surprise would be difficult.

On a signal from Michael they pulled out their weapons and inched forward, Edward taking the lead, then Michael and Nigel at the rear. When only ten feet from the house, bathed in light from above the door, a loud hissing and a yowling was heard as two cats began to fight. There followed the clatter of a garbage lid tipping onto the cobbles. From the window above them a head appeared to see what the noise was about and noticing the three men crouched against the wall shouted, '*Achtung, attacke,*' to his comrades inside. Michael aimed the Welrod at the light above the door and pulled the trigger. The bulb shattered and the street was plunged into darkness but the advantage had been lost.

There was nothing for it but to press on with the assault. Edward stood and faced the door. To keep his balance he drove the heel of his standing foot into the ground, lifting his other leg he kicked the weakest part of the door where the lock was mounted. It stayed firm. He kicked it again and the wood began to splinter, he kicked it for a third time, the door flew open on its hinges. As it did a hail of bullets came from the hole in the wall at the top of the stairs. Edward, hit in the chest and stomach, fell to the ground. Michael knelt, leaned forward around the doorway, aimed the Welrod at the hole in the wall and pulled the trigger. He saw a man above fall backwards. Stepping over Edward, Michael entered the building and crouched down. He quickly looked around the ground floor and seeing no one else he turned his attention again on the hole at the top of the stairs. Raising the Welrod to cover the hole in case someone fired through it, he shouted, 'All clear,' to Nigel.

Nigel entered the hallway and briefly attended to Edward; he was dead. Nigel picked up Edward's pistol and stuffed it into his own jacket pocket. In the silence Michael heard some noise along the street. The street's residents had been woken by the noise. It would not be long before the police arrived to investigate the disturbance. Still crouching in the hallway Michael noted there were two doors on the ground floor. He indicated to Nigel that he would open the door nearest to him and that Nigel should cover him from further fire from the hole at the top of the stairs. Nigel pointed the crossbow up the stairs.

'Ready?' whispered Michael.

'Ready,' Nigel whispered back.

Michael went down onto his haunches and turned the door handle. He opened it and threw himself onto the floor. He saw a man had taken cover behind an upturned leather chair, a pistol was pointing towards him. The man fired. The bullet went wide and Michael was showered in plaster as the bullet embedded itself into the wall. Michael fired back but harmlessly hit the chair. From the top of the stairs a man's head appeared in the hole in the wall. A pistol swivelled in Michael's direction. He was now caught in crossfire. Nigel raised his arm, aimed the crossbow and pulled the trigger. The tension on the thick rubber bands was released; the thin metal bolt flew through the air up the staircase imbedding itself between the German's eyes. The man remained in the hole, frozen for a full second, before falling back into the room. From the downstairs room another shot was fired. It too went wide and Michael was sprayed with more plaster. To steady his own weapon he placed the Welrod against the doorframe and waited for the man to appear from behind the leather chair. There was no movement. Michael waited. Then half a face appeared. Michael squeezed the trigger; the man slumped to the floor.

Nigel looked at Michael. 'You all right, your head's bleeding?'

Michael rubbed his temple and looked at his hand; it was streaked in blood.

'Flesh wound, that's all.'

Nigel indicated to the door on the right side of the hallway. Turning the handle he pushed the door open. It revealed an empty kitchen and at the far end an open door leading into the back courtyard.

'Upstairs or through the kitchen?' said Nigel.

'Upstairs, John's covering the back.'

As Nigel covered him with his crossbow, Michael took the stairs two at a time. At the top he paused. The landing was empty. He kicked in the first door; the room was empty. He kicked open the final door and found the two dead men in a large room that Michael assumed was the master bedroom. He rushed downstairs and, followed by Nigel, ran through the kitchen and into the courtyard. Beside a large pile of books and household possessions they saw an open gate leading to a small alleyway. Arriving in the alleyway they found John slumped on the flagstones. He was conscious and pressing his hands against his chest.

'You all right?' asked Michael as he bent down.

'I've been stabbed and I guess they left me for dead. It hurts like buggery but I'll be fine,' answered John.

'How many of them and which way did they go?' asked Michael.

'Three, Bernstorff was one, turned right at the end of the passageway. I guess they're moving towards the river.'

Michael and Nigel left John, turned right at the end of the passageway and ran through the small piazza and onto the road running along the bank of the River Tiber. They both looked up and down but didn't see the three men.

'Which way?' asked Nigel.

'The Ponte Palatino, it's the nearest bridge. If they cross that they'll be able to disappear into the Roman ruins in the Forum and we'll have lost them,' shouted Michael and began running down the road towards the bridge. As they began their pursuit the uneven cobbles and the danger of them taking a tumble made progress painfully slower than they wished.

Fifty yards further on Michael looked through the gloom of the night and noticed three men begin to cross the Ponte Palatino. Even with one of them limping, Michael knew they had a head start and were unlikely to be caught.

Suddenly Michael felt a hand stop him, he looked to see Nigel standing, one leg in front of the other, with his head at an angle aiming his crossbow.

'If I aim an inch above our target and half an inch in front, that'll compensate for the movement of the target and the wind,' he said matter-of-factly.

Nigel pulled the trigger. The bolt flew forward. Michael watched as it disappeared into the darkness of the night sky.

The men on the bridge continued to run.

'Damn it, I've missed.'

'They're too far away to fire another. We've lost them,' sighed Michael.

Suddenly the man with the limp stopped running. They watched as he stumbled forward and then bent down as if in pain. The two men with him seemed not to notice and continued running for a few yards. Then the man seemed to recover, lifted himself up and staggered towards the side of the bridge. He crashed into the wrought iron balustrade, only just waist height, and slowly tipped over the balustrade, tumbling thirty feet before splashing into the black waters of the Tiber. They watched as the body floated down the river, surrounded by hundreds of pieces of paper. The two men on the bridge ran back to the railings and seeing there was nothing to be done ran off in the direction of the Foro Romano.

'Good shot,' Michael said as he slapped Nigel on the back.

Michael and Nigel returned to the house on Via dei Salumi. The neighbours, concerned at the commotion, had called the Carabinieri who had begun to arrive at the front of the house. Michael and Nigel worked their way up the narrow streets to the rear of the house and found John. They helped him back to their hotel where they telephoned Armando who arranged for a doctor to attend.

A day later Armando joined Michael at his hotel for breakfast. He'd brought with him a copy of *Il Messaggero* and translated the newspaper's report on page three:

> *'Investigating reports of a group of fascists taking refuge in a house in the Trastevere area of Rome the Carabinieri became involved in a heavy gunfight. In the ensuing gunfight a number of wanted fascist criminals were killed. The leader of the gang*

was later hauled out of the river. The chief of police told our reporter the man had committed suicide rather than be arrested. The Carabinieri suffered no casualties.'

Armando put down the newspaper. 'So what now?' he asked.

'Bernstorff's dead. The group is broken up and as far as we can tell the money he was carrying has floated down the Tiber and into the sea. Now we go back to London,' said Michael.

'It's a shame, I'll miss the excitement,' said Armando smiling.

Michael smiled back. 'Father, there is something you can do for me. The money I found in Bishop Hudal's safe didn't belong to him. It most probably belongs to Jews murdered by the Nazis. I was wondering if you could arrange for it to be used to help those who should properly benefit from it.'

'It's a generous thing that you do. You could have kept the money for yourself,' said Armando.

'No Father, I couldn't. The money was stolen once by the Nazis. It would be compounding the sin if I kept it and besides knowing where it came from would bring me no happiness or comfort.'

'Then I will pass the money on to the Tempio Maggiore, it's the Great Synagogue of Rome. I know the rabbi well. He will know how to use the money in the best way.'

'Thank you, Father,' said Michael.

Armando said, 'Throughout this war I've wondered how often men have deceived themselves on their motivations for fighting. Many told themselves it was for racial purity, others for God when, in fact it was for their own anger and fears. But when peace comes men can't return to a contented life if they are feeding an inner demon, when instead they should be feeding inner angels. I think this war has brought you many troubles. Would you like to talk about it?'

Michael looked at Armando; the priest's eyes showed the same gentle concern his mother had when she spoke to him as a child. Soothed by the tone of the words more than the actual meaning Michael intended to say that such a conversation wasn't necessary but the words he spoke were different.

'Yes, Father, I would,' he whispered to the priest.

Many hours passed as Michael talked about the pain over his mother's death, the death of his unborn baby and Peter's murder. It all poured forth and he talked of the war and his part in it; blowing up the train in France, throwing Molotov cocktails into German vehicles, killing the old man in the forest, the events in Switzerland and others earlier in the conflict. When it came to an end Michael was exhausted but felt a relief from the burden he'd carried on his shoulders for so long, his demon had gone away.

Eventually Armando said, 'Now it's over, I hope you can find the peace you are seeking. Would you permit me to give you my blessing?'

Michael looked at Armando. 'Thank you Father, you're going to make a fine priest and your blessing would be most welcome.'

Armando raised his right hand and made the sign of the cross on Michael's forehead.

'In nomine Patris, et Filii, et Spiritus sancti.'

'Amen,' whispered Michael.

Chapter Forty-Seven

London

Michael arrived back in London in the first week of July. Tim Wilson updated him on the events in Italy.

'The two surviving men with Bernstorff were arrested by the Italian police as they tried to cross the border back into Switzerland. Under interrogation they told us the bearer bonds that floated down the Tiber with Bernstorff were destined to finance a new Nazi party. To date, none of the bonds have been recovered though I suspect there are some pretty happy Italians somewhere.'

'What about the Swiss bank account?' asked Michael.

'The only person to know the number was Bernstorff. The information died with him and the Swiss aren't playing ball to help us recover the money. The fact that no one else can use the money is probably as good a result as we can hope for,' answered the colonel.

At the end of the debriefing Michael smiled, 'There is one more thing, sir. Before the war I'd begun a career with the Tagleva bank, now the war's over I'm resigning my commission. I'm going back to work in the family business.'

'I thought you'd say that, and I won't stop you, but if Britain ever needed you in the future may I contact you?'

'You can ask, but if I see you first you can expect me to run in the opposite direction. You and the Nazis have spent much of the last five years conspiring with each other to neglect my wife, and I now intend to put that situation right.'

Tim Wilson laughed.

'Very good, old man, your discharge papers will be sent on to you.'

An hour later Michael pressed the doorbell and waited until the door was opened by Dorothy. Seeing him she rushed forward, gave him a hug and pulled him into the hallway, and asked him, 'Are you home for good?'

'I am,' he answered.

She firmly told him, 'Now stay here. I want to be the first to tell everyone you're home.'

Walking to the bottom of the staircase Dorothy picked up the felt hammer and began to hit the dinner gong again and again. The flat surface vibrated sending a 'crash', rather than a tuned note, around the house. Summoned by the unexpected noise Philip, the twins, Juliette and the servants appeared from various parts of the house and the family began to hug Michael. Once he had recovered from all the attention he announced that he had left the army and was home for good.

'I'm so pleased my boy, the bank needs you, but more importantly, the family needs you,' said Philip.

That evening Michael and Juliette were in their bedroom, dressing for dinner, when Michael gently took her hand, led her to the bed and sat her down.

'I have a lot to apologise for. When you told me you'd lost our baby I was already angry over my mother's death. Losing our baby was like a stab to my heart. It might have seemed as if I blamed you, but I didn't. I became self-absorbed and withdrew for some stupid reason, wallowing in a selfish aggressive rage and never understood that you were hurting too. I'm so sorry for that, particularly as I know you worked so hard at showing me how much you loved me. I hope it's not too late for you to forgive me.'

Juliette stroked Michael's cheek.

'My darling, there's nothing to forgive. My work with the Foundation has shown me how people react to grief in very different ways. Some get angry, some find it difficult to relax, some can't stop talking about their anger and others avoid talking to anyone about their experiences. I knew you were upset. I just had to wait until you were ready to talk about it.

I've never stopped loving you. How could I? You're everything to me.'

Juliette took his hand in hers. 'But, if it helps, I forgive you and will always love you Michael Tagleva, with all my being.'

'I don't deserve you,' Michael whispered.

Michael took Juliette's head in his hand and began kissing her, she pulled him to her and they fell onto the bed.

They would be very late for dinner.

Postscript

Five years after the end of the war, in the splendour of Salon Vert of the Élysée Palace, Philip Tagleva watched as President Vincent Auriol awarded Jean-Claude the Légion d'honneur, France's highest order of merit, *to recognise his remarkable acts of courage that contributed to the Resistance against the enemy.*

When Jean-Claude eventually retired from Tagleva he and Sébastien went to live in their villa in Nice, in the South of France, where they could often be found at the Negresco hotel drinking champagne or enjoying a meal with friends.

In the winter of 1952, aged seventy-seven, Philip Tagleva caught flu. Despite the doctor's best efforts it developed into pneumonia and two weeks later, surrounded by his family and closest friend Jean-Claude, he lapsed into a coma and died. Ten days later he was buried next to his beloved wife Sophie. Each year, on the anniversary of their meeting in St. Petersburg in Russia, twenty-four white roses are placed on their graves.

Following his retirement from the army Michael joined the Tagleva bank eventually becoming the head of the London office. He and Sophie had two children, a boy and a girl. Every year Michael's family holidayed in a house they bought overlooking the picturesque fishing village of Port Isaac on north Cornwall's Atlantic coast. It was there Michael and Juliette taught their children to swim and to enjoy the delights of crab salad and Cornish cream teas. Juliette continued to run the Tagleva Foundation until they both retired.

In 1948 Samuel emigrated to live in the newly established State of Israel. A year later he met and fell in love with Sarai, also a concentration camp survivor. They were married and lived in an apartment overlooking the sea in Tel Aviv.

After leaving university Dorothy joined the Tagleva bank ending her career as Chair of the Board of Directors. She never married but adopted two orphans, one German and one British. In 1992 she travelled by private jet to Moscow. In an intimate ceremony in the Kremlin Dorothy handed over a leather box, embossed with the Imperial Russian eagle, to Boris Yeltsin the first popularly elected president of the Russian Republic. Inside were the jewels Philip and Sophie Tagleva had brought out of Russia for the last Tsar. Three days later rubies the size of hens' eggs, a gift to the Russian monarch from the Shah of Persia, ten huge cut diamonds, two diamond and ruby bracelets, four diamond and sapphire necklaces and a platinum chain set with a huge emerald studded with diamonds that had once belonging to Catherine The Great were added to the display on the ground floor of the Kremlin Armoury Chamber that house Russia's Crown Jewels. In accordance with the wishes of Countess Sophie Tagleva the Romanov jewels had been returned to the heirs of the imperial family: the people of Russia.

In the late 1990s Edgar Bronfman Senior, the chief executive of the family drinks firm Seagram and president of the World Jewish Congress, championed for the restitution of all the assets stolen by the Nazis and held in Swiss banks to the Holocaust survivors. Under international pressure the Swiss authorities identified over three hundred and sixteen million dollars of gold deposited by the Nazis in Swiss banks which was estimated to have been looted. It was agreed to release all Swiss banks and the Swiss government from future legal claims regarding the Holocaust in exchange for one and a quarter billion dollars paid to victims.

In the same year *Time* magazine asked the Vatican about rumours that it also held money for 'safe keeping' on behalf of the Nazis. A spokesman for the Vatican bank declared, 'There is no basis in reality to the claims'.

Detail on the actual historical events, locations and characters behind the story

The Nazi ratline organisation

The system of escape routes developed by some priests within the Vatican allowing Nazis and other fascists to flee Europe at the end of the war to havens in Latin America as well as Switzerland, Australia, Canada, and the Middle-East. A leading organiser of the ratlines was Bishop Alois Hudal, the rector of the Pontifical Istituto Teutonico Santa Maria dell'Anima in Rome. A second escape route was the San Girolamo ratline with headquarters at the Pontifical College of St. Jerome, also in Rome, and operated by members of the Franciscan order.

Operation Werewolf

In late summer of 1944, Heinrich Himmler ordered SS Obergruppenführer Hans-Adolf Prützmann to organise an elite troop of volunteer forces to operate secretly behind enemy lines. It was supposed to have at its disposal a vast assortment of weapons, from fire-proof coats to silenced Walther pistols but in reality this was merely on paper; it was starved of funds and most units manned by unseasoned soldiers. Nevertheless Allied troops and intelligence units were deployed to defeat the units. All Werewolf units were quickly defeated.

Operation Red House.

Begun at a secret meeting at the Maison Rouge Hotel in Strasbourg on August 10, 1944 where Nazi officials developed a plan for Germany's post-war recovery and the Nazis' return to power.

Locations and weapons

The church of Santa Maria dell'Anima

The German national church and hospice in Rome was founded as early as 1350, as a private hospice for German pilgrims. The Collegio Teutonico, often referred to by its Latin name Collegium Germanicum, is one of the Roman Catholic Colleges of Rome established for the education of future ecclesiastics of the Roman Catholic Church of German nationality.

St. Ermin's Hotel

Close to Buckingham Palace and the Houses of Parliament, during the Second World War it was a meeting place of the British intelligence services and was notably the birthplace of the Special Operations Executive (SOE).

Trent Park

Trent Park is an English country house in north London. During the war it was used as a POW camp for eighty-four German generals and some staff officers for the purpose of listening in on their conversations.

All the vehicles and weapons described in the story, including the hand crossbow, were used by British or German forces during WW2.

Details on historical characters mentioned

To satisfy readers who wonder 'what happened to…' I include a few details of the historical characters mentioned in the story.

Vatican State

Bishop Alois Hudal

For thirty years Hudal was head of the Austrian-German congregation of Santa Maria dell'Anima and an influential representative of the Austrian Catholic Church. In 1937 he wrote a book *The Foundations of National Socialism* in which he praised Adolf Hitler, and several sources claim Hudal was a Vatican-based informer to German intelligence. After the war he is credited with helping war criminals including Josef Mengele and Adolf Eichmann, among others, to find safe haven in overseas countries. In his memoirs Hudal said of his actions, 'I felt duty bound to devote my charitable work to former National Socialists, especially to so-called war criminals and I thank God He allowed me to help them escape…'. In 1960 Pope Pius XII banned him from the Vatican and he withdrew to his sumptuous residence in Grottaferrata near Rome. He died in 1963 and is buried at Campo Santo dei Teutonici, adjacent to St. Peter's Basilica in the Vatican City.

Domenico Tardini

A long-time aide to Pope Pius XII in 1952 he was named Pro-Secretary of the State for Extraordinary Ecclesiastical Affairs. In 1953 Pope John XXIII named him Cardinal Secretary of State and, in this position, the most prominent member of the Roman Curia in Vatican City. He died in 1961.

England

Charles Sydney Gibbes

Gibbes was born in Rotherham in Yorkshire. He moved to St. Petersburg, Russia, and came to the attention of Tsarina Alexandra and was appointed English tutor to the Tsarevich. After the revolution Gibbes left Russia. He joined the Russian Orthodox Church in April 1934 and later became a priest. In 1941, Father Nicholas, as he was then, established St. Bartholomew's Orthodox Chapel near Oxford where he displayed several icons and mementos of the imperial family that he had brought out of Russia, including a pair of the Tsar's boots. These items are now in a private collection. Gibbes died in 1963.

Sir John Cecil Masterman OBE

Best known for organising the scheme that controlled German double agents in Britain during WW2 it's widely believed Ian Fleming, himself a wartime intelligence officer, adapted Masterman's name for the character of Jill Masterson in the James Bond novel *Goldfinger*. He died in 1977, aged eighty-six.

Sir D'Arcy Osborne

Envoy Extraordinary and Minister Plenipotentiary to the Holy See between 1936 and 1947. During WW2 he was one of a group of priests and diplomats who concealed some four thousand fugitives, Allied soldiers and Jews, from the Nazis in Rome. His role was portrayed in the 1983 film *The Scarlet and the Black*, starring Gregory Peck. He died at the age of seventy-nine in 1974, and is buried in the Protestant Cemetery in Rome.

Marguerite Patten

During WW2 Marguerite hosted the BBC radio programme *The Kitchen Front* when she suggested nourishing recipes using the rationed food. After the war Patten published cookery books and in 1961, a time when they were illustrated in black and white, she produced with her publisher Paul Hamlyn a glossy cookery book in colour. It influenced all later cookery publications and the famous chef Gary Rhodes describes her as 'one of his two culinary heroes'. She died aged ninety-nine in 2015.

Germany

Heinrich Himmler

Himmler was obsessed with racial purity in Germany and was responsible for the attempted elimination of Jews. At the end of the war Himmler tried to escape using a false identity of a Sergeant Heinrich Hitzinger, of a Special Armoured Company. Captured by the British he committed suicide on 23 May 1945 while in custody. Himmler is buried in an unmarked grave in the forest near Lüneburg.

A list of some of the Nazi war criminals who escaped using the Vatican ratlines

Adolf Eichmann

SS-Obersturmbannführer (lieutenant colonel). Eichmann managed the logistics of the mass deportation of Jews to extermination camps. After the war he fled to Argentina but was captured by the Israelis in 1960 and smuggled to Israel where he was tried and executed on 1 June 1962.

Franz Stangl

Nicknamed 'The White Death' he was the commandant of Sobibór and Treblinka extermination camps. He escaped to Brazil. He died in 1971 of natural causes.

Gustav Wagner

Deputy commander of Sobibór extermination camp, where more than two hundred thousand Jews were gassed. Due to his brutality, he was known as 'The Beast'. He fled to Brazil. In October 1980 he was found in São Paulo with a knife in his chest. The authorities deemed he had committed suicide.

Klaus Barbie

SS-Hauptsturmführer *(equivalent to army captain)* and known as the 'Butcher of Lyon'. He took pleasure in personally torturing French prisoners of the Gestapo. After the war he fled to Bolivia. In 1983 he was extradited to France where he was convicted of crimes against humanity. He died in prison in 1991.

Erich Priebke

Participated in the Ardeatine massacre in Rome in 1944 when three hundred and thirty-five Italian civilians were executed in retaliation for a partisan attack that killed thirty-three men of a German SS police regiment. In 1973 the story was dramatised in the film *Massacre in Rome* starring Richard Burton. After the war Priebke fled to Argentina on a Vatican passport. Fifty years later he was extradited to Italy where he was convicted of war crimes. He died in prison in 2013.

Eduard Roschmann

Known as the 'Butcher of Riga', Roschmann was commandant of the Riga ghetto where he was responsible for the deaths of eighty thousand people. After the war he escaped to Argentina where he became an Argentinian citizen using the name Frederico Wagner. In 1976 West Germany requested his extradition to face charges of multiple murder. He fled to Paraguay and died there in 1977.

Aribert Heim

An Austrian doctor known as 'Dr Death'. He served at Mauthausen concentration camp, torturing and killing inmates by injecting toxic compounds into the hearts of his victims. He disappeared in 1962.

Ante Pavelić

A Croatian fascist dictator who led the Independent State of Croatia established in occupied Yugoslavia. While in power, Pavelić pursued genocidal policies against ethnic minorities including Serbs, Jews, and Romani. After the war he escaped to Argentina. He died in Spain in 1959 from wounds sustained in an assassination attempt.

Walter Rauff

The creator of the mobile gas chamber. He is thought to have been responsible for the deaths of a hundred thousand people. As late as the 1980s, he was arguably the most wanted Nazi still at liberty. He died in 1984. At his funeral in Santiago in Chile, the pall-bearers included his son and grandson, and it was attended by hundreds of old Nazis. As his coffin was interred in the ground many shouted *Heil Hitler* and gave the Nazi salute.

Josef Mengele

A doctor at Auschwitz concentration camp. Mengele was responsible for the selection of victims to be killed in the gas chambers. After the war, he fled to South America, where he evaded capture until drowning in 1979 while swimming off the Brazilian coast.

About the Author

Stephen Davis began his writing career in his twenties with his own column in the *South Wales Echo*. Since then he's become an award-winning writer, a broadcaster and the author of two business books. His articles have been featured in nearly thirty business magazines, including *Accountancy Age*, *Training Journal* and *People Management*. An energetic entrepreneur, Stephen runs a successful business consultancy and is regularly invited to speak at business conferences and meetings.

The Tsar's Banker was the first novel in the Tagleva trilogy and *I Spy the Wolf* the second story. The trilogy follows the fortunes of Philip Cummings and his family as they battle for survival through two world wars and beyond.

When not working, Stephen enjoys golf, swimming, cooking and travel.

Also by Stephen Davis

The Tsar's Banker

Philip Cummings hated change. When his high-flying job at the Bank of England takes him to Russia he's caught up in the chaos, turmoil, violence and vengeance of the Bolshevik Revolution. Philip must survive double-cross and cold-blooded murder if he's to bring the beautiful Countess Sophie Tagleva, her wounded brother, a chest full of the Tsar's jewels and secret papers out of Russia and escape from the clutches of the fighting factions swirling around if he's to expose those who betrayed him.

'A thrilling novel painted in glorious period and geographic detail with the real life conspiracy theory of Dan Brown and the glamour of Ian Fleming at his best. It compels you to turn the pages to find out how Philip Cummings and the British Empire are embroiled in the destiny of Tsarist Russia. I loved it.' **Caspar Berry – Poker Advisor on Casino Royale**.

I Spy the Wolf
  The secret they don't want you to know...
  Michael Tagleva is the eldest son and heir to one of the wealthiest banking families in Europe. When visiting Germany he is welcomed as a distinguished guest by the Nazis and recruited into the Nazi party, but not everything is as it seems. Michael soon finds himself in a labyrinth of deceit and double-cross. In a breathtaking race against time Michael must uncover the plot and thwart those that conspire to destroy his family and force Britain to surrender to Germany...

- Who are the British aristocrats who conspire with the Nazis against Britain?
- How is the Bank of England involved in the plot?
- What is the identity of the sinister figure in London?

And why is the story still classified as TOP SECRET?

'Stephen Davis wonderfully captures the atmosphere, the confusion and the tragedies at the start of the Second World War in Nuremburg, Paris and London. It compels you to turn the pages to discover if Britain and the Tagleva family can survive the onslaught that's directed against them.'